Coffee Girl

Coffee Book 1

Sophie Sinclair

COFFEE GIRL

Copyright © 2019 by Sophie Sinclair
Print Edition

Editor: Michelle Morgan, www.fictionedit.com
Proofreading: Michelle Morgan
Book Cover: Carrie Guy, Shawna Montague

All Rights Reserved

To A & S,
You are kind, you are smart, and you are beautiful.
Never forget that.

If you don't like the road you're walking,
start paving another one.
– Dolly Parton

Chapter 1

HAVE YOU EVER had that moment when you lean in for a first kiss and butterflies explode in your stomach, because you really, really like the guy? He's funny, cute, smart, has a great job, and he's really in to you.

And when your lips touch...

Nothing happens.

Zilch. Nada. Niente.

You feel nothing.

Oh God, this is really, really, bad. So bad I start thinking about random things, like if I left my straightening iron on, or if I remembered to record *The Bachelor*. The kiss that's barely a kiss is so bland and bad, it feels like I'm kissing my brother.

Cue the vomit.

It's so awful, when his slimy little tongue tries to break apart my sealed Fort Knox lips, I reflexively lift my knee up to his groin. *Abort, abort!*

I push back from Ethan, my nose crinkling in disgust

and disappointment. His smirk tells me he thinks he's a pretty badass Romeo. I try to smile back, but I'm pretty sure I just threw up a little in my mouth.

I look into his twinkling, golden-brown eyes, his perfect, square jaw, his sexy smile… Dang it, should I try again? I quickly peruse his face one more time. The answer is no. No, I should not.

It's like I'm looking at him in a whole new light. He's still a good-looking guy, but I no longer have the desire to jump in bed with him. Not that I would on the first date. I mean, we could get handsy for sure, but I'm not a let's-sleep-together-on-the-first-date kind of girl…at least, not with Ethan.

I run my fingers through my hair, preventing him from leaning in for a second kiss. All I want is to go home and get in my jammies. Another failed date that I'll have to rehash with my best friend in the morning.

"Listen, Ethan. I, um, had a great time tonight, but I have to wake up super early for a meeting in the morning. I'm just going to call an Uber and go home. I hope you understand."

I quickly take my phone out of my coat pocket and stare at the black screen. I try to swipe up, waiting for my password entry to appear. Nothing. I swipe at the blackness a hundred more times, and then I shake it like an eight ball, hoping it will magically come to life.

Shit, it's dead.

"Oh, oh yeah, totally. I'll ride with you." He quickly taps open the app.

"No!" I yell a little too loudly, a little desperately. "I

mean, I, uh, I live in the opposite direction, it would be really inconvenient for you."

I do not want a continuation of the worst make-out session I've ever participated in, or for him to try and cop a feel in the back of the Uber. My karate moves are less than stellar.

"I already punched it in my phone. It's no big deal. It's done. He'll be here in a minute." He smiles confidently as he slides his phone back in his coat pocket. His self-assured demeanor I found attractive about an hour ago now grates on my nerves.

"Ha. Okay, great," I murmur weakly as I look anywhere but at him. *Shit, shit, shit.*

He leans into me and the scent of his cologne tightens my throat, suffocating me. His perfectly gelled hair and cocky smile make my eyeballs twitch. "Listen, I really like you and would like to start dating exclusively."

"Oh, um…wow," I squeak as I press my hand against his chest to prevent him from getting any closer. "I'm, um… I'm not sure what to say. I mean, we've only had one date."

"Well, when you know, you know, right?" He smirks as he leans into my neck.

Is he sniffing me?

I cross my arms, taking a step back and glance up and down the empty street hoping the Uber driver screams in on two wheels, running me over at this very moment.

Now!

I crane my neck. Nope, no Uber driver in sight. Still alive.

Just Ethan invading my personal space, giving me the

creeps.

"Look, Ethan, I'm just not looking for anything serious right now. You're great, but I just—"

"Seriously, Kiki? Fucking unbelievable! You're breaking up with me?" he huffs as I take another step back.

"Technically, one date doesn't mean we were dating," I mumble as Ethan shoots daggers at me. Gone is the overly charming smile—in its place a sour grimace. Just then, the Uber driver pulls up to the curb.

"Really? Couldn't have arrived two minutes ago?" I mutter under my breath. I start forward to get in to the car.

Ethan grabs my arm and pulls me back. "Get your own ride," he snarls as he slides in and slams the door. The Uber driver rolls down his passenger window, looking at me with a mixture of pity and amusement.

"You riding?"

Ethan is on his phone pretending like I don't exist.

"Just go," I say miserably. "Oh hey, wait! Can you come back and get me?" The driver nods and they quickly take off, leaving me on the curb.

And…it starts to rain.

Just fucking great.

Chapter 2

Kiki

"SO…HOW WAS THE date?"

TJ, my best friend, sidles up to me in the break room. TJ and I work as stylists at the men's magazine, *Cufflinks*. You could say he strikingly resembles Prince Harry, if Harry were extremely loud and gay. We have the same witty sense of humor and similar fashion sense. When I told him on my first day that I adored his polka-dot bow tie and he complimented my one and only beloved pair of Louis Vuitton skyscraper heels, we became inseparable.

"Yeah, thanks for setting us up. Where did you find that winner?" I roll my eyes sarcastically as I jam a coffee cup into the Keurig.

"Oh no! Deets, honey! What happened?" TJ giddily looks over his mug of coffee as he squirms in his seat.

"Don't look so excited that I had yet another disastrous date, you evil twat."

"I love it when you talk dirty," he whispers dramatically. "Come on! Give me the DL!"

I shrug and peer at the new horn-rimmed tortoise shell glasses he's sporting. "Are those prescription?"

"What? Oh, these? Adorbs, right? No, they're fake. I found them downstairs in the December issue stash. I thought Trent in accounting might take my passes more seriously if I looked more bookish."

"Trent is gay? Huh, who knew?"

"Totes, he just doesn't know it yet. Ugh, don't distract me. What happened?" He slams his hand on the table.

I blow on my coffee as I lean against the counter. "I don't know. He was good-looking, funny, a perfect gentleman. I mean, we had fun at dinner, but then when he kissed me, I didn't feel a thing. Remember when Michael kissed Oscar in that episode of *The Office*?"

"No!"

"Yes. It was that bad." I flick his ear as I pass by him, heading back to my desk.

TJ scrambles out of his seat and jogs beside me. I'm tempted to stick my foot out and trip him, but that would just be too mean this early in the morning. I also don't want to risk spilling my coffee.

"Well, what happened after you kissed him?"

I huff at the annoying memory. "Uh, let's see…well, my phone died. Ethan called an Uber but wouldn't let me ride with him because I turned down his offer to date exclusively, so then I asked the driver to come back and get me, but of course he never did, and it started to rain. So I ran a couple blocks and waited under a bus stop shelter until a cab came by about an hour later. I looked and felt like a freezing, drowned rat." I shake my head in irritation. "And you want to know the worst part? When I got home and charged my phone I had a freaking Venmo request for my half of the dinner bill from him. Who does that?"

"*No.*" He's trying so hard not to laugh, but failing miserably. "Do you think you'll have a second date?"

I roll my eyes. "Go away, pest."

"Did you wear those suede Tory Birch booties I wish they made in my size?"

"You know I did. You picked out my outfit."

"I'm about to cry."

"Me too…for letting you set me up on a date in the first place," I grumble as I reach my desk.

"I meant about the shoes. I'm sure they're totally ruined now."

"I should have tripped you when I had the chance." I roll my chair out and sit down.

"I swear, Stacy said he was super sweet. He's a client of hers." TJ leans against my cubicle wall.

"Who is Stacy again?"

"My facialist."

I put my coffee on my desk and turn on my computer. "Well, why the fuck isn't *she* dating him if he's so great?"

"Oh honey, no. She likes the boobies," he whispers dramatically as if anyone around us cares.

"Ugh, go! I've got work to do and you're too much for me to handle before my morning coffee."

"Are you going out with us tonight?" he asks as he looks around the other cubicles to make sure no one is listening.

"I have no plans as of yet."

"My place to pick!" he sing-songs as he shoves away from

my wall.

"I said I didn't have plans *yet*. Besides, the last time you picked, I ended up in Los Angeles at RuPaul's DragCon."

"Nothing wrong with that, sweets! Loud and proud!" He whistles as he walks away.

I throw my pen at his retreating form. "You still owe me for the plane ticket."

My boss steps out of his corner office and makes his way to my desk.

"Kiki, can we have a moment in my office? You won't need your laptop."

"Uh, sure, Jordan. Can I bring my coffee?"

He smiles weakly at me. "Please, by all means."

My stomach clenches because Jordan looks like someone just told him that *Cufflinks* was turning into a *Guns N Ammo* magazine.

Chapter 3

LOUD BOMB SHELTER sirens rip me from a deep, dreamless sleep. I sit up in my bed like a rocket, scared shitless as I clutch my sheets to my chest. Why the fuck are sirens going off in my bedroom? It takes me about thirty seconds to realize I forgot to turn off my work alarm from the day before. I fumble for my phone on the nightstand and swipe at the screen until it silences. I fall back on my fluffy pillows after I blearily look at the time. Six a.m.

Fuck. My. Life.

I can't even manage to sleep in on my first day of unemployment. I'm just a big, fat failure all around. I turn over on my side and hide under the covers, blocking out the early-morning sun trying to peek through my blinds.

God, I'm thirsty. My mouth feels like I stuffed a hundred cotton balls in it last night. I must have had at least…

Oh God, don't think about it. Don't even say the name in your head, Kiki. Don't you dare…

Tequila, tequila, tequila!

Goddammit. Even my brain has turned against me.

I think I'm going to hurl.

Tequila straight. Tequila and salt. Tequila on the rocks. *Gah!*

I throw back the covers and stumble to my kitchen, which is twelve feet away from my bed in my tiny San Francisco studio apartment. I drink a glass of water and then swallow a couple Tylenol. Well, now that I'm up, I might as well make a quick cup of coffee. I throw in a Keurig pod and the amazing smell of coffee brewing quickly fills the air. I take my coffee and shuffle back to bed. My cat Oreo jumps up next to me and bumps his head against my hand, spilling coffee on my pajama pants.

"Fuck, shit! That's fucking hot! Dang it, Oreo, chill out, dude. I'll feed you in a minute. Give Mommy a break. I'm seriously hungover." I toss a catnip ball off the bed and he immediately chases after it. I sit back against my cloud of pillows and nurse my hangover with my steaming cup of coffee. I open up my phone and scroll through social media. Several pictures of my sister and her Martha Stewart-esque family life fill up my Instagram feed.

I slide through the pictures. No one can be that perfect. She looks like she has her hair and makeup professionally done for every family photo…even the ones of them in their morning, matching plaid pajamas, making pancakes with homemade maple syrup. The caption reads: *Early bird gets the pancake! We even tapped our own maple syrup!*

"Puh-lease, Brooke, we all know the syrup is from Trader Joes—who are you fooling? This is San Francisco, not freaking Vermont," I scoff as I tap the heart under the picture to "like" it.

She's older than me by five years, and it's safe to say we aren't exactly close. She's more concerned with how many likes she gets on her Instagram photos than real-world problems. Don't get me wrong, I love my sister, but there's only so much I can tolerate of her desire to be perfect. I'm closer to my brother Cameron. He's three years older than me and has always treated me like a friend, not a bratty baby sister. I sigh as I heart all the pictures of my nephews like the good sister and auntie I am and continue to scroll down. My finger freezes and my eyes bulge.

Oh no, he didn't. I'm going to kill TJ!

I call his phone as I stare at myself in the image, obviously wasted, holding two margarita glasses up to my mouth while TJ and my other former co-worker Darren twerk on either side of me. Pink liquid is dribbling down my chin and leaving wet stains all over my dress.

Hideous.

I don't remember any of this.

I quickly swipe to favorites and call his number, but get his voicemail. "This is TJ!" he says loudly in a sing-song voice. "Call me maybe!"

"Goddammit, TJ, take that awful photo down! I'm going to keep calling and texting until you wake up! My mom follows me on IG!"

I drown myself in self-pity all over again, remembering why I'm not at work right now, throwing baby carrots at TJ's head. First my disastrous date with Ethan, and then the next morning, I get fired. Karma is a bitch, and I'm wondering what on earth I did to make her take a swing at me.

I can't believe I was fired. Well, technically "let go" for budget reasons. I was at *Cufflinks* magazine for five years as a fashion stylist. When the company got bought a couple months ago by a larger magazine, changes were made and my position was given to the other magazine's stylist. He had tenure, a male's perspective, his thumb up some higher-up's ass… I don't know, the list goes on and on.

Devastated doesn't even cover what I feel. I'm in total shock. It was my first job right out of college and I worked my ass off on the photoshoots, always looking for the hottest trend in men's clothing, working my way up through the ranks. I was damn good at my job, and my boss concurred. But apparently, the mothership company wanted to use their current staff, so my job was eliminated.

TJ cried in the bathroom for an hour after I told him. I ended up being the one to console him that everything would be okay. We left work halfway through the day, because, let's face it, TJ was useless and I was jobless. We decided to drown our sorrows in a little retail therapy before going out. After our dinner at a little Mexican restaurant, the rest was history.

I text TJ.

Me: *Take the photo down, TJ, or I'm going to post the one of you when you had orange perm extensions and brac-es…and I'll even tag my brother on it. I mean business.*

As much as they drive me crazy, I really am going to miss working with TJ, Darren, and the rest of the guys. They met up with us after dinner, against my better judgment, and we partied like it was our job.

Unfortunately for me, the party's over. Now I'm hungover, single, and unemployed.

Chapter 4

Tatum

A WARM BODY presses against my back as I stretch, slowly waking up from her soft snores. I grimace as I glance over my shoulder at the body curled up next to me. *Fuck me.* I have no idea who this chick is. Must be a groupie the guys let crawl into bed with me. The previous evening runs on fast-forward through my brain as I try to recollect what happened once we got back here.

Right, she came in, tried to give me a lap dance, but she was too drunk…or I was too drunk, and then she blew me off before I passed out.

How am I going to get her out of here? I don't want any more blow jobs, and I definitely don't want to return any favors. I mean, I obviously didn't mind it last night. I'm single and a guy, but I never like waking up with a random girl in my bed.

Shit, Savannah is coming over to my suite this morning to sign some papers. I need to get this girl *out* before she sees her. I'm on a tight rope with my ex-girlfriend right now, and the last thing I need is to have her catching me in bed with another girl.

I sit up, trying not to disturb her, because nothing is more awkward than trying to make small talk with some chick the morning after a drunken fuck-fest and you have no clue what her name is. You just want her gone. I hold my head in my hands, trying to put pressure on the raging headache pounding in my brain. My thoughts drift to Savannah.

Since our recent breakup, my relationship with Savannah Edwards has been strained, to put it mildly. We grew apart the last year we were together. Our careers took off, and we went in different directions...literally and figuratively.

A couple months ago, a mutual friend approached me and told me Savannah was sleeping with one of her producers. I confronted her and she denied it vehemently, but the friend was a reliable source, and I knew deep down it was true. Part of me was pissed, but a larger part was relieved to finally have an out of our high-profile relationship.

Our relationship took a further hit after a huge fight a few weeks later. She wanted to move back in and try to work out our issues, but our problems were beyond fixing at that point. That night, I went out and partied with the band and ended up in bed with two random fangirls. Savannah came by the next morning to hash it out again and walked in to find them tangled in my sheets. She went apeshit, and I had to have my bodyguard escort her out. Wasn't exactly a high point for me, but technically, we *were* broken up.

I thought at that point we were officially over, but our publicists begged her to "stay" with me until after the

American Country Music Awards, once our tours were in full swing. No one wanted to see the "hottest couple of country" not make it, especially before we were supposed to sing a duet together on the ACMs.

That was four months ago.

We're on speaking terms, but barely. Our relationship is awkward and complicated at best. She could win an Oscar for her duplicitous personality as the Ice Princess and America's Country Sweetheart. Pretending for the audience that we're desperately in love is causing a lot of stress on me. Thus, the all-night bender and nameless girl currently in my bed. I groan as I slide my hands down my face, trying to rub the memories away.

I quickly slide out of bed and pull on my boxer briefs. I look over my shoulder, but the blonde is still passed out. I throw on a T-shirt and jeans and grab my cell phone, quickly moving across the suite to the adjoining room. I stop short, turn around, and quickly snatch her phone off the nightstand. I'll have Lee or Jimmy remove any pictures she might have taken last night.

I open the door quietly and sigh in relief when I see my bodyguard and my assistant having their morning coffee in my living room suite.

"Uh, hey, Brad. Morning, Jimmy. Um, I kind of have a girl in my bed who needs to be removed."

Jimmy arches an eyebrow and smirks. "Kind of?"

I grin sheepishly. "Uh, yeah, okay, there's definitely a girl in my bed who needs to be nicely removed before Savannah gets here. Maybe we can give her VIP tickets to the next show or something."

"Or something," Brad mutters as he hauls his hulking body toward my bedroom door. "I'll take care of it, boss."

I reach for the coffee carafe. "Thanks, man. I'll get you VIP passes too." I wink at him.

Jimmy chokes out a laugh as Brad grimaces at me. Brad is *not* a fan of country music. I'm not sure he's really a fan of anything.

"Don't do me any favors," he grumbles as he heads into my room.

I hand Jimmy the girl's cell. "Make sure you guys get the password to her phone when she's up. I don't need any pictures in the press."

"Ten-four."

I shoot back some aspirin with a bottle of water while I read the paper. Jimmy follows Brad into the adjoining room. The main door to the suite opens as my manager and good friend Lee strides in.

"What's going on, Lee, my man?"

Lee is not just my manager. He's also my babysitter, my wingman, and my coach. If shit is going bad, without a doubt, I'd call Lee. If the world is my oyster, this guy's shelling it for me.

"I just got a call—we're at number one on the charts this weekend." He pumps his fist in to the air.

"What? That's incredible!"

"You guys are on fire! Next week is the ACMs, where you'll be performing the new song with Savannah. Then we go on tour, man! I see Entertainer of the Year in your near future." He grabs a cup of coffee and sits down on the couch, and we fist bump.

"That's so awesome, man, just awesome. I think you're right. We've got this in the bag."

"*You've* got it in the bag. You've earned it, Tatum. Just don't screw it up." Lee looks up as Brad enters the room with the disheveled blonde. His jaw slackens. "And for God's sake, keep it in your pants if you can until we go out on tour. We don't need any more shit from Savannah's camp." He shakes his head as Brad and Jimmy escort the girl out.

The blonde spots me and frantically starts to wave around Brad's bulky body. "Call me, Tatum! Can we have a picture together? I love you. Last night was unbelievable!"

Brad ushers her out with Jimmy assuring her that I will.

"Yeah, I don't even know what that was about." I wave a hand, dismissing the girl. "This whole Savannah thing has got my balls in a knot."

Lee smirks and shifts in his seat. "Entertainer of the Year, my friend. Keep it in your pants. We don't need the wicked witch of country ruining it all."

"That's my sole focus, Lee. I got it. I haven't worked this hard for it to all go to shit."

Chapter 5

Kiki

"KINKY, IT COULDN'T have been that bad. You're being *so* extra." TJ ignores my death stare as he puts a packet of Splenda in his coffee.

I continue to scowl as I pull my laptop out of my bag and plunk it on the coffee table. I don't know what I was thinking, letting little Ms. Matchmaker across from me set me up on yet another disastrous date.

"Will you stop calling me 'Kinky'? You owe me way more than a latte, by the way. It was up there with worst date in history. Not as bad as Ethan, but definitely a close second. And can I just say out loud—put it out there into the universe—that you are never, *ever* allowed to set me up on another date ever again."

"*Pfft*, you're so dramatic."

"Well, that's calling the kettle black, Mr. Pot." I sign in to the coffee shop Wi-Fi and wait for the computer to sync.

"I'll help you today on one condition. I want a play-by-play of your date last night."

19

I roll my eyes. "If I tell you, will you shut up so we can do some job searches?"

He claps giddily as he boots up his laptop. "Darren said he was a nice guy."

"Darren thinks everyone is nice."

"Okay, spill the rice."

"It's beans. Spill the beans."

"Whatevs. I think I've already aged about forty years waiting for this story."

I sigh. "So he picks me up, and he's a cute guy. Tall, brown hair, brown eyes. Plaid button-down and khakis."

"So in other words, bland and possibly a virgin," TJ interrupts.

I shrug. "I mean…just a normal guy. He didn't sweep me off my feet, but he was friendly."

TJ huffs and motions for me to speed up the story.

"Okay, so we get into his super-clean, black Mercedes Benz."

"Nice! The virgin yuppie has a sweet ride."

"Er, yeah. So we decide to go to an Indian restaurant over off of Hollister. But he turns to me as we're chatting about the weather and tells me he has to make a stop first."

"Uh-oh."

"I try to play it off as cool, like, 'okay, don't freak out, Kiki,' but I've got 9-1-1 cued up on my phone just in case."

"Good call, and you remembered to charge your phone this time, right?"

"Yes. So we pull up to this house and this couple comes out and gets in and gives him an address to a bar."

TJ spits coffee all over his computer. "*No*, he didn't!"

"Yes, he did. He was Uber-driving during our date." I sigh as I drink my latte.

TJ is shaking from laughing so hard he has a hard time wiping up the coffee. "Wha—Ah God, sorry, what did you do?"

"What could I do? I was furious, and the couple in the back kept asking us like a hundred questions, because they've never had a couple drive Uber before. It was so awkward!"

"Did your date think it was weird?"

"No! He answered their questions as if we were an actual Uber couple!"

"Did you go to the restaurant after that?"

"No! Another ride popped up on his app and apparently it was a 'really good fare' and he just had to take it. It was a mom and two bratty kids whining about going to a birthday party at the roller-skate rink. I finally asked him to take me home, and you know what he had the nerve to say?"

"What?" TJ whispers excitedly over his laptop.

"He said, 'I'm going to have to charge you since you're forfeiting our date!' First of all, who says forfeit like we're competing in *The Amazing Race*? I said 'forget it,' and got out of the car at the skate rink and called another driver to get back home."

"No! Did you at least get your skate on?"

I roll my eyes. "You are *not* allowed to set me up on any more blind dates. *Ever*. In fact, I'm done dating. I'm just going to become a nun."

"I can't believe he took you on his Uber runs." TJ wipes tears from under his eyes.

"Almost worse than my date with Ethan. Almost. Never

again. I'm never letting you set me up on a blind date again."

"You've said that three times now."

I throw a piece of blueberry muffin at him. "Well, this time I mean it."

"Ah, I'm sorry, but I wish you would give it another go. It's such good entertainment for me."

I purse my lips at him. I'd had a handful of boyfriends after college, but I never felt a serious connection with any of them. I've had a hard time finding the one that makes my heart beat faster. At this point, it seems like I'll never find him.

"Okay, so enough about bland Uber boy and my non-existent dating life. Since you offered to help, what have you found for me on the job front?"

TJ sinks back into his chair. "Well, Thomas from shoes said Bloomies is hiring."

"For a personal shopper position?" I brighten up. "I could handle that!"

"No, for the shoe department stockroom."

I completely deflate. "This is hopeless."

"Dress Warehouse is hiring off El Camino."

I give TJ a shady eye glare. "I am not going from a stylist position to working at Dress Warehouse."

"I mean, muumuus could be coming back in to style…"

"So are onesies. Doesn't mean you should wear them."

"Good point. Ooh! You could get me some jazzy free socks if you worked there."

"Socks? Why on earth would you need a bargain bag of socks… Ew, no, never mind. Don't answer that."

"Kinky, that's sweat socks, and that was *so* high school

ago. People like my fashion-forward colorful sock choices. I can't help it that I'm a sock rock star."

"And by people, you mean…"

TJ ignores me as he picks up a pen. "Okay, so we'll put Dress Warehouse down as possibility numero uno." He writes it down in all caps and underlines it three times at the top of a tablet.

"Somehow I feel like you are secretly enjoying this."

"That hurts, Kinky!" He wipes a non-existent tear from under his eye. "I am Patrick to your SpongeBob, Laverne to your Shirley, Monica to your Rachel." He takes a deep breath and leans across the table and whispers loudly, "*I am Gayle to your Oprah*, and don't you forget it, sister."

"Oh geez, okay, I got it. I'm sorry, I'm just cranky."

"Apology accepted. So did you apply to other magazines?"

I take a sip of my coffee. "I applied, but most of them are based down in LA and so far, I haven't gotten a response from any of them," I say glumly. "It's hopeless, TJ. I'm going to be a nun working at Dress Warehouse."

"That does sound pretty tragic." He at least has the decency to sound sad. "You can always become an Uber driver."

I lovingly kick him under the table and wonder what the heck I'm going to do with my life. I'm twenty-six, single, and jobless—with no prospects in either department. Even though I got a severance package, my bank account is dwindling and soon, I'll be homeless too.

Talk about depressing.

Chapter 6

Kiki

"Kiki, what are you doing?"

I groggily roll over on my back, falling off the couch. I quickly sit up and wipe the drool off my cheek.

"Sleeping. What does it look like, Brooke? How the heck did you get in my apartment, anyway?"

"Was that drool you just wiped on your sleeve? That's disgusting."

"How did you get in? The door was locked." I glare at my sister as I fix my wild hair and lounge back down on the couch.

"Um, remember, you gave me a key?" She stands in front of me, her arms crossed, tapping her foot.

"Yeah, but you've never used it before. Where are the boys?"

"With Mother. She sent me over here to check on you."

I groan. "I'm fine. Just tired."

"Uh-huh. Well, you've been sleeping for two weeks now." She looks around my apartment. "Is that your *bed* in the corner? Ugh, this is so…utilitarian." Disgust drips off the last word.

"Well, that's what a studio is—one room." I wave my hand around my palatial palace like a *Price is Right* model.

She nudges my knee with her hand, indicating she wants to sit down. The last thing I want right now is to hear how perfectly Brooke's life is going. I refuse to move my legs, much less sit up, which makes my sister huff as she sits down in the opposite chair. She's perfectly dressed in size-zero white skinny jeans with a taupe cashmere sweater and matching suede booties. Even her Birkin is taupe. Her long, blonde hair is perfectly curled, her makeup flawless. She even smells expensive.

Ugh, I hate how perfect she is. I feel ratty next to her with my disheveled hair and sweats I've slept in for three days straight.

She frowns at me. "You're such a spoiled brat, do you know that?"

"Wow, first you barge into my apartment, waking me up from a nice nap, and then you call me a brat? I'm waiting with bated breath to hear what you're going to say next."

Brooke huffs as she looks at her manicured nails. She takes her phone out and starts typing. "Don't be such an asshole, Kiki. Mom and Dad are worried about you, and I'm here to offer you a proposition and ease their anxiety. I need a nanny, and since you're out of a job, I figured…" She shrugs.

"Um, why do you need a nanny? You're a stay-at-home mom."

"Well, Kiki, some of us have lives, you know."

I roll my eyes.

"I have tennis club, book club, and my weekly girls' night out. I need someone to shuttle the boys to their after-school activities, someone to do laundry and walk Bailey..."

I hold up my hand as I sit up. "Whoa, whoa, wait a minute. So you not only want me to drive the boys all over town, but you want me to be your maid and dog-walker?"

Brooke looks up from her phone and shrugs. "Hello, isn't that what I just said? You need money, I need the help, it's a win-win! And we have a maid, Kiki. Geez, like I wouldn't." She continues tapping away on her phone, completely oblivious to my mouth hanging open. "You'd just be helping her. Oh! And one more thing. Can we not mention to my friends that you're my sister? Let's just keep that between us. Do you speak French? Of course you do, you're in fashion. I'll need you to speak to me only in French when we're around them. Charlotte is going to be so jelly!" Brooke squeals and claps her hands.

I sit up straighter and tuck my legs under myself. "Hold up. Before you start spreading the news, I need some clarification. What makes you think I want to be your nanny? I'm in the fashion industry. I have a degree from the Art Institute of San Francisco in fashion design. I don't even think I like kids."

"Kiki, don't be so dramatic. Mom thinks—"

I groan. "Oh, now I get it. Mom put you up to this. Fuck me."

"Kiki, don't be so vulgar, it's not very ladylike. Mom may have mentioned it and I hated the idea at first, because I didn't want you influencing the boys in the wrong way, but then I thought, well, my poor little sister is down on her luck, and as a Christian I need to help those who are more unfortunate than me."

"I'm not unfortunate," I mumble, picking lint off my throw pillow, as she talks over me.

"And furthermore, you can be my personal shopper, which would save me a lot of time. That way you can still do that cute little fashion thing you like."

I close my eyes and count to ten, as I start to defend my "cute little fashion" career, but she cuts me off by pulling a black leather-bound binder out of her Birkin.

"Here's my list of dos and don'ts Graham and I put together. Oh, and here's your schedule." She hands me the binder.

I want to protest immediately and throw it back at her, but curiosity has me opening up the cover. The first page is a glossy eight-by-ten photograph of Brooke and Graham hugging each of the boys with the title, *Loving, Living, Life with the Parkers.* The second page is a non-disclosure agreement.

"Seriously? An NDA? Why? It's not like you guys are famous."

She sniffs haughtily. "Just read it and sign it, Kiki. You can never be too careful. Graham has a lot of prestigious clients at the law firm."

"Graham's a douchebag," I say under my breath. Brooke ignores me as she rifles through her bag for a pen.

The third page is a list of *please dos* and *don'ts* with a creepy picture of Brooke holding up her index finger.

Please call us Mr. and Mrs. Parker.

Please wear your uniform, pressed and cleaned, daily.

Please clean and pick up after the boys.

Please only buy fresh organics from Whole Foods.

Please have my tennis uniform pressed every morning by 6:30.

I turn the page.

Don't leave fingerprints on any of the stainless-steel kitchen appliances.

Don't forget to wash your hands every thirty minutes.

Don't park your car in the driveway. Please park it at the park and walk to the house. (This is approximately two miles away.)

Don't enter the house without putting scrubs over your shoes.

Don't make eye contact unless spoken to.

Don't forget my morning lattes at approximately 6:35 a.m.

Don't read my magazines, mail, or look at our family pictures.

Don't enter my bedroom unless you're putting away my laundry, and then you must ask permission.

The list continues and I'm so nauseated, my eyes start to glaze over. Is this for real? Am I being *Punk'd* right now?

I look around, waiting for my brother, TJ, or Ashton Kutcher to jump out. Nothing but my evil, Burberry-clad sister applying lip gloss across from me. Even though I'm totally disgusted by this book, curiosity has me flipping to the next page, which is the itinerary.

Please arrive at approximately 5:45 a.m. (Don't forget the scrubs on your shoes!)

5:50: Make organic lunches for all three boys.

Does she have another child I'm not aware of? Oh wait, she means the boys and Graham. Over my dead body will I be making that asswipe lunch.

6:05: Walk Bailey down to the park and back.

6:25: Wake the boys up and make sure they brush their teeth and get dressed.

6:35: Please gently tap on the door to let me know my latte and pressed tennis ensemble are ready.

6:45: Feed boys breakfast. (Organic free-range eggs and organic turkey bacon with homemade French toast drizzled with organic maple syrup)

7:00: Drive boys to school.

I look up at Brooke, who is engrossed with something on her phone. Her best friend Charlotte probably got another lip injection or some other earth-shattering event.

"I'm sorry, but what on earth are shoe scrubs? And how the hell am I supposed to walk the dog a total of four miles in twenty minutes?"

Brooke sniffs. "Shoe scrubs are paper shoes you put on over your shoes so as not to bring in dirt and germs. And Kiki, twenty minutes is adequate time to walk Bailey to the park. If you find that you are lacking in time, then you must take her for a jog. Geez, when did you get so lazy?"

"What's this about no eye contact? I'm your fucking sister, for God's sake!" I ignore her lazy comment as I skim her dos and don'ts list again.

"Language, Kiki, seriously. You can't speak like that in my house. God forbid around my children! And the no-eye-contact rule is just to keep employer-employee boundaries. I mean, *obviously* this was written for employees we don't know. I'm sure we can make some exceptions with you— Agh! What is that?"

Oreo jumps up on the couch and starts kneading my leg. "Um, it's my cat, Oreo, remember?"

"That's not a cat. That thing is bigger than Charlotte's teacup Yorkie! Ugh, gross. I hate cats. I'll make sure to have a roller brush on hand before you enter the house. Graham is allergic." She sniffs as she reaches into her purse for a tissue. "Hee-choo! Oh great, I must be too. Hee-choo!"

Her sneezes sound like a high-pitched hiccup. We grew up with our cat Mittens, so I know for a fact she's not allergic. I side-eye her as I toss the book on my coffee table. I've had enough and I want her out. How on earth am I even related to this person? I would never treat another human being the way she's proposing to treat me—her sister!

"Okay, well, thanks for checking in. I, um, I'll think about your proposal."

Right after I throw it in a dumpster.

Brooke stands and grabs her bag. "Well, don't think too long. I have a waiting list of applicants who would *die* to be in your position."

"I'm sure you do," I say drolly. I eye her as she heads to the door and sneezes one more time for good measure. "Oh, I almost forgot. What would the pay be?"

"Well, I wouldn't pay you as much as I would a domestic because you *are* family, but I think eight dollars an hour would be more than sufficient. *Hee-choo!* Or you could move into our guest room and that would be your pay. Then you could get rid of this dump. Oh, but *sans* cat, obviously."

I almost choke on my water. No way in hell would I move in with Graham and my sister.

"Right, how could I pass that up?" I mumble sarcastically.

"Exactly! Oh, it'll be so fun. You can sit with me while I get my nails and hair done, and I'll let you hang out at another table while my girlfriends and I have lunch. It'll be just like old times," she gushes. "I mean, after you complete your chores, of course."

"Right." *When did we ever hang out?* The answer is never. Cam and I always joke that my parents adopted her and then they had us. She's blonde while we both have dark chestnut hair. She's stick-skinny, while I have curves. She's married to an asshole, uppity lawyer, while I am not.

"Okeedoke, well, I'll let you know. Byee." I give her a fake smile as I stand up.

"Tomorrow, eight a.m. sharp! Hee-choo. Ugh, you need to bathe that thing or get rid of it." She's out the door without a kiss or a hug before I can blink.

I sit back down and glare at the big binder of suck on my coffee table while I absentmindedly rub behind Oreo's ear.

"I'd never get rid of you, Oreo, my handsome boy. Don't you listen to that mean, old, wicked, Martha-Stewart-wannabe witch."

Oreo meows in agreement as he stretches out on the back of my couch.

Chapter 7

Tatum

"GODDAMN, TATUM, IS it so hard to hit that note? Do we need to prerecord this?" Savannah slams down her microphone.

"No, Savannah, I'm just tired. I'll get it."

"Maybe if you weren't banging every girl in sight every night, you wouldn't be so tired," she says snidely.

I stop in my tracks and whirl around on her. She's standing with her fists on her hips, a sneer on her lips after her malicious remark. I've been rehearsing our duet for the ACMs all afternoon with her, and I'm exhausted. Her attitude is the last thing I need right now. I walk slowly toward her, glancing to my right and left to see if anyone is eavesdropping. I get within a foot of her.

"You and me? We're over," I whisper fiercely. "That was *your* doing. So who I see and who I bang is none of your damn concern. Now, I'm a little under the weather today, so I'm going to take my tired ass home and sleep. I will hit that note—don't worry your pretty little tits about that. And keep your mouth shut about us until after the ACMs, and everyone in both our camps will be happy. Think you can manage that, Vanny?"

"Don't be such an arrogant asshole, Tate. I know what I have to do," she huffs as she sashays away to her personal assistant and throws her microphone at the tech guy.

I watch her retreat and reflect on how it went so wrong. Savannah Edwards is gorgeous, in a plastic too-much-makeup, Barbie-doll kind of way, but damn if she isn't a piece of work. We met at a label party featuring up-and-coming new artists about three years ago. There was an immediate physical attraction, but not much of an emotional one. We respected each other professionally and sounded good together. We had budding careers in common, and when our stars both started to rise, the media and fans went nuts over our relationship. The label encouraged our relationship—even forcing us to go public. We were lovingly called "Vanum" by the press.

I hated all the attention, the nickname, the constant barrage of paparazzi, but Savannah ate it up. With mounting pressure from the press and the label, Savannah constantly nagged me to take the relationship further by moving in together. I relented and after that, things started to go downhill. We toured separately and rarely saw each other. Award shows seemed to be the only time we spent together as we walked the red carpet. That's when the rumors started floating around that she was sleeping with the record producer.

"Tatum, I need to do a fitting for the show," says Jess, my wardrobe assistant.

"Not now, Jess. I think I have the flu."

"But, Tatum, I'm down a person. I need to get this done sooner than later."

"Talk to Lee. I'll stop by the studios tomorrow. I just can't right now." I ignore her and slam out the studio door to head back to my house. I can't wait for all this Savannah bullshit to go away once and for all.

Just have to get through the ACMs—and I'm done.

Chapter 8

Kiki

"OH MY GOD, no!" TJ bites his knuckles as he continues to read. *"Do: fold his boxers into a perfect square after ironing them. Is this forizzle?"*

I grimace as TJ reads another line from the black binder of bullshit. "I would shoot myself if I ever had to touch Graham's underwear." I shiver in disgust.

"Do: disinfect our toothbrushes every morning for approximately ten minutes." TJ looks up at me, trying desperately not to crack up. "So, are you supposed to do that after you iron her tennis outfit or before you make the boys French toast from Paris in between your four-mile jog with the dog?" He snorts at his own joke.

"Seriously, it's totally ridiculous. I'm thinking about showing it to my mom so she can see how mental Brooke is. Who asks someone to disinfect someone else's toothbrush?"

"Um, the more suitable question is, who asks to have their underwear ironed and folded into a perfect square?" A knock on my door has TJ throwing the book on the table like it's on fire.

I laugh. "It's not Brooke, goof. It's Cam. Will you let him in?"

"Oh my God, Cameron's here? Why didn't you tell me he was coming over? Do I look okay?" He quickly runs his fingers through his hair and down his chest. I roll my eyes.

TJ's been crushing on my brother since the first time he met him at a family dinner four years ago. It's a very one-sided crush since Cameron is straight, but I don't have the heart to destroy TJ's fantasies.

"You look fine. You know, if you're trying to go for the whole Ronald McDonald thing." I wave my hand around my head and smirk.

"What!" TJ shrieks as he runs for a mirror. I love giving him shit over his strawberry-blond hair. He's terrified of looking like a carrot top or having Ronald McDonald hair. He's actually the hottest ginger I've ever met, but I'll never give him the satisfaction of revealing that little nugget.

I open the door to my smiling brother.

"Hey sis, I see you're still living in this rat trap."

TJ sighs as Cameron waves at him.

"Hey TJ, how's it hanging, man?"

TJ squeaks and spins in a circle as he runs into my bathroom.

"Uh…that was weird. Is he all right?" Cameron gives me a hug.

I laugh. "Yeah, I just gave him a wedgie. He'll be fine."

Cameron chuckles. "You two have an odd friendship." He flashes me a brilliant smile as he reaches into my fridge and extracts a beer, then settles on the couch. TJ walks quickly out of my bathroom and huffs, glaring at me as he sits on the couch next to Cam.

"I'm better now."

"Well, thank God. *Drama.*" I smack him on the head. He quickly smooths his perfectly coiffed hair while giving me the evil eye.

"All right, Kiki, what's the big emergency? Why am I stopping by to check on you instead of going on a hot date tonight?"

"Ooh, a hot date? Do tell! You do smell delicious." TJ leans in, sniffing Cameron's shirt.

Cam looks up at me and cuts his eyes towards TJ as he shifts a little away from him.

"TJ, quit hitting on my brother and grab the black binder Brooke brought over."

His face lights up as he grabs the book and sits back down on the couch next to Cameron, showing him the tabbed chapters of the binder.

Yes, chapters.

"What the fuck is this?"

I lean against my kitchen bar. "My next job. Brooke wants me to nanny for her and that's her binder describing all of my duties. Oh, and she's graciously paying me eight dollars an hour, or I can move in with them."

"The fuck it is." Cam looks through the pages. "You are not going to be her nanny. That dickweed Graham probably typed this up."

"Did you know he folds his underwear into a perfect square? There's even a diagram with pictures," TJ whispers dramatically as he tabs to that particular chapter.

Cam smirks as he skims over the pages. "Not surprised. This is so fucked up. Is this for real? Does Mom know about this?"

I nod solemnly. "It was her idea. Can you help me, Cam? Please? Don't you know of anyone who needs a fashion consultant? A blogger? Anything besides this? I'll even bartend at your place with that skeezy Charles if it could get me out of this."

My brother, the brilliant entrepreneur of the family, owns three upscale bars in San Francisco, Chicago, and Los Angeles. Charles manages the San Francisco bar. He hits on everything that walks with boobs—including his boss's little sister—and it makes my skin crawl. But, desperate times call for desperate measures, and I'll do anything to get out of the proverbial noose Brooke has wrapped around my neck. At this point, I may even have to apply for that position at Dress Warehouse. I shudder at the thought.

Cam looks up from the binder. "Just tell her no. What's the big deal?"

"I tried. Mom and Dad are fully on board, supporting Brooke, and I don't have any other prospects. I'm going to have to move in with Mom and Dad soon if I don't find something."

"Ugh, Kiki, I don't know." He starts flipping through his contacts on his phone. TJ scoots closer to him on the couch and gazes longingly at him.

"Did you get a haircut?"

"No." My brother continues to scroll without looking up.

"You look tense. Would you like me to massage those

muscular shoulders?"

"No."

"If you want to come by my place I could totally style you for your date."

"No."

"Well, when you're ready..."

"Wait a minute," Cam says, and TJ sits up excitedly as my brother leans forward. "My friend Lee might know of someone. He's a manager for a country singer."

"Ugh, country music? Their fashion taste isn't exactly what I was going for. Lots of bedazzled fringe jean jackets."

"And cowboy boots and bad makeup," TJ adds as he sashays to the kitchen. "But I do love me some Dolly."

"Exactly."

Cam sighs. "Do you want my help or not?"

"Yes, yes, sorry! Whatever it is, I'll take it."

"Okay, let me make some calls. In the meantime, burn this shit." He chucks the binder into my kitchen garbage and TJ swoons dramatically against the fridge.

Chapter 9

Kiki

"OREO, WE'RE NOT in Kansas anymore," I whisper to my frazzled cat, who's meowing loudly in his cat carrier. From my window I see a funny building with two towers—it looks like Batman. Nashville is bigger than I expected, and really humid! My hair isn't used to it and it's frizzing out in protest.

I read a little about my new home in a magazine on the five-hour plane ride. Nashville, Music City USA, is the heart of country music, showcasing musicians at places like the Grand Ole Opry and the Ryman Auditorium, which is housed in a retro, old, red-brick church. They even have a replica of the Parthenon in Greece, which is crazy-cool. Batman buildings and humidity aside, I can't wait to check out all there is to do in the city. I am really nervous, but excited at the same time for something new.

The Uber driver pulls up to my new apartment in downtown Nashville and helps me unload my luggage on the sidewalk. People are walking everywhere and restaurants and bars are flashing neon signs declaring "Good Eats Here." Alone on the sidewalk I'm suddenly feeling overwhelmed and unsure if I made the right choice to move here. I don't know anyone, and the crowded sidewalk isn't helping my sudden anxiety. With that bleak thought, I drag my luggage and Oreo's carrier into the modest-sized lobby, take the elevator up to the sixth floor, and unlock the door to my new place.

Wow, I expected mediocre like the lobby, but this place is posh and looks brand-spanking new. I wander through the apartment in complete awe. This apartment is four times the size of my old studio. Granite countertops in the kitchen, new appliances, an open floor plan that opens up to the living room, and there's a fireplace. Oh my God, this makes my studio look like a cardboard box. Floor-to-ceiling windows span one of the living room walls and opens to a small patio. There's even a litter box and Oreo's food set up in a little hideaway cabinet in the spacious bathroom. I let Oreo out of his carrier and immediately call Cameron.

"Hey Kiki, how's Nashville?"

"This place is freaking amazing! Did you have a hand in this? Because this definitely is not in my pay grade."

"I may have helped a little. I asked Lee's assistant to get everything ready for you. The cabinets and fridge should be fully stocked."

"Cam, you've done enough!" I groan. "You did *not* have to do this."

"Yeah, well, while you're on tour, I thought about staying at your place and checking out Nashville for a new location for one of my bars. I'm thinking of selling the

Chicago and Los Angeles locations."

"Wow, seriously? That's awesome! This is perfect—we're going to be roomies!" I squeal.

"Not quite." He chuckles. "Remember, you're going to be on the road for the next couple of months."

"Oh right, how quickly I forget," I deadpan.

Cameron's friend Lee is the manager to a big-time country music singer named Tatum Reed. I've heard of him, but not being a big fan of country music, I don't know any of his music. I've vaguely heard of his girlfriend Savannah Edwards, who's starting to cross over from country to pop, but that's the extent of my knowledge. Anyway, Tatum's fashion designer for his tour needs an assistant and so, here I am! It's shit pay and I'm like the assistant to the assistant to the band, but it's a job, and a chance to get my foot back in the fashion door. Plus—and this is the best reason—I am *far away* from Brooke.

She's furious with me that I turned down her nanny position. She refused to go to the farewell dinner my parents had for me. My mom shared with me that she had told all her friends she was hiring this amazing French nanny and now she has egg on her face. Since I don't speak French, she would have looked like an ass regardless.

"Well, Cam, I can't thank you enough for all your help. I'll call you after I get settled in at the new job."

"All right. Be careful out on the road, Kiki. And call me if you need anything, okay?"

"K, love you."

I call Lee next to let him know I arrived and to find out my schedule. After I get off the phone with him, I dance around the kitchen. This is the real deal. I'm officially living in Nashville and going on tour with Tatum Reed. *Holy shit!* Maybe this is meant to be.

I giddily slide across the wood floors in my socks to look out the windows. The sunset over the city landscape is glorious. Gone are the nerves from just fifteen minutes ago. For the first time in a long time, I feel so happy and sure of myself.

This job is going to change my life.

Chapter 10

Kiki

GOD, *THIS JOB sucks.*

It's only been a week, but I'm pretty much a glorified delivery girl. I'm the assistant to Jess, Tatum Reed's fashion stylist advisor, and help his PA Jimmy. Pretty much I'm a paid intern, which is kind of insulting since I paid my intern dues back in college. But I have to keep reminding myself it's a job. A job that I need so I can stay current on fashion trends and get my foot back in the door. Let's face it, no one wants to hire a has-been stylist who sleeps on her parents' couch with no job prospects. Who knows what opportunities might open from this?

Jess doesn't like me very much, from what I can tell. I overheard her telling the receptionist at the label that Lee hired me as a favor to my brother. She didn't need an assistant, nor does she want one. As far as she's concerned, I'm just taking up space. I need to prove I belong here, and I'm not just someone's coffee-and-sandwich bitch.

"What are you doing, Mackenzie?"

Ugh, that's another thing I hate. Jess keeps insisting on calling me Mackenzie, my given name, even though I've been known as Kiki my whole life. It irritates the hell out of me. I've asked her to call me Kiki several times, but she just ignores me.

And let's be honest, I'm a little scared of her.

"I'm hemming these pants like you asked me to."

She strides over to my sewing machine and puts her hand on her wide hip. "That should have been done already. I'm jonesing for a latte. Please go to the coffee shop on Broadway and pick one up for me. See if anyone else needs one too. Chop-chop!" She claps her hands in my face, causing me to jump. She grabs the pants I'm working on. "Give me those. I would've had them finished hours ago."

"Then maybe you should have done it yourself," I say under my breath as I grab my raincoat and purse.

"What was that?" She gives me the stink eye.

"Oh! Just saying how much I love lattes!" I say breezily as I quickly exit. I make sure the company credit card is in my wallet. At least that's one perk—free coffee.

SO, HERE I am again, walking around Nashville with about sixteen drink orders spilling over onto my white tank, sweating like a pig because although it's April, it's an unseasonably warm spring and it's drizzling. My pale-pink rain jacket that felt cozy this morning now feels like I'm wearing a straitjacket in a sauna. I carefully balance the trays of coffee as I reach for the studio doors, when they suddenly bang open, causing me to jump back.

"Watch out!" I cry as hot coffee splashes over my hand, burning like hell. I almost drop the trays and start cursing the idiot who's not looking at where he's going.

"Sorry." The guy doesn't even glance up from his phone, much less hold the door for me as he brushes by. It starts to swing back in as I turn sideways to catch it with my elbow, hot coffee sloshing everywhere.

"Shit!"

Suddenly the door stops and is held open by someone from behind me. I glance over my shoulder and smile in appreciation, but my smile freezes because I'm suddenly captivated by the most gorgeous green eyes I have ever seen.

"Th-thanks." I swallow and move through the open door.

"No problem. Looks like you have a little coffee on you. Um, do you need help?" he whispers as he holds the phone he's talking into away from his ear. He looks me up and down with an adorable dimpled smile. Straight white teeth compete with his perfect, pink lips. His dimples rival those of Josh Holloway's. His dirty-blond hair curls up under the edges of a baseball hat. I don't usually go for blonds, but goodness gracious, this one is to die for.

"No, I'm good, thanks!" I gush gratefully at him. He winks at me as he walks toward the bank of elevators, continuing his conversation on the phone.

The blast of sudden air conditioning makes me shiver. I stand staring at the retreating figure of Mr. Gorgeous Green Eyes. He is tall and well-built with muscular broad shoulders that taper down to a trim waist. Worn Levi's mold to his perfect ass, making me want to sneak a pinch like a pervy old lady. His soft-cotton, army-green T-shirt shows off well-defined tan arms and clings to his body perfectly. I could imagine those arms holding me tight. I could imagine those arms doing much more. I want to squeeze those biceps.

Just once.

I'm still standing by the door lost in my porno day-dream, ogling him like an idiot, when he looks over his shoulder at me and gestures to the open elevator. I shake my head no quickly, because there is no way in hell I could ride up in an elevator alone with him. I would melt down the side of the wall onto the floor.

Chicken? *Totally.*

He flashes another killer smile and winks. He looks so familiar to me, like *The Fast and the Furious* actor, but before I can place him, he gets onto the elevator and then he's gone.

Pretty sure my mouth is hanging open. And what was it he said? I have coffee on me? I look down to see that the front of my white tank and jacket is soaked in coffee, my jeans have coffee on them and even my white Chucks have coffee splatters. I might as well have bathed in it. *Fuckin' A.* Seriously? I meet the man who's going to have my babies someday, and I'm covered in coffee?

So humiliating.

I rush over to the bank of elevators and push the up button. I look at my reflection in the gold, mirrored doors and cringe. I'm sweaty, grungy, and my cute French braid from this morning has frizzled out.

"Oh God," I whisper to myself as I notice my mascara

has melted away giving me smudged, little raccoon eyes. I sigh heavily as I step inside the crowded elevator to make my deliveries. I drop my first tray of coffees off at the production management's floor and then head on up to the studios, where I distribute two more trays. Fortunately everyone lets me know I have coffee all over myself, as if I wasn't aware.

Finally, I get to the wardrobe department and find Jess hanging clothes.

"Mackenzie, where the hell have you been? And oh my God, what happened to you?"

"I got coffee like you asked. Had a little accident. Sorry, your grande latte is now a tall."

I'm not sorry.

"Ugh, figures. You just missed Tatum Reed. He came in for some measurements and has lost some weight, so we need to take in a few things." She dumps a pile of clothes on my chair. "I need these done before we leave for Vegas tomorrow."

I eyeball the pile of clothes that would normally take me about four days to alter, but I just nod because I need this job, and I can't let my brother down. I'll just have to take it home with me and work on it while I watch something mindless like *The Bachelor*.

"Hey, Jess, I just saw the hottest guy downstairs. If Paul Walker had an identical twin, I swear it would be him. Do you know—"

"Mackenzie, seriously, I don't have time for this. Just get your work done. I have to go pick up Tatum's suit. And don't forget, we leave at seven a.m. sharp for the ACMs in Vegas. I'll have a car pick you up and take you to the airport."

"Got it." I nod, suddenly very homesick for TJ. "I'm just going to head on out, then, and take this stuff with me. Unless you want me to go run errands with you?" I ask with a tiny note of desperation in my voice. A little shopping therapy with a friend would make me feel less homesick...even if it were with just Jess, who's more like a frenemy. If that.

"No, I'd rather you take in the clothes. Mackenzie, don't let anything happen to them or it's on your dime. Got it?"

"Got it." I'll have to make sure Oreo doesn't go anywhere near this stuff.

I call TJ on my way home.

"It's five o'clock somewhere!" his obnoxious new recording chirps.

"It's three o'clock where you are, slut. Call me back. I really miss you." I hang up and daydream about the cute guy with green eyes as I trudge home.

Chapter 11

Tatum

VEGAS.

The up-all-night, bells-ringing, girls-drinking, partying, crazy-shit-happens kind of city.

I hate it.

Don't get me wrong, I have some very fond memories of times in Vegas with my friends, but it truly is the city that never sleeps, and it gets old after a while.

Because you don't fall asleep in Vegas—you pass out.

My band guys are itching to gamble and party after the awards show tonight, but I have a feeling I'm just going to want a quiet place to drink. Savannah and I are about to walk the red carpet and pretend like we're the happy "it" couple. Then there's the performance. I'm nervous and irritable. Savannah can be unpredictable, and I want tonight to be over and done with.

I finish getting dressed in a black Armani suit that fits me like a glove when a knock at my suite door signals Jess and Sarah, the hair-and-makeup stylist, have arrived.

"I need help with my tie," I say to Jess as she enters with Sarah.

"Sure, no problem." She reaches up and begins to work on the tie. "I have my assistant at the MGM getting your outfit ready for the performance."

"Okay, cool." I stand back and look at my now-perfect tie in the mirror. "Oh, can you help with my cufflinks too?"

Jess attaches the cufflinks as I sit down in the makeup chair. Sarah covers my shirt and starts to style my hair.

"Looking pretty good, Tatum."

"Pretty good?" I cock an eyebrow at the two women.

"Okay, damn good, you cocky bastard." Sarah smiles and Jess grumbles in annoyance.

LEE AND I walk to the limo. The driver opens the door and I'm met by a pair of sleek, toned, tanned legs. Savannah Edward's legs, to be exact. She's wearing a short, pink-sequined mini dress with some kind of long, flowing, gauzy contraption on the back. Well, this will be a pain in the ass down the red carpet. If I step on it, I could bring her down. Not a bad idea actually...

"Savannah." I smile bleakly at her.

"Tatum." She bares her teeth like a barracuda.

"All right, kids, let's get this party started!" Lee climbs in behind me, grinning at both of us. The tension is so thick you could cut it with a machete.

"How are you, Savannah?" Lee tries to engage her, but

Savannah ignores us both as she taps away on her phone. Lee shrugs and we fall into easy conversation about the upcoming tour as the limo heads to the MGM Grand.

"You're welcome, by the way," Savannah breathes out like a rabid dragon a few minutes into the ride.

"Um, I'm sorry, did you say something?" I lean forward.

"I *said*, you're welcome." She speaks louder as she continues to type on her phone.

I look over at Lee to see if he knows what she's talking about. For the past few months it's been like stepping around hidden land mines with Savannah because you never know what's going to set her off.

"Uh...thank you?"

"Jesus, you're such an asshole, Tate! I just finished taping my part of our duet for your tour," she seethes.

"Oh, great, thank you so much. I'm sorry, Vanny. No one told me for sure you were doing that for me. That's incredibly awesome of you."

"I'm not doing it for you," she scoffs and then rolls her eyes. "Whatever, just stop talking to me." She continues to text.

I look over at Lee and he looks like a deer caught in headlights. I give him my *say fucking something* eyes and he immediately jumps into action.

"Savannah, I'm so sorry, your agent didn't mention you were doing that for... Uh, anyway we really appreciate it. It'll be awesome to play during the concert. Hopefully it'll launch the song to number one."

Savannah sniffs as she looks out the window. "Well, it's better than having some half-ass, first-string newcomer trying to take a hack at it."

She is unfairly referring to Maddie Macon, one of my opening acts for the tour. Her career is starting to blow up, and she has two singles out right now that are climbing the charts at a fast pace. Savannah feels threatened by her. That's one thing that drives me crazy about her. No matter how big her career gets, she still acts incredibly insecure around her peers. She's insecure about everything. In the past, I always had to reassure her in our relationship, and it quickly got old. I personally feel offended by her attack on Maddie because that "hack" is not only a part of my tour, selected by me, but she's also quite talented.

"I think that *hack* will be singing her single tonight," I say icily.

Savannah shoots daggers with her eyes and then starts to fake laugh. "Oh, this is rich! You're fucking her too, aren't you, Tate? You're screwing your opener. I'm sure she's eating this up, thinking a relationship with you will skyrocket her career. She's just using you, you know."

I look at her as if she's suddenly gone batshit crazy, which in all honesty, she has.

"Wow, Savannah." I chuckle without humor. "You really think a lot of me, don't you? Not that it's any of your business anymore, but no, I'm not screwing Maddie, nor do I have future plans to screw her. In fact, if I might bring us back to the reason we're in this predicament, it's because *you* stepped out on *me*. So keep your fabricated, fucked-up fantasy stories to yourself, and have the decency to leave Maddie out of this."

Silence fills the space between us.

"If looks could kill, you'd be flat-lining right now," Lee mumbles next to me as he shifts uncomfortably in his seat.

Savannah chooses to ignore me for the remainder of the ride to the MGM, which is probably for the best. We both need to cool down. The limo pulls up in front of the venue, but before Savannah can reach for the door, I grab her hand.

"Listen, I'm sorry. I don't want to fight with you. We just have to get down the red carpet, take a few pictures, and then sing our duet. We can still be friends, Vanny," I say, gently squeezing her hand.

"Fuck you, Tatum." She rips her hand out of mine. "You're nothing to me."

And with that, the driver opens the door and helps her out of the limo. I'm crestfallen that things have gone so sour between us. Her words are like a slap in the face. I really did like her once—I don't think I ever loved her, but I liked her very much early on in our relationship, before fame got to the both of us.

Lee claps me on the back. "Sorry, man. Just slip on your charming smile and take your own advice. I'm right behind you."

I nod as I exit behind Savannah. She's waiting for me on the red carpet with a big dazzling smile, cameras flashing behind her like lightning, and paparazzi shouting our names.

Chapter 12

Kiki

I'M STEAMING TATUM Reed's shirt when Jess walks in to the large dressing room. I'm exhausted from staying up into the wee hours of the morning taking in the clothes she gave me yesterday, and then having to catch an early-morning flight out to Vegas.

"Crazy that I haven't met this guy yet," I say. "I don't even know what he looks like really, except from pictures, but even then he's always wearing a big cowboy hat."

Jess stops and stares at me like I'm from another planet.

I shrug. "What? I'm not a country music fan."

She snorts. "Yeah, but country fan or not, everyone knows who Tatum Reed is."

I shrug. "Well, not this girl, but I guess I'm about to find out."

"You better get used to it because Tatum Reed is a brand. He's everywhere. You're about to go on his tour and it's all country."

"Is he really going to wear this...um, blouse thingy?" I

wrinkle my nose as I look at the floral button-down with pearl snap buttons.

Jess grabs the steamer from my hand. "Yes, it's country-sexy. You've got a lot to learn, little girl, before you start spouting your ideas about what a major artist like Tatum Reed should wear. Didn't you work at a men's magazine?" she asks snidely.

Whoa, did she really just call me "little girl"? What on earth did I do to get on this woman's bad side? Tears burn behind my eyes, but I'm not about to let her see me cry. I want to ask her what her problem with me is, but right now isn't the time to hash it out.

I take a deep breath as I move across the room to take his cowboy boots out of the box and stand them next to his jeans.

"What will Savannah be wearing?"

Jess sighs loudly, as if talking to me is so tedious. "I'm not sure. She has three dresses to choose from."

"Wow, I bet it's fun to be her stylist."

"Oh, I don't know. I've heard she can be really picky and indecisive. I'd hate to have to make three dresses and then have her go in a totally different direction. Girls are a lot of work." She gives me a pointed look. I tilt my head and stare directly back at her. What the fuck is that supposed to mean?

"Now, remember the paperwork you signed when you were hired. Tatum will be here in a few minutes and getting undressed in front of you. If you can't handle yourself properly, then you need to tell me now."

"I can handle myself just fine," I snap.

Seriously? Does she really think I'm going to go fangirlcrazy and throw myself at this guy? Give me a little credit. I mean, I worked at a men's fashion magazine for five fucking years surrounded by good-looking—albeit mostly gay, but still attractive—guys. Ugh, Jess is grating on my last nerve.

The door opens and a petite blonde with violet streaks in her hair pokes her head in and smiles. She opens the door wider and comes in, hauling a large case.

"Hey, guys! I'm Sarah, Tatum's makeup artist. You must be Kiki. I've heard so much about you!" She cheerfully holds her hand out to me.

"Hi, Sarah. Nice to meet you."

"It's so nice to meet you. Welcome to the team! You've got beautiful glossy hair and killer eyebrows. Oh, and your skin, it's so dewy. Ooh, I'm so going to have to do your makeup when we go on tour." She gives me a big hug as I stand there awkwardly.

I laugh. "Um, thanks. Okay, I'd love that!"

I instantly like Sarah. Not only because she's so sweet, but because she is sunny and exudes positive energy, unlike the other person in the room. If Sarah is rainbows and sunshine, then Jess is a dark rain cloud that shits out drizzle.

"Okay, hair-braiding time is over. Mackenzie, I need you to find the silver oval belt buckle."

I head toward the rack we brought that holds different belts, pants, and shirts in case of any wardrobe malfunctions. My back is to the door when it opens and the infamous Mr. Reed strides in.

"Ladies, I'm in a foul mood, so let's get this over with as quickly as possible. I'd like my dressing room cleared out so I can have some alone time before I perform."

God, talk about sounding like a diva asshole. His voice is sexy, though, a deep, smooth baritone.

Now where's the silver oval—*Ooh yes, found it!*

I turn around and nearly drop the belt on the ground as I stumble. Standing in front of me dressed in the sexiest black suit, looking like a *GQ* model, is the guy from the lobby yesterday. He's loosening his tie when he notices me.

He does a double take and the corner of his mouth slightly curls up. "Aren't you the girl that had coffee all over her?"

I'm totally speechless as I stand there ogling him. Again.

"Oh, sorry. Tatum Reed, this is my assistant, Mackenzie Forbes. She'll be going on tour with us," Jess lamely introduces.

He smiles but it doesn't reach his eyes. He looks stressed.

"Nice to meet you...again. Mackenzie." My name rolls off his tongue like liquid silver, making me shiver.

"Um, I...me, Kiki," I fumble. Cheese and rice, I'm acting like an idiot. I inhale and exhale. "Nice to meet you again. And thanks for your help yesterday."

He glances at me again, his lip lifts up into a sexy grin, and then he turns to Jess and frowns.

"Jess, help me get these damn things off." Tatum thrusts his wrists at her.

I step back wiping my hands on my dress as I take the cufflinks from Jess. God, I sound like such a moron. *Thanks for your help?* He held the door open like any gentleman would. I can't *believe* Hot Guy is actually Tatum Reed. *Pull it together, Kiki.*

I look over at Sarah and she smiles giving me a knowing

look: *he's totally hot, right?*

Jess starts to hand me the articles of clothing he's discarding, and... *Oh my fucking God, he just took off his shirt.*

I try to look away, I really do, but when he's standing there stripping down, you just can't look away from a body that beautiful.

He's tan, long, and lean. Not overly bulky muscular like a football player, but just the right amount of lean, ridged muscle that lets you know he's a man who works out and takes care of his body. He must work out *a lot.* Golden hair dusts his muscled chest and then forms a hot little line that runs into his boxer briefs. Yes, that's right, he has now stripped down to his black boxer briefs, and I'm just standing there watching as Jess piles his discarded suit into my hands.

"Getting a good show, Coffee Girl?"

I look up from where I'm drooling over his six pack to see him smirking at me.

Someone, please kill me now. I can't believe he caught me ogling him. I feel my face turn bright red as I spin on my heel and begin to hang his suit up on the rack. I clear my throat and try to think of something to say to salvage the moment.

"I've seen it all before, Mr. Reed. Don't go getting your tighty-whities in a knot," I sass as I secretly die on the inside of utter embarrassment.

He grunts in amusement or irritation, I can't quite tell. "You've got a good point. Maybe I shouldn't wear...what did you call them? Tighty-whities? They're actually black, but who needs them, right?"

I bite my lip and close my eyes. *No, no, no, no!* Please God, please don't let him take off his boxers. I most likely will lose all self-control, jump on him and violate my non-disclosure agreement, and end up in jail.

Sarah laughs. "Jesus, Tatum, leave the poor girl alone. You don't need to scare her off on her first night."

"Here, stop flirting and put this on," Jess deadpans, bringing the whole room back to business.

"Such a killjoy, Jess." He smirks.

"So I've been told."

Sarah quickly fixes his hair and blots his face. I glance up at him as I finish hanging his suit up and see him watching me in the mirror. I blush furiously as I busily start cleaning up.

Tatum stands and pulls on his jeans, and they are the tightest damn pants I have ever seen. I mean, those suckers look painted on. They show everything, and I mean every. Thing.

"How can you breathe, much less sing, in those things?" I blurt out before I can stop myself.

Tatum looks at me and smirks. "I can breathe and sing just fine, Coffee Girl, but thanks for the concern."

"Mackenzie, Sarah, let's give Tatum some alone time. Now!" Jess barks.

I roll my eyes and chuckle, following a glaring Jess out the door.

"Why does he keep calling you 'Coffee Girl'?" Jess demands once Tatum's door closes shut.

"Come on, Kiki, come with me and we'll watch from the side stage." Sarah loops her arm in mine and steers me away from Jess before I can answer. "Don't worry about Jess. She's just bitter because she hasn't gotten laid in years."

I laugh. "Well, I'm glad it's not just me. I was beginning to get a complex."

"She's good at keeping the boys in line, but she's got zero personality. The guys call her Brunhilda behind her back."

"Sarah, I think you and I are going to get along just fine." I squeeze her arm and grin as we head toward a crowd mingling backstage. Thank goodness I have Sarah in my corner now.

Backstage is mayhem with producers, stage hands, and singers milling about. Music stars I don't recognize are dressed in dazzling gowns. Hot guys in tuxes with cowboy hats, and some who just think they're hot, strut around and shake hands, sizing up their peers. Several interviews are being given behind the stage, and handlers and PAs zip in and out of the throng of talent. There is a lot of bling and lace, and a helluva lot of tacky. It's like a car wreck—you just have to stop and stare and hope everyone makes it out okay.

"Go big or go home, right?" Sarah whispers in my ear as we pass a female singer in a see-through, full-length, blush-pink crystal gown with ostrich feathers.

"Ugh, I guess…so many bad decisions," I murmur as another young female singer struts by in a leather-and-denim studded halter pantsuit.

"That girl over there looks like a cross between a tissue box and a toilet bowl brush." I subtly point out a woman in a light-blue tulle dress with puffs of tulle coming out of every angle and crevice. It's seriously disturbing.

"I know, it's awesome!" Sarah gleefully claps and drags

me along. "Come on, we'll watch Tatum and Savannah's performance from the side here. Besides, you have to be on hand in case there's a wardrobe malfunction."

"Seriously?"

"Oh yeah, it happens more often than people realize. Just make sure you keep your earpiece in if Jess needs you."

I touch my ear and feel the little bud Jess gave me earlier. "Got it. Thanks for being so nice. You're the first friendly face, besides Lee and Tatum, who actually wants to talk to me."

"Aw, of course. I've been where you are. I know how lonely it is when you don't know anyone, especially when you're working for a bitch like Jess. I'm just so glad we'll be on tour together. I was dreading being alone for weeks on end with Jess."

I sigh. "Yeah, she's not that friendly."

Sarah snorts. There's a flurry of activity behind us and I turn to see some tech guys handing Tatum an earpiece and a microphone. God, he really is gorgeous. He may be the only guy I know who can pull off a floral button-down shirt and cowboy boots and make them look so damn sexy. Guess Jess is right—this girl does have a lot to learn.

He takes a drink of water and passes the bottle to Sarah as he passes us. "Wish me luck, Coffee Girl," he whispers and winks at me as he takes his place on the dark stage.

I seriously think my ovaries just burst.

Sarah nudges me with her elbow and whispers, "You are definitely going to have to tell me about this nickname."

My cheeks heat and I nod as the band starts to play. A willowy woman crosses the stage from the opposite side and stands toward the front. Her red hair is poofed out and curled, blowing from a fan somewhere on the stage. She is stunning. Her amazing body is sheathed in a tight, sequined mini dress. She is *made* for the spotlight.

"That's Savannah Edwards," Sarah confirms.

Tatum is still hidden in the dark shadows as she starts to sing. A spotlight slowly turns on directly over her and the crowd goes wild. I mean, freaking-lunatic, ear-splitting wild. My eyes go wide as I look at Sarah. She smiles at me and mouths, *Just wait.*

When it's Tatum's turn to sing, a spotlight bathes him in golden light as he walks towards Savannah. The crowd goes ballistic. I have to cover my ears, it's so deafening. Sarah laughs at me. I've never been to a concert where the crowd goes this crazy.

They meet in the middle of the stage and fireworks go off behind them as they sing their duet. They are good. Seriously good.

It's a love song about losing their connection and trying to find their way back to each other. Their voices hit all the notes and they put their heart and soul into the song. It's only three minutes, but I'm totally carried away and mesmerized by the music. They really do have good chemistry together. As they sing the last notes, a single tear tracks down Savannah's face. Tatum reaches out with his thumb and wipes it away, keeping his hand under her jawline. It's heartbreaking and beautiful.

The song ends and the lights go out, and the crowd goes nuts again, giving them a standing ovation. Tatum leans down and kisses Savannah's lips, and then they take a bow.

Savannah and Tatum exit the stage opposite us holding hands, and I'm a little crushed that I don't get to see him up close again. I turn to Sarah, my head buzzing, and she takes my arm and leads me back through the throng of people toward the dressing room.

"Wow. That was just...wow. I think I'm a country fan!"

Sarah chuckles. "I know, right? Want to go get a drink?"

"Uh, sure, if you don't think Jess will mind."

"Nah, we're done here. They're headed out to after-parties after this."

"So what's the story with those two, anyway?" I look over my shoulder to where Tatum and Savannah have exited, hoping for one more glance at the superstars.

"Well, they've been going out officially for about two years. But, I know for a fact they've been over for the last couple months. They haven't announced it to the public yet."

"What? Why? How do you know?"

"Because my cousin is Savannah's makeup artist, and I'm Tatum's." She laughs and shrugs. "We swap stories with each other of she-said, he-said. It's gotten pretty bad. Anyway, they are a very adored public couple, so when they do finally announce their split, it's not going to be pretty."

"Oh. That's sad. They're... cute together. Are you sure? I mean, he just kissed her."

"Nah, that's all an act. They just look good onstage together. She's a bitch and really insecure. Tatum could do so much better. Besides, I think he likes flirting with a particular coffee girl."

I blush again as we wind our way through throngs of

people. "Nah, I have a feeling he's a big flirt to anything with boobs."

Sarah laughs. "True. That's pretty accurate. He's a natural charmer, and it doesn't hurt that he *is* sinfully good-looking and can sing the panties off my eighty-year-old grandma." She winks as we walk back into the dressing room.

"Sit down and tell me all about coffee while I do your makeup, then we'll go get a drink. You have beautiful eyes. Sometimes they look gray and sometimes almost purple."

I sit down in her makeup chair, my heart deflating a little as Sarah babbles on about my eyes. Not that anything would ever become of a country superstar like Tatum and little ol' me, but I did feel kind of special when he flashed his gorgeous smile my way in his dressing room and backstage.

Oh God, seriously, who am I kidding? He just broke up with Savannah Freaking Edwards. I doubt I'm even a blip on his radar. I'm just "Coffee Girl" because he can't remember my name.

"Earth to Kiki." Sarah snaps her fingers in my face and I blush, caught daydreaming about Tatum.

"Sorry, guess I zoned out for a sec."

"S'okay. So, tell me. I'm dying to know why Tate calls you 'Coffee Girl.'"

Sarah cracks up when I tell her about my first meeting with Tatum. "Oh my gosh, I wish I could've seen you."

"Yeah, I'm sure I was a real showstopper." I chuckle.

"Wow, Kiki, you really are beautiful, you know that? I don't think you do, that's why I keep saying it. If you did, you'd act like Savannah, and Lord knows she's had a few enhancement surgeries."

I flash her a timid smile. "Oh, well…growing up, my sister was always the beautiful one and I was the tomboy, but thank you." I quickly change the subject. "So, what kind of enhancements?"

"Oh, you know, the usual—new nose, teeth, boobs, butt. You name it, she's had it tweaked. She's not even a real redhead. You, on the other hand, are the real deal. You've got beautiful olive skin, gorgeous glossy chestnut hair, and amazing large gray eyes. And I believe your boobs are real." She's eyeing my boobs like she's about to reach out and squeeze them. I quickly cross my arms over my chest.

I snort. "Do you have a little crush on me, Sarah?" I wink at her in the mirror.

"Oh, gosh, no, I don't go that way. Never had any desire. I kind of like a guy in the band. But I appreciate natural beauty when I see it."

I chuckle. "I…I was just kidding… Never mind. So who do you like? I miss girl-talk," I say sadly. Even though TJ isn't technically a girl, he likes to gossip like one.

"You can girl-talk with me whenever you want. I'm so glad they hired you. Jess is such a drag. She's so serious all the time. All work and no fun. I seriously think she'd be a different person if she loosened up and got laid. Anyway, enough about her. Just talking about her is depressing. Okay, you can't tell anyone in the band, but I kind of have a thing for Tatum's lead guitarist, Lex Ryan." She blushes.

"Oh, I met him the other day when the guys came in for measurements. He kind of reminds me of David Beckham when he did that 'Sexiest Man Alive' *People* shoot. So hot.

He's really cute in that bad-boy rocker kind of way. I was actually surprised he was in a country band. I love guys with accents—is he Scottish?"

"I know, me too. He's Irish, and his accent makes my toes curl. I can kind of see David Beckham thing, except Lex has dark hair." She sighs. "I think he's so sexy. I'm so jealous you'll get to see him naked. Hands off on that one. He's my little man-crush."

"Naked? I, um…I don't think that'll happen."

"Probably will. Those guys don't care. They'll strip down right in front of ya." She smacks her gum as she applies eyeliner.

Oh God. What have I gotten myself into? I just picked out the clothes at the magazine for the photoshoots. I never actually physically dressed the guys. I get the feeling this gig is an entirely different beast than what I'm used to.

"No problem, hands off and eyes averted," I say seriously.

Sarah laughs. "You and I, Kiki, are going to get along just fine."

"Are the other guys friendly?"

"Oh yeah, all the guys are great. The drummer, Will, is like a big ol' teddy bear, and Matt, the bass player, is a prankster, but really nice. You'll hear them call me Sunshine. I guess because I'm always smiling." She beams. "They're all so cute in their own way, it's amazing to me that none of them are tied down yet."

"Well, that's good, since we'll be spending a lot of time on tour with them." I smile.

"Oh yeah, totally cool guys." She applies some gloss to

my lips. "All right, hot coffee girl, let's blow this popsicle stand and go out!"

I turn to look in the mirror and am awed by my makeup. She's given me a smoky eye that make my eyes pop. I have a faint blush to my cheeks and the rosy gloss she put on my lips make them stand out.

I stand up and hug her for making me feel so pretty and put-together. For the second time since moving to Nashville, I feel like things will be okay.

Chapter 13

Kiki

THINGS ARE *NOT* okay. I had no idea touring with the band meant living on a tour bus filled with racks and racks of clothes…and Jess. I'm not sure what I was expecting…I thought we would be staying in five-star hotels and flying private jets to where the band needed us, not living on a bus.

Luckily, Sarah is here too, and I'm rooming with her, but sharing confined quarters with Jess is my worst nightmare. The only saving grace is that she's allowed me to bring Oreo. At first, she was pissed when I brought him on the bus, but I told her I didn't have anyone to take care of him. It was either let Oreo go with us, or lose her bitch—me.

I snuggle with Oreo on my bed as we watch the landscape blur past us. Oreo mostly stays on my bed. He stays clear of Jess, but he's quickly warmed up to Stan, our driver. Stan let him ride shotgun with him this morning. I think he secretly loves Oreo, and the feeling is mutual. I caught him having conversations with Oreo last night. I almost busted out laughing, ruining the moment between the two, before I quietly tiptoed back to bed.

Oreo is an attention-seeking whore.

I share a bunk with Sarah. I'm on the upper bunk and she's below me. Thankfully we can close our microscopic "room" off to the bunks across from us that house Jess and the personal assistant to Maddie Macon, the other touring musician. Her name is Allie and she's very quiet, takes her job seriously. She's usually on Maddie's bus at her beck and call, so she isn't around much. Mainly it's just Sarah and I gabbing away, driving Jess nuts.

We start the tour off in Boston and then will make our way out west, ending in Los Angeles. Twenty cities in all. I'm kind of excited to see all the cities we're heading to, even the ones in the middle of nowhere.

As I absently stroke Oreo's fur, I think maybe it won't be all that bad. I feel like a wildflower floating along, going where the wind takes me. Well, in this case where the bus takes me. Way better than being Brooke's pretend French nanny. Also, Cam told me after working for Tatum Reed I wouldn't have a problem finding a stylist position. I have to remind myself of that—keep my eye on the prize. And I can't forget about the super-cute eye candy I'll get to see almost every day. I haven't seen Tatum since Vegas, and I'm excited to be on his tour despite these tight living quarters.

I pull out my phone to text TJ my new outlook on this career change.

Me: Things are looking up, TJ Maxx.
TJ: You're sleeping with the cowboy!
Me: What?! No!

TJ: *I'm going back to sleep then.*

Me: *Don't you want to hear my new outlook on life?*

TJ: *Zzzz...unless your outlook includes Tatum Reed's fine ass, no.*

Me: *Well, there goes your chance at meeting him...*

TJ: *Your empty threats don't scare me.*

"Mackenzie, I need to talk to you. Up front. Pronto!" Jess yells from the other side of our curtain enclosure.

"God, she sucks, Oreo," I whisper as I kiss his head, and he meows in agreement as he stretches. I climb down from my bunk and stretch too.

I walk down the bus hallway and sit down at the kitchen table across from Jess, who is furiously scribbling in her notebook.

"Um, do I need my notebook?"

"No. So, I just got a text from Lee that Maddie and The Wake Brothers are going to need us to dress them while out on tour."

"Wow, okay, what will we have to do?"

Jess waves her hand, dismissing my comment. "The Wake Brothers will be simple. They both wear white T-shirts and black jeans for every single concert."

"Well, that's kind of monotonous and unexciting."

"Yes, but makes our jobs easier. The tough one who'll be a lot more added work for us will be Maddie. Have you met her yet?"

I shake my head. I've Googled her to see who would be on tour with us, but all I know about her is that she's an up-and-comer that has a strong voice. From the pictures she dresses a little trashy.

Jess leans closer, looking over my shoulder toward the hallway. I assume she's looking to make sure Allie isn't eavesdropping.

Are Jess and I finally bonding? Holy shit, miracles do exist. Maybe she'll let me wax her eyebrows. They're like hairy little caterpillars. I stare at them as I lean closer.

"Well, she has made horrible fashion choices in the past," she whispers. "She likes skimpy clothes and anything that has rhinestone-studded bling. She's never used a stylist and it shows on the red carpet. She wore a red, leather bondage-type dress to the ACMs, and apparently there was nip showing...on purpose." Jess presses her thin lips together in judgment. "She's even modeled topless in *Clover*."

"What's *Clover*?" I whisper.

"Kind of like a country version of *Playboy*."

I cringe. "So we have our work cut out for us. Where do you want to start, and how are we going to fit more clothes in the back?"

"We'll be fine as far as fitting the clothes on the bus. When we stop in Boston in the morning, we'll meet with her to discuss her style and guide her in the right direction. This is where your fashion styling experience will come in handy. We need to make her see the light of good fashion versus the hideous horrible fashion she's currently sporting. I'm putting you in charge."

I crack a smile and do fist pumps in my head. *Yes!* I'm finally going to get my moment to shine. I mean, I'm not about to point out to Jess I was a stylist for men for the past five years. Can't be that hard, right? I'm a woman, for God's sake. I know what's in style and what's not. This will be cake.

"I'm on it. I'll start Googling some of her past looks and then we can make some suggestions."

"Already done. Tatum Reed is a wholesome brand. He has a lot of women at his concerts, but he also brings in a lot of younger kids. I need you to rein her in, Mackenzie. She can still be sexy, but not trashy. Here are a few printouts of her past looks."

Jess hands me the photos and I almost bust out laughing. I bite my lip hard and quickly scan the sheets. High-waist pleather jeans with bedazzled, mock turtleneck cut-out bodysuits that do nothing for her figure. Just because the Kardashians do it doesn't mean Maddie should. Sequined, cutoff jean shorts with cowboy boots and halter tops. Tight pleather dresses that are too small. *Is that tinfoil?* Yikes, she looks like she's wearing a parachute in this one.

Oh my. I really do have my work cut out for me. It's not that she isn't cute. I mean, she has potential with a major makeover. She kind of reminds me of a country version of Ke$ha: clothes, teased-out, eighties rocker hair, and a bad attitude.

I sigh. "Wow, okay. I'll do my homework and be ready for tomorrow."

THAT NIGHT WE all meet up for dinner. Lee has rented out the top floor of a local steakhouse in Boston. Tatum is here with his whole band, Maddie, The Wake Brothers and their drummer. I sit down next to Sarah at the long, wooden trestle table that barely manages to fit all of us. I sneak a peek under my lashes to the opposite end of the table to watch Lex and Tatum banter back and forth. He's better-looking than I remembered. His green eyes connect with mine and I immediately duck my head and pretend I wasn't just staring at him. I quickly pick up my menu, which is heavier than it looks. The momentum causes the menu to swing forward, banging me in the forehead. Sarah snorts beside me.

Oh God, I pray he didn't see that. I slowly lower the menu and casually glance over to see him smirking at me until one of his bandmates grabs his attention. I melt in my seat with mortification. I can't believe I made an ass out of myself in his presence, *again.*

Lee stands up and chimes his glass with a dinner knife. "Hey, everyone! Tatum, the boys, and I want to thank everyone for coming tonight. We're so excited to have you on board with us, and we're going to rock this tour!" Everyone cheers and claps. "Tatum, the table is all yours." Lee smiles as Tatum stands up.

He's wearing a faded, blue, plaid button-down over worn Levi's. His sleeves are rolled up past his tan, muscular forearms. His strong jaw has a hint of scruff, and his dimples make an appearance as he smiles with his beautiful lips. He's like a work of art I could study and sketch every day for the rest of my life. His green eyes sweep across the table, taking us all in. His dark, honey-blond hair is artfully disheveled like someone just ran their hands through it. What I wouldn't give for it to be my hands.

He's so pretty, it's unfair.

He smiles and quickly flicks his tongue over his lips to moisten them, and I'm pretty sure I groan out loud. I quickly glance around, but everyone's attention is focused on him.

Sarah gives me a strange look.

"Stomach just growled." I whisper to her as I return my attention to Tatum.

"I'd also like to thank y'all for being here tonight. We wouldn't be able to put on a successful show without all of your hard work. Lex, Matt, Will, and I really appreciate your dedication to making this three ring circus run smoothly for us. The tour is sold out and I can't wait for all of us to work as a team to deliver a kickass show to our fans. Maddie, Tuck, and Harrison will be opening for us, and we couldn't be more excited."

Claps and whistles go around the table. Maddie lifts her arm up over her head and gives the peace sign with a pouty smirk.

"There are some new faces here, so why don't we go around and introduce ourselves." He sits back down and smiles at the table.

Oh shit. I hate this kind of crap.

Lee jumps up. "Great idea, Tatum. Let's start at the back table with Jess's team."

Crap crappity crap.

Jess stands first, but everyone already knows her so her introduction is about ten seconds long. Sarah is second, but her quick dialogue is over in a blink. Then she elbows me in the arm.

"Ow!" I hiss.

"It's your turn," she whispers as she nudges my leg under the table. I look up, and the whole table is staring at me. I start perspiring as I uneasily get to my feet. A blush spreads across my cheeks as I zone in on Harrison Wake's salad plate.

"Hey, I'm Kiki." I give a lame little wave. "I'm Jess's assistant. You may hear Jess calling me Mackenzie, but I prefer Kiki."

Ha! Take that, Jess!

"Um, I'm from California and used to be a stylist at *Cufflinks* men's magazine. I'm super excited to be on tour with you guys." I fidget as I sit back down and reach for my water.

Tatum shouts down the table, "Or you can call her Coffee Girl." He smirks as I choke on my water. Everyone at the table chuckles as I glare at him.

"There is that...if you want to get punched in the face," I mumble under my breath.

I'm super pissed that Tatum told everyone to call me that. Not only does it make me feel like a simple errand girl, but now people will be asking me left and right to get them coffee. Ugh, I am going to slowly kill him.

"Nice!" hoots Matt, Tatum's bass player, as he leans back putting his hands behind his head. He grins and winks at me.

I *hate* Matt the bass player.

"Coffee Girl, you have my permission to call this jackass Tater Tot." Matt slaps Tatum on the back who scowls back at him.

Sarah snorts and whispers, "Tate hates that nickname."

I *love* Matt the bass player.

I pocket that tidbit of info to mull over at a future date as I smile and take a big drink of my water. I eye Tatum over the rim of my water glass as the next person stands up for introductions. His green eyes laser into mine. He quirks one side of his mouth up into a sexy smirk, but his eyes reflect something else…guilt, maybe? At least, I hope he feels guilty for throwing me under the bus.

I give him a half smile as the server reaches for my menu and asks what I'd like to order, thus breaking the trance Tatum's eyes have me under.

The rest of dinner goes without a hitch. The bandmates pass stories back and forth, and I find out these guys are really nice and funny. And it's also refreshing they genuinely like one another, unlike some bands you hear about that are constantly at one another's throats.

I excuse myself midway through the evening to go to the bathroom. After leaving the restroom, I see Tatum waiting out in the hallway. Is he waiting for me? Couldn't be. He's texting on his phone, but looks up and zeroes in on me when he hears the door swing shut.

I suddenly feel nervous and giddy all at once. Being alone with him makes my heart beat wildly. I cross my arms and lean up against the hallway wall, pretending to be as chill as he looks.

"Coffee Girl."

"Tater Tot."

He huffs out a laugh. "I guess I deserve that." He moves closer to me and rests a hand on the wall over my head, partly caging me in. Butterflies erupt in my stomach.

"Listen, I hope I didn't make you uncomfortable. I don't know why I shouted that out loud. I'm...sorry." He runs a hand through his hair, seeming nervous.

But there's no way this sexy tall man leaning against the wall next to me could be nervous. I, on the other hand, am completely frazzled and feel like a deer in headlights. I swallow, my throat suddenly parched. He's so close to me I feel warmth emanate from his skin, and his masculine, woodsy scent is sharp in my nose. Whatever aftershave or cologne he has on makes my brain defective.

He is so delicious.

"Uh, it's...it's no big deal."

He reaches out to touch a lock of my hair, rubbing it absentmindedly. I freeze because holy shit, Tatum Reed is touching me. And just as quickly, he steals his hand back and rubs the back of his neck.

"I kind of liked it just being mine, but now it's out there, I guess." He winks as he straightens from the wall and walks by me, leaving me utterly speechless.

He liked it being his? He liked what being his? What the hell did that mean?

I realize I'm still holding my breath as I exhale and push back from the wall to head back to dinner, feeling confused and frustrated about Tatum Reed even more than before.

THE NEXT MORNING I'm lying in my bunk with Oreo curled up next to me when my phone chirps, announcing an incoming text. I grin as I grab it, ready to read whatever craziness TJ has been up to. He doesn't disappoint.

TJ: *I'm going to murder Jonathon in his office. He's totes nutcray.*

Me: *What did he do?*

TJ: *He called me kitten and asked me to go fetch him a tuna sandwich.*

Me: *Gross. Who eats a tuna sandwich for breakfast? I'd tell Becky in HR he's calling you Kitten. That violates a hundred different HR rules and regulations.*

TJ: *Right?! I told Becky. He calls everyone kitten. It's so creepsadoodle.*

Me: *Creepsadoodle is not a word.*

TJ: *Anyway, I told him I'm not a dog and I don't fetch, I sashay. I also don't do food for people, you know that. Seriously nutcray.*

Me: *What is nutcray?*

TJ: *Nutcray is crazier than cray-cray. Duh Kinky.*

Me: *You made that up didn't you.*

TJ: *It will catch on*

Me: *It won't*

TJ: *Kiki why can't you ever believe in my hopes and dreams? You're just like Jonathon.*

Me: *Your hopes and dreams are to come up with new slang words?*

TJ: *Not all of us can work for a sexy 'get me in your pants and I'll do magical things' hunky cowboy.*

I laugh as a text pops up, but it's not from TJ. It's from an unknown number.

Unknown: *Hey Coffee Girl. How old are you?*

I check the number, but it just says private. Who is this? One of the guys from the band? Tatum? How on earth did he get my number, and why is he texting me at 11 a.m.? Tatum wouldn't be texting me. That would just be crazy. My heart thumps against my ribcage.

Me: *Ok, I'll play along. Who is this?*

Unknown: *Your favorite country singer*

Me: *No way…Is this really Kenny Chesney??*

Unknown: *Ha, you're funny. So?*

I quickly switch back over to my text conversation with TJ.

Me: *TJ! I think Tatum Reed just texted me! He asked me how old I was…at least I think it's Tatum. Shit, what do I do? Should I text him back? Should I ignore him? Agh! Help! I don't want to sound lame.*

TJ: *Jesus Kiki, keep your boobs in your bra. Tell him you want to lick your tongue over every inch of his body, in particular his hot package, and then let me know what he says! Don't tell him you're older than 25, that's super grandma territory for a stud like him.*

I reread the text from unknown caller and then switch back to TJ.

Me: *First of all, my boobs are swinging free in all their glory right now. Second, TJ, you know I'm twenty-six and that's not even close to cougar territory. And you're one to talk, pining after Justin Bieber the way you do.*

Me: Jesus, can you imagine if I said I wanted to lick him from head to toe? Let's be honest, I'd do more than just lick. There would probably be some biting and hair-tugging...maybe some other parts tugged.;) Grrr.

I smile as three little gray dots appear.

Unknown: Uh...I'm not sure how to respond to that...

Wait. What?

No. Oh my God, no. *No*!

Did I just text that to the unknown number? I hug my cell phone to my chest and get on my knees as I stare up at the ceiling, silently praying as I try not to hyperventilate.

Please God, I will become a nun for the rest of my life and give all my money to charity... I'll even give up coffee and swear words and be kind to Brooke if you somehow make it that I texted TJ and not the unknown caller.

I peel the cell phone away from my chest. *Please, God, please tell me I didn't just text Tatum that I want to lick him all over and that my boobs are swinging around like a hippie dancing with her bongos.*

Me: TJ, is this you? Please let it be you.

Unknown: Only my sister calls me TJ.

Me: Thomas Jean?

Unknown: Tatum James...gotta run. See ya around Coffee Girl.

Me: As in my boss, Tatum Reed?

Unknown: lol, is there any other? ;)

Me: OMG. I am SO sorry. I'm hyperventilating right now. I thought you were someone else. I'm so embarrassed.

Unknown: *I figured.;) It was definitely entertaining. Better go get a paper bag, CG, before you bite or tug something you shouldn't.;)*

I freeze before I type out another humiliating message. No need to dig myself further into a pile of crap. How did that even happen, anyway? Gah! I hate freaking cell phones and TJ for making me say and do stupid shit. It's all his fault. How did I switch text messages and not realize it? Oh my God, that wasn't *my* TJ. That was…

I quickly Google Tatum Reed, and his Wikipedia page shows, sure enough, Tatum fucking James Reed. TJ!

Oh crap.

I sounded like a total lunatic. Did I really tell him that I want to do more than lick him, bite him, and tug certain appendages? I quickly text *my* TJ and tell him what happened. He replies with a hundred laughing-crying emoji faces. Literally a hundred. I counted.

I throw my pillow over my face and scream.

Kill me right fucking now, please.

Chapter 14

Kiki

"NOPE. NO. UH, no. Lordy, no! What else you got?" Maddie smacks her gum as she flips through some sketches and a mini look book I compiled for her. She tosses the book back onto the table, looking bored. Jess shakes her head in frustration.

"Maddie, please tell us what it is you don't like about these looks." Jess pushes the book back toward Maddie.

"Um, they're too...I don't know...country club." She smirks as she speed-flips through the look book again.

"Country club?" I ask incredulously. Jess places a hand on my arm. I disliked Maddie the instant she stepped on the bus and gave me an obvious, head-to-toe contemptuous stare.

"Okay, well, tell us what direction you were thinking," Jess says soothingly.

"Well, I don't see what's wrong with what I've been wearing." There's nothing worse than trying to help someone who thinks they have great fashion sense and actually has zero. You might as well pull the plug.

"Mackenzie?" Jess turns to me with a questioning look.

Um...

"Uh, well...sure. So, tell me whose fashion you really like in Nashville or Hollywood. We'll start there."

She smacks her gum again. "I don't know. I mean, if I had to choose, I think Miley really rocks it. Katy Perry wears some killer stuff onstage. Cardi B, Kim Kardashian."

"Kim Kardashian pre- or post-Kanye?"

Jess gives me a weird look. I give her my big eyes and try to convey mental telepathy to just hang on because this is an important, valid question. Before Kanye, Kim dressed somewhat normally. After she married Kanye, her fashion choices went to hell.

"Post."

"I see." Oh God, this is more serious than I thought. "Okay, so if we did some shorter styles, more dazzle?"

"Yeah, um, okay. And maybe some mesh or some see-through dresses? Kim Kardashian really rocks that. Bedazzled bodysuits would be amazing."

"Well..." I chew on my thumbnail, avoiding eye contact with Maddie. "Probably not. That's not really Tatum's brand." I start making this up on the fly. I have no fucking clue what his brand is yet, just that it's supposed to be wholesome.

"Oh, huh. Never thought about his style."

"Exactly. I mean, we can do lots of bright colors with you and lots of sparkle to make you pop on stage, but I think we should keep you kind of covered for all the little kids that might be in the audience."

"Well, I guess. Maybe I should discuss it with Tatum."

"No need. He gave us his opinion on what style direction he wants the show to go in." Total bullshit spewing from my mouth. I see Jess from the corner of my eye, nodding at me with her mouth slightly agape.

Maddie looks from me to Jess and then to Allie, who just shrugs. I can't imagine cardigan-clad Allie would want Maddie walking around with her boobs and vag hanging out, but hey, what do I know?

Jess nods. "Maddie, you can dress however you want in between the shows, but on stage, take our direction. We're professionals and know what we're doing. Savannah Edwards doesn't look the way she does by doing her own styling."

That hits the nail on the head.

Maddie lifts her chin up and sniffs. "Okay, fine. But I want final say."

Jess looks at me and subtly nods.

"Deal."

Chapter 15

Kiki

OH. MY. GOD.

Who would have guessed part of my job description would be to wipe down Tatum's body in between songs? I mean, I must have missed that in the fine print. But when Jess tells me to grab a couple of towels and two clean shirts to have with me on the side of the stage, I'm thoroughly confused.

"Um, what do I need to do with the towels?"

Jess gives me a strange look. "You have to wipe the sweat off Tatum in between song breaks. If he needs a new T-shirt, then have one ready for him."

I wrinkle my nose. "Wipe his sweat off? That sounds disgusting."

Sarah snorts. "I don't think you'll mind it much."

I shrug my shoulders and grab the towels. "Whatever, sweat is sweat. Still sounds nasty."

MY NERVES HUM as the concert starts. Lights crisscross all over the stage. Behind the scenes, crew members run back and forth with instruments and set props. But I'm completely mesmerized by what's going on onstage. Tatum, Lex, Will, and Matt are captivating and have the arena's crowd eating out of their hands. The energy bouncing off the audience onto the stage is an amazing rush.

Tatum jumps around all over the stage with Lex and Matt and I'm completely fascinated by the amount of energy they all have. The man can move...and sweat. Holy cow, can he sweat. After the opening song, he's drenched. It doesn't help that it's June in Boston and super humid. He sings two more songs, then suddenly jumps off to my side of the stage, where we're hidden from the audience. He winks at me.

"Hey, Coffee Girl," he pants.

He peels off his shirt and throws it to the side as he stands in front of me. I stare at him dumbly. Holy mother of pearl. His washboard abs and perfect pecs glisten with a sheen of sweat. I want to run my tongue up and down his body. Did I say sweat was disgusting? Sweat is goddamn amazing.

"Hello?" He waves his hand in front of my face zapping me out of my trance. "This is where you're supposed to jump into action, give me a water, and wipe the sweat off me, and then hand me that clean T-shirt...quickly." He smirks.

"Right! Right, shit, I'm sorry," I mumble as my face

heats up, probably an embarrassing shade of tomato-red.

I hand him his water and immediately take the towel and wipe off his muscular arms. The vein on his bicep is so incredibly sexy. Who knew a damn vein could make me salivate? I run the towel over the hard ridges of his abdomen. I wonder if he'd notice if I quickly flicked my tongue out and licked him.

No, Kiki, down, dog. That would be a very bad idea. I'm pretty sure he would notice. Right?

He turns around as he talks to his sound guy, and I wipe off his shoulder blades and lower back. It doesn't escape my notice he's totally unaffected by me wiping him down, but I'm a simpering wet noodle barely keeping it together. Oh sweet Jesus, who knew a muscular back could be so fucking sexy? I'm pretty sure I'm panting. I start humming the song "Slow Hands" by Niall Horan as I concentrate on the task at hand so I don't pass out or, God forbid, drool on him.

I finish up and throw the towels to the side and hand him his shirt. He hands me his empty water bottle and quickly pulls the shirt over his head.

"Thanks, Coffee Girl." He jumps back onto the stage as Lex plays a solo intro to their next song. What seemed like a thirty-minute wipe down took less than thirty seconds. I quickly clean up the towels and throw them into a laundry bag. I secretly want to smell his discarded sweaty T-shirt. That's sick, I know, but his scent makes me want to do stupid things.

Damn. If I knew being the assistant to the fashion coordinator required me to clean off Tatum's body, I would've signed up for this gig a *long* time ago.

They open the next set with Tatum and Lex covering Justin Timberlake's "Sexy Back" and I have to say, it's amazing. The crowd roars with approval and I agree, Tatum has definitely brought sexy back. He is positively drool-worthy.

I'm totally mesmerized by the performance when Maddie saunters up to my side and flashes me a fake smile, which quickly disappears. A tech guy hands her a cordless mic.

"I'm not thrilled with this outfit, Kiki."

"Maddie, you look awesome. It's very flattering on you."

"There's no cleavage," she whines.

She's wearing a sparkly, dark-plum knit dress I picked up in Boston this morning. It hugs her curves in all the right places. The tank dress has a scoop neckline. The back opens down to her derriere. She looks pretty damn hot.

I try to placate her. "Just because there isn't cleavage doesn't mean it's not sexy. You look awesome."

"It's not short enough."

I want to strangle this girl. I look down and see that the hem of the dress hits upper-thigh. Any shorter, and everyone would think she's channeling Sharon Stone in *Basic Instinct*.

"It's plenty short. Just go out there and rock it. You're amazing!" I clench my teeth as I try to mollify her.

She huffs as she turns towards the stage. Tatum introduces her and she walks out, smiling and waving. They sing an upbeat duet together and I've got to say, they do a pretty good job.

Maddie may be a fashion tragedy and a pain in the ass, but the girl can sing.

Chapter 16

Kiki

TONIGHT WE'RE IN New Jersey, and we have the night off. I'm so excited because we get to spend a blissful evening at a fancy hotel. I even get my own room, which Jess says never happens. Thank you, God, I don't have to share one with her.

Sarah and I had dinner earlier, and now I'm feeling happy as a clam as I stretch out on my gorgeous, snow-white duvet cover. The room is small but decorated in soft, muted grays and blues. I just showered and threw on a comfy tee and leggings. I can't wait to just have an evening off and chill out.

Stan is happily watching Oreo for me on the bus because I didn't want to confuse him with another new room. My phone buzzes on the night stand as I flip to the movie channel and find *Pitch Perfect* on. Ah, bliss. I reach over and check my messages.

TJ Hotness: *Hey Coffee Girl.*

Chills run up my arms. *Play it cool, Kiki.*

Me: *Hi. Great concert last night!*
TJ Hotness: *Thanks. What's your status?*
Me: *What's my what?*
TJ Hotness: *Are you seeing anyone?*

Is Tatum Reed seriously asking if I have a boyfriend?

Me: *Um…is this a work related question?*
TJ Hotness: *Possibly*
Me: *Who gave you my number anyway?*
TJ Hotness: *Most girls would die to have me texting them.*

I roll my eyes and smile.

Me: *I'm not most girls.*
TJ Hotness: *I'm finding that out. So, what kind of music do you listen to?*

What the heck?

Me: *A little bit of everything. You?*
TJ Hotness: *Same. What are you doing right now?*
Me: *Um…watching a movie.* Pitch Perfect.

Shit, did I really just admit that?

TJ Hotness: *What's* Pitch Perfect?
Me: *Um, just a chick flick. Nothing important. What are you doing?*
TJ Hotness: *Ssh…I'm reading the reviews on it. Wow, surprisingly 95% of Google users liked this movie.*

Me: *I mean, it's not terrible…*

TJ Hotness: *80% Rotten Tomatoes. I think I need to take you to a real movie.*

Did he just ask me out? *Oh my God, oh my God. Okay, get a grip, Kiki.*

Me: *And what's considered a real movie?*

TJ Hotness: *Deadpool is a good one.*

Me: *Dead what? Sounds like a Baywatch movie gone wrong.*

Oh Kiki, just shut up, you moron.

TJ Hotness: *Hmm, not quite. I'll talk to you soon. Night Coffee Girl.*

Me: *Night Tater Tot.*

TJ Hotness: *I'm going to kill Matt.*

That was the most random text conversation I've ever had.

WAS THAT A knock on my door? I turn down my TV and climb off the heavenly bed to look through the peephole.
Holy shit.
My heart thuds in my chest at an unnaturally rapid rate. I open the door and there's Tatum with one arm stretched up on the door jamb, looking sheepish. He's wearing a navy Henley, dark jeans, and his dimples. He looks incredibly

delicious.

"Hi, Kiki."

My tongue feels stuck in my throat as I soak him in. "Uh…hi," I croak.

My heart is now at a full gallop in my chest. What on earth is he doing at my door?

"Can I come in?" he asks quietly. My eyes dip and I watch his thumb as he glides it across his lower lip. I'm completely mesmerized.

I stare at him dumbly as thoughts race through my muddled brain. What is he doing here? Why is the superstar-sex-god of country standing at my door?

I shake myself out of my stupor. "Are you lost?" I look down the quiet, empty hall.

He chuckles as he clenches the door frame and runs his other hand along his scruff. "I don't think so. Can I come in? Please?"

I stare into his mesmerizing green eyes, my body swaying slightly toward his like two magnets coming together. I lick my lips and try to assess the situation rationally, but curiosity wins out over logic.

I open the door farther, unsure what I should say or do. Is he sure he has the right room? I've got to be dreaming right now, because shit like this doesn't happen to me in real life. I take a deep breath as I close the door behind him.

"What's up, Tatum?"

He looks around my room, taking in the small suite with its queen bed. "Do you want to go back to my room?"

"Um…" *What the fuck?* "That's probably not a good idea."

"Shit, sorry, that didn't come out right." He smiles guiltily at me. "I meant my room is four times the size of this. Thought we could hang out if you want. But here's good." He sits down at the end of my bed.

He wants to hang out? I stare at him like one of those Looney Tunes characters whose eyes bug out and tongue rolls out a mile long. Tatum fucking Reed wants to hang out with me? Tatum Reed, multi-millionaire, platinum recording artist is sitting on my bed in my hotel room asking to hang out...with me. What twilight universe did I land in?

My heart is drumming so fast I have to silently will it to calm down. My back is ramrod straight against my closed door and my hands are perspiring against the wood, but I can't seem to move away from it. Tatum looks up at me with a question in his eyes and quirks one eyebrow up. So goddamn sexy, I can't even breathe.

"You want to hang out...with me," I repeat slowly like I've got peanut butter on my tongue. His beautiful grin has my skin breaking out in goosebumps. Then reality slams into me. His version of hanging out and mine are probably immeasurably different. I huff out a laugh as I run my fingers down my ponytail.

God, I'm such a dumbass.

"Right...um, I don't really know how to say this, but I'm not..."

"I thought we could just talk. You seem like a cool girl, and I have a lot on my mind. I need a distraction, and you make me smile," he says smoothly. Too smooth.

It doesn't escape my attention that he just called me a distraction.

"Just talking." I eye him suspiciously as I chew my bottom lip.

"Yeah." His eyebrows shoot up suddenly and he smirks. "Coffee Girl, honest to God, I just came here to hang out and talk. No funny business." He holds up his hands innocently.

"Funny business?" I smirk. "Is that what country people call hookups?"

He chuckles. "Country people?" His dimples deepen, and my panties dissolve. "Are you suggesting you want to hook up with me?"

I blush hard and squeal, "No! *What?* No!" Whoa girl. Bring it back down to a normal pitch that won't make dogs howl. "No! I did *not* say that."

"Easy, CG, I'm just teasing. Maybe once you unglue yourself from the door we can listen to some music. I think you're a cool girl, and I'd like to get to know you better. I'll even let you call me Tater Tot."

"I call you that anyway." I smirk as I quickly cross the room and slide into the small desk chair next to the window. It's as far away from the bed as I can get without going into the bathroom.

"Do I smell funny?"

I'm intently studying my fingernails trying to calm myself down to the fact that Tatum Reed is sitting on my bed. *My bed!* Agh! My head snaps up at his question.

"Huh?"

"Why are you sitting over there?" He pats the bed.

Jesus, Mary, and Joseph, I'm going to have a coronary.

"Ah, ha. I think I'm good right here."

He kicks his boots off and stretches back against my cloud of pillows and sighs. "Suit yourself."

I just stare at him as he pulls his phone out. "How did you figure out my room number?" My eyes dart around the room as I look for my phone. Shit, it's on the opposite nightstand from where he's lying.

"I know everything."

I roll my eyes and try to guess how fast it would take me to stride to the other side of the bed and then run back to my chair. Maybe I could hurdle jump over him without him even noticing. Like a ninja.

"What's wrong with your eye?" He's staring at my left eye that I have scrunched closed as I think through different strategies on how to quickly grab my phone.

"Who? What? My eye? Nothing!"

Real smooth, Kiki.

Could I sound or look like more of a weirdo? Here I am, a jumble of nerves, and he's lying over there cool as a cucumber. I clap my hands loudly like a spazzy preschool teacher trying to control her class.

"So...what do you want to talk about?" I yell.

Seriously, someone please just shoot me now.

He looks at me strangely before returning his gaze to his phone screen and chuckles. "What kind of music do you like?"

"Who, me?"

He lazily looks over at me and grins. Ugh, those dimples. "Is there someone else in here with us?"

Heart stops. Brain wills heart to beat again.

"I'm sorry, what did you ask me?"

His smile widens. "What kind of music do you listen to?"

"Uh, a little bit of everything I guess. Not much country, though." I smirk. "I'm not really into dump trucks, dirt roads, losing your dog, beers after tears…"

"You mean pickup trucks?"

"Huh?" I wave my hand dismissing his smirk. "Oh whatever, same thing."

His fist thuds his chest right over his heart. "You're killing me, Coffee."

I just stare at him dumbly. I'm still trying to process the fact that Tatum Reed is lying on my bed asking me about music. The sexiest man I've ever seen is lying on *my* bed! Alone…with me…on purpose. I wonder if he'd think I was a total freak if I took a picture of him stretched out and lounging. I can't take my eyes off his Henley, which is slightly pulled up, exposing a sliver of his tan, muscular abs. I groan, imagining my lips placing little sweet kisses along those beautiful ridges.

TJ would blow his cute little carrot top right off.

"You okay, Kiki?" Tatum stares at me with a grin on his face.

"Yeah, why?"

"Because you just groaned. Are you sick?"

Oh Jesus, did I actually groan out loud? *Inside head voices, Kiki! Come on, pull yourself together!* My cheeks flame as I quickly nod. This can't get more embarrassing, that's for sure.

"Not sick. I was just clearing my throat."

He stifles a laugh as he plays a song on his phone.

Twangy music starts playing.

"Ugh, what is this crap? This is exactly my point about trucks and beer."

Tatum grins. "Just playing you some Joe Diffy. He's an icon in country music."

Joe croons on about being a pickup man.

"Did he really just sing about how he met his wives in a traffic jam? In a truck? And not just one wife, but he said plural, implying he's been married lots. People listen to this?"

Tatum laughs. "Joe Diffy is the man."

"Uh-huh, I'm sure." I smile at him as I shake my head.

He gives me a lopsided grin and I want to lick it right off his face.

"Okay, your turn. Play me something."

"Me?" I squeak out.

"Yeah." He chuckles, and I shift in my seat because he makes me want more. More of what, I'm not exactly sure. Just more.

I slowly get up and walk over to the other side of the bed and reach for my phone. I sit on the edge of the bed and unlock my phone. Tatum quickly pinches it from my grasp.

"Hey!" I protest weakly.

"See, I believe music tells a lot about someone. A window into their soul."

"Are you trying to tell me you're a womanizing pickup man who likes traffic jams?"

"Haha. No, I was just playing a classic country song." He chuckles as he plays a song from my Pandora playlist.

I swing my legs up onto the bed and throw a pillow over my head as Shawn Mendes starts singing "Nervous." Hell, yes Shawn, I *am* fucking nervous and excited around this guy. The song changes to Jason Derulo, who starts singing about it being too hard to sleep. Oh geez, Jason, you're right, there's nothing I wouldn't do to get up next to this dude. After a minute, he switches to the next song. As Jonas Brothers' "I Believe" plays, he slowly peels the pillow from my grasp. My eyes are squeezed shut, but I feel him leaning over me. His smell is intoxicating. Like woods and mint. Minty woods with waterfalls and sex. Lots of sex. I inhale deeply.

"Why are you hiding, beautiful?" He chuckles. "It's just music."

I shake my head as I peel my eyes open. "I think you're right. It does feel super personal."

He shifts toward me and stares into my eyes. He's seriously a beautiful human being. "What do you play when you're sad?"

I huff out a laugh. "When I'm sad? Uh, it depends on why I'm sad. Breakups are different from losing a job." I shrug. "Breakup songs are Taylor Swift."

"Ah, good ol' Swifty. She's got that down to a science."

I laugh and hit him playfully with the pillow. "I guess, when I'm moody I like to listen to John Mayer, Maroon Five, and Coldplay. Adele and Norah Jones when I'm feeling quiet. Anything upbeat when I'm at the gym. When I'm happy, whatever's on the radio. I don't know, I love it all."

I shrug, feeling like I just stripped my soul to this gorgeous stranger lounging a foot from me. I look up into his eyes and see his lopsided grin. Butterflies erupt in my stomach.

"Everything but country," he deadpans.

"Yeah, well, I guess I'm gonna have to work on that."

"What's your number-one song? The song you never get tired of?" he asks quietly.

"Oh gosh, I can't. It changes all the time."

"Come on."

I puff out a breath. "It's embarrassing."

"Try me."

I sigh. "'Songbird.'"

"Fleetwood Mac? Great band."

"Yeah, my mom used to play them all the time. I was one of the lucky ones who had a happy childhood. Whenever I hear Fleetwood Mac songs, it brings me to a happy nostalgic time."

"It's a great song."

I blush and smile as the music changes to "Thinking Out Loud" by Ed Sheeran. He looks over and grins at me as we listen to the music. I can't describe this moment we are in, staring at each other, but it's intimate and completely soul-baring. I feel vulnerable as his eyes sear into mine. My cheeks heat as I glance back down at my phone.

Sharing your favorite music with someone is like standing naked in front of a room of strangers. Completely exposed. Your deepest, darkest thoughts beat in time with the lyrics as they play out, tapping on the rhythm of your soul.

"Okay, your turn." I nudge him.

He plays Shinedown's version of "Simple Man."

I turn and stare at him. "I so had you pegged as a country-music-only kind of guy."

He chuckles. "Well, I mostly am. But I like all kinds of music too." He plays me a Keith Urban song called "Parallel Line," and I swallow as he tucks a lock of hair behind my ear as we listen to Keith croon about being careful with his heart he's putting on the line. My own heart beating furiously. I swallow at how true the lyrics ring.

He puts on Pandora and we listen to country hits. He talks about the different artists, telling funny little stories of the ones he's friends with. One of his songs comes on and he quickly changes it.

"Hey, that was yours!"

"Yeah, just because I sing it doesn't mean I want to listen to it," he says absently as he looks for another song. "I've written songs with a lot of these artists."

"Wow, that's pretty cool. Why don't you sing all the songs you write?"

"Some of them I do, especially if Lex and I write together, but sometimes the song just isn't meant for me. Like, I wrote one for Lady Antebellum. It needed their voices to bring the lyrics to life. Does that make sense?"

"Want To" by Sugarland starts to play. I nod, totally entranced by his bright-green eyes. The moment is not lost on me that we are being very intimate without actually touching each other physically. I haven't been like this with a guy ever, not even my last serious boyfriend.

Sugarland sings about wanting to take the jump into a relationship, but unsure of what the other wants—just one kiss could change everything. Tatum sings along with the song and my heart beats erratically. Having Tatum sing softly to just me? About a love song?

I think my heart just combusted.

"Have I swayed you yet on country music?" he asks huskily.

"I'm learning to appreciate it." I smile back at him. It's hard not to. His smile is infectious.

Chris Stapleton's "Tennessee Whiskey" starts to play. I swallow nervously. "Can I ask you a dumb question?"

He grins and rolls to his back as he stares up at the ceiling, stealing the moment away with him. For a brief second, I miss the closeness we just shared.

"Of course," he says.

I roll to my back, mirroring him. I laugh and poke a finger into his rock-hard abs. Holy shit, it feels like poking a piece of granite. "Aren't you supposed to say there are no dumb questions?"

He chuckles. "Oh, but darlin', there are."

I give him a big, shit-eating grin as I turn to face him. "Okay, smartass, well, now I feel pressure." I blush. "So, um…do you like being a big, super-duper country star?"

"You meant sexy."

I raise my eyebrow at him in question.

"You said super-duper, but you meant to say super-sexy."

I smirk at him. "Are you always such an ass? I didn't mean—"

He sits up on his elbow and stares down at me with his gorgeous, dimpled smile, putting a finger on my lips, silencing my protest. He turns serious as he considers my question, his smile sliding off his face. He twirls a lock of my hair around his finger.

"I like performing, but I love singing and writing the

songs. The other stuff just comes with it. There's a lot of pressure to stay on top once you get there. I'm always feeling the constant pressure from the fans, the label, from Lee... Some days, it's hard to just be myself.

"I have to put on a certain persona for everyone around me, and it gets damn lonely at the top. You never know who you can really trust. It gets old, but I certainly wouldn't want to go back to being a struggling singer/songwriter. No one ever wants to struggle. Listen to Jason Aldean's song 'Crazy Town.' That's a pretty good representation of what we go through."

He sighs and is quiet for a moment before his devilish smile returns. "The sexy part just comes naturally."

He absently swipes his phone. Foo Fighters starts to play "Times Like These."

I roll my eyes. "Are you always this cocky?"

He dazzles me with his pearly whites. "Is that a deal breaker?"

I laugh. "Are we making deals here, Mr. Reed?" His eyes twinkle as I poke his dimple with my finger. "Never mind. Don't answer that."

"I love making you blush." He traces his finger down my cheek.

My hands fly to my cheeks. "Don't say that, it'll make me blush harder."

He chuckles. "Let me ask you a question."

"Shoot."

"Do you like being on tour?"

"So far, it's okay. I mean, it's not what I want to do with the rest of my life, but it's exciting and fun."

"For now."

I smile. "For now."

"What do you want to do for the rest of your life?" he asks.

I swallow and I can hear how small my voice sounds when I answer, "I don't know yet."

He's silent a beat. "What song would you play if you were happy?"

"Hmm. Probably 'Feels' by Pharrell."

He tucks a lock of hair that has slipped from my ponytail behind my ear. "And when you're sad?"

"Wait, it's my turn!"

"You can ask me in a bit. I'm getting to know you."

"Through what songs I equate with my emotions?"

His face lights up. "Exactly. Sad."

"'Maybe' by Emeli Sandé."

"Depressing." I shove him playfully. And he laughs. "I actually have no idea who she is."

"My turn now. Happy."

"Any of my songs."

I scoff. "Puh-lease. That's a copout."

"What? As long as I hear my songs playing, then I know I'm still floating along."

I snort. "Floating along? I think more like sailing out of a gale-force storm, but whatevs. Okay, sad?"

"'Dark Horse' by Devin Dawson. It haunts me," he says softly.

"Play it for me?" I ask.

He finds the song and plays it.

I stare into his beautiful, golden-green eyes, seeing the

real him for the first time. He hides behind his charm and good looks, but deep down, there's much more substance to this beautiful man stretched out beside me.

He clears his throat, breaking the spell once the song ends. "My favorite is anything by George Strait. He's the king."

"Ah, another one I'll have to brush up on."

He stares at me for a beat. "You're killing me, sweetheart." He smirks. "What's your sexy song?"

I laugh. "What do you mean?"

His smile spreads across his face, making my insides erupt like a volcano. "Like, when you're getting ready to go out. What song makes you feel sexy?"

I blush. Hard. He's lying less than a foot away from me and wants to know what my sexy song is? Shit.

"I mean...I can't really pull one song out of my head..."

He quickly snatches my phone and starts swiping. *No!* I try to reach for it, but he keeps it out of arm's length.

"Give it back, Tater Tot!"

He holds me at bay with one arm, and damn, he's strong.

"I knew it! It's even titled *Going Out Playlist*." He grins hard, his dimples winking at me. I suddenly go weak like a limp noodle as he starts my going-out playlist. "Wasabi" by Little Mix starts to play. This is so embarrassing. He side-eyes me and changes the song after a minute. Kid Rock's "WCSR" starts blasting.

"Oh Jesus, change it!"

Tatum starts laughing. "The Kid? Didn't see that one coming. Especially this song."

I sniff. "I like Snoop Dog on that one."

He grins as he changes it. The next song is Cyndi Lauper's "Girls Just Wanna Have Fun." I feel so freakin' stupid right now. I throw my hands over my eyes to hide.

He chuckles. "Is it true? Is that all girls really want?"

"Yep. They just wanna have fun," I deadpan.

"Kiki...look at me."

He takes my hands from my face and rolls me towards him so that we're facing each other. He hits next on my song list. "Delicate" by Taylor Swift starts to play. This just keeps getting worse.

"I know Tay. She's a sweet girl."

"Really? Wow, that's crazy." I fidget, looking anywhere but at him.

He watches me as I struggle with my embarrassment. A beat of silence hangs between us.

"Would you want to hang out with some of these people we're listening to tonight?"

"I mean...sure. Who wouldn't? But honestly, this is more my speed. This is kind of nice. Just hanging out with you," I say quietly. I see a brief respite of relief in his eyes before he smiles.

"Me too." His eyes are hooded as he leans toward me. I'm enveloped in his scent, hypnotized by the way it seduces me and pulls me under. The chorus of the song beating in between us.

I know I'll regret this when it's over.

He reaches out to skim his fingers along my cheek and lips. I move closer, my body on autopilot. My leg slides in between his, my hands going to his chest.

What the fuck am I doing? the rational part of my brain screams, while my hormones flip it off.

His lips brush my jaw, and I'm paralyzed as if I've been stung. I can barely breathe as he skims down my neck, breathing me in.

Holy shit, do something, Kiki! You need to stop this. Taylor sings on about not making promises.

My fingers thread through his silky hair and I sigh, arching in to him.

"God, Kiki, you drive me crazy," he whispers. He's kissing his way to my lips when my phone starts playing TJ's ringtone, breaking the spell. Michael Jackson's "The Way You Make Me Feel" blasts between us, dumping ice-cold water on my brain.

I push back from Tatum as if I've touched fire.

"Shit, shit, that's TJ. I, um, I've gotta take this." I quickly scoop up the phone and answer it.

"Hey!" I pant as if I'd been running a marathon.

Tatum sits up on the bed and runs his fingers through his hair. He's so fucking delicious. Why on earth did I just let TJ cock-block him? What is wrong with me?

Oh right. Because one: I'm way out of my league, and two: I didn't want to be another notch on his post.

Ugh, but it was *so* good.

"You sound all panty-licious. Are you making out with that hunk of cowboy meat?"

"What?" I shriek. "No! I'm just watching TV."

Tatum smirks and rubs his jaw as he looks at me over his shoulder. He gets up, leans over, and gently kisses my head. I close my eyes as I hear him quietly open the door and leave my room.

TJ prattles on as I replay the night in my head. "*Hello,* Kinky, did you hear anything I just said?"

"Hmm? Oh, sorry, TJ. Can I call you tomorrow when we're on the road? I'm suddenly really tired."

"Sure thing, skank cakes. Tell the sexy rhinestone cowboy I said hi."

I mumble bye and throw myself down onto the cloud of pillows. All I can smell is Tatum's delicious scent. I bury my nose into the pillow he was just lying on. I wonder if the hotel will notice it's missing, because I am going to be a total creeper and keep it.

I run my fingers over my lips, remembering Tatum's scruff as he dragged his lips along my jaw. Fuck. I can't believe that just happened. Did he regret it? Do I? It definitely complicates things, that's for sure. I can't believe I freaked out—I'm in way over my head.

Shit, did I just fuck everything up?

I toss and turn, unable to get his green eyes out of my mind.

Chapter 17

Tatum

ARE TATUM REED and Savannah Edwards calling it quits?

For those of you who love the dynamic country duo, they just announced through their publicists today they have parted ways. After their performance at the ACMs we for sure thought the next headline would be he put a ring on that finger. So what does this mean for country fans? Tatum Reed plans to finish out his sold-out tour, and Savannah is asking the public to give her time and space to move forward. Obviously, this wasn't a mutual decision. Rumor has it, Maddie Macon, headlining on Tatum's tour, might just be stepping into Savannah's cowboy boots. Those will be some hard boots to fill, Maddie. We took the news to the public and 95% of the fans are crushed Savannah and Tatum are over. There is 5%, though, who would like to see him with Maddie. Only time will tell! This is Candace Foley for E News.

LAST NIGHT'S CONCERT in New Jersey went off without a hitch. I'm super-pumped the band is gelling so well together. I'm also relieved to be out on the road and away from all the drama back in Nashville.

Savannah and I have officially released a statement to the press of our breakup, and social media has gone crazy. Rumors run rampant, and I just have to let my PR people handle it. According to the latest story splashed on the gossip sites, I left Savannah for Maddie. That should go over real well with the public. Savannah probably leaked it herself to make her look like the victim. After our successful performance at the ACMs, I thought maybe Savannah and I could part as friends, but she wouldn't even acknowledge me at the after-parties. That tear on her cheek after our duet was pure gold. It's what Oscar performances are made of, and she should have walked away with her very own golden statue. It's disheartening, but it's her choice.

So, here I am, relieved to be on the road again, our buses having reached New Hampshire for the next two nights.

The June afternoon is humid and warm when I head toward my tour bus after going for an eight-mile run along Lake Winnipesauke. I drink the rest of my water and wipe the sweat off my brow and chest with my T-shirt. I see Kiki walking across the parking lot where we have parked our buses for the show tonight, carrying a tray of coffees. I hesitate, wanting to head toward her, but I know I should just leave it alone.

After the other night, I should stay far away from her, for a number of reasons. The first being she's in a relationship with some other guy coincidentally named TJ. It's a bitter pill to swallow hearing her tell him she was alone watching TV. I'm not into being someone's side game while out on the road. Besides, I'm going through a PR nightmare at the moment. I don't need extra drama. I need to concentrate on getting Entertainer of the Year and keeping my personal life squeaky clean. No complications. But like a moth to a flame, I turn and head toward her. We could just be friends, right?

"Hey, Coffee Girl. Got one for me?" I smile at her as she whips around, almost dropping the tray.

Jesus, there's something about her that has me hooked. She's beautiful with curves in all the right places. Her eyes are the color of storm clouds. She's goofy and cute. I just want to reach out and skim my thumb along her full, bow-shaped lips. Those lips that are smiling at me right now.

"Hey." Her voice is raspy as if she were screaming at a concert all night. Maybe she was screaming for me. That thought does something funny to my insides.

"Let me help you with this." I take the tray from her before she can protest. "Why is it every time I see you, you're carrying coffee?"

"My name is Coffee Girl, isn't it?" She rolls her eyes and then looks down at her Converse.

I laugh. "So it seems. Again, I'm sorry for telling everyone. Hope it didn't make them think that's all you do around here."

She shrugs and gives me a half smile. "It's not as humiliating as Tater Tot."

I huff and place my hand over my heart. "That's just mean."

She eyes my chest and then quickly looks toward her

tour bus like she's about to say goodbye.

But I don't want us to part ways just yet. I want to make her smile again.

"So, um, I just finished my run and I need a shower, but would you want to walk over to my bus with your coffee and hang out for a little bit?"

"Oh, uh…if Jess doesn't need me…sure." She looks over at her bus and then at mine, avoiding my eyes. I wonder if she regrets what happened the other night.

"Wow, my dog acts way more enthusiastic than that when I mention the word 'walk.'"

She blushes and laughs, and she's fucking beautiful. I want to make her blush all the time now.

"Are you comparing me to a dog?" she deadpans, her lips curving up into an impish grin.

"What? Jesus, no, I—shit."

"I like seeing the cool confident Tatum Reed flustered." She blushes again as if she's revealed too much. Her eyes flicker from my eyes to my bare chest and back again.

I give her my real smile, and lean closer in to her. "Trust me, beautiful, I'm not flustered."

"Rattled," she breathes.

"Exactly," I murmur as I stare at her lips, closing the gap between us.

She sucks in her breath and takes a step back, as I watch her pupils dilate. At least I know I affect her the same way she does me, boyfriend be damned.

She subtly nods as if shaking herself out of a trance. "I'm not sure if I can go. I've got to check with Jess."

"Well, I'm Jess's boss and I say it's okay. Which coffee is

yours? Let's see." I grab the tray from her before she can protest and look at the names. "Um…Keepy? Did they really write Keepy down as your name?"

"I think the guy might have smoked a few before his shift." She shrugs one shoulder up, blushing again and chuckling.

I grin. "Come on, Keepy, it won't take me long to change out of these sweaty clothes." I slide her coffee out and quickly run the tray to her bus, depositing it on the steps and knocking. I quickly steer her toward mine before anyone protests. Truth be told, I am a little scared of Jess. I open the door to my bus and help her in. She looks around in awe.

"Wow, this is beautiful, and spacious!" She trails her fingers along the glossy wood paneling and granite counter-tops. "It's like a house in here. Is that mother-of-pearl backsplash in the kitchen?" She walks over and examines it.

I smirk. "Thanks. It helps I get it all to myself."

"One can only dream," she mutters as she sits down on a plush creamy leather couch with her coffee.

"You can wait here or come back into my room. I'm just going to take a quick shower in the bathroom."

"Are you trying to lure me into your back room, Mr. Reed?" she asks innocently, but her eyes dance with humor.

"Gorgeous, if I wanted you in my back room, you'd be there." I wink at her and her cheeks flame again.

"Are you always this confident and cocky, Tater Tot?" She arches an eyebrow up and purses her perfect, plush lips.

God, she is fun to tease. Any other girl would be all over me at this point. It's refreshing that she isn't.

"Always." I give her my cheesy paparazzi grin as I walk

backward toward my bedroom door, catching her rolling her eyes at me as she nervously fidgets in her seat. I'm about to say screw the boyfriend at this point—all is fair in love and war—when I open the door to my back bedroom and freeze.

"What the fuck?"

On top of my bed is a topless Maddie Macon.

"Oh! Hey, Tatum. I read the news about you and Savannah. Thought you might need a little comforting," she purrs.

I hear Kiki gasp from behind me. My arm automatically goes up to block the door, shielding her from God knows what, since she's obviously already seen Maddie. The damage has been done.

"Oh my God. Wow, oh, shit I'm just going to, um, skip the um—uh, thanks anyway, Tatum." Kiki dashes down the hallway and out the door.

"Kiki, wait!" I shout over my shoulder, but it's too late. She's gone.

Fuck my life. I run my hands through my hair and hold my head. The last thing I want is Maddie in my bed, and for Kiki to see that. If anyone sees Maddie on my tour bus, much less *naked* on my tour bus, I'm screwed. The press will eat me alive, and Savannah will look like an angel.

Shit, I'm so naive. I didn't even look around to see if paparazzi were skulking around when I innocently invited Kiki on the bus. I need to be more careful because of all the Savannah drama, and apparently, I need security outside my door.

"Get dressed and get out of my bed, Maddie," I growl as I throw my sweaty T-shirt at her.

"But, Tatum—"

"I said, get dressed and get out or you're off the tour."

That spurs her into action as she scrambles off my bed to grab her top from the floor. She slides by me, making sure her tits brush against my arm.

"You're going to regret this. You and I could be *real* good together. And you will get lonely on this tour. *Real* lonely," she purrs as she runs a fingernail down my arm.

I don't say a word. I can feel my nostrils flaring as I keep my lips pressed tightly together. I'm so fucking mad, it's best I don't say anything I'll regret later. I don't even look at her as she exits the bus. Only then do I start to curse.

Fucking Maddie Macon.

Chapter 18

Kiki

I'VE MANAGED TO avoid everyone for the afternoon by hiding out in the back room of the tour bus, folding laundry. I'm kind of glad I skipped hanging out on Tatum's bus because I have a ton of laundry I need to do.

Yep, that's what I keep telling myself. The bus has stackables on it we're fortunate to get to use, but unfortunately, that also means we launder everyone's clothes.

We. Ha! I mean, *me.*

I tap my lips as I wait for the dryer to finish, replaying the earlier scene in my head.

The last person I thought I'd see in his bed was Maddie Macon. How could he go from Savannah to that? Wait, strike that. How could he go from Savannah, to me, to that? I rub at my heart because I really feel like such a fool to think he wanted more than just a hookup with me. *God, Kiki, you are so naive.* The tabloids are probably right. He's screwing around on Savannah with Maddie.

I mean, duh, the writing was on the wall, or should I say

bus, this afternoon. I'm so confused. Why would he ask me up onto his bus if Maddie was there? It didn't make sense. Unless he didn't know she was in there. He did seem surprised and confused when he opened the bedroom door. I didn't hang around long enough to see if he joined her or kicked her out.

I sigh as I fold my jeans and load them into the basket.

Maybe Maddie is the kind of girl he likes. I mean, he is a country superstar and he's single. I'm sure he screws anything that moves. I'm definitely not the type of girl who can get naked in some guy's bed in the hopes of getting laid because he's a country star. There are lots of girls like that on the tour, and I just can't compete with that. Not to mention he's sinfully good-looking. Jesus, sweaty Tatum with his shirt off just after a run? I was practically hyperventilating as I was talking to him.

Why am I even entertaining this idea? Like I even have a chance with Tatum Reed.

Maybe after the other night in New Jersey he regretted being with me and thought this would deter me. Or, maybe he was just using me. A hot piece of ass, ready and willing. I mean, I practically was grinding into him on my bed. Jesus, I don't want to think what I would have done if TJ hadn't called and interrupted. But I didn't even kiss him. I panicked and chose my phone call over him. No wonder he's got Maddie in between his sheets. He obviously thought I was a prude. Maybe I've been friend-zoned and don't realize it.

God, I'm so dumb. Of course he doesn't want a relationship with anyone right now. He just called off a very high-profile one with Savannah Edwards, a practical goddess in country music. If I were him, I'd be screwing every hot piece of ass on tour too.

I laugh without a trace of humor as I furiously fold a T-shirt. *Why* am I obsessing over this, and getting upset over something that hasn't even begun?

Well, whatever. From this point on, I can turn off my little crush. I'm not going to dangle myself like a carrot in front of him anymore to play with. He's so full of himself, anyways. I've never met someone as cocky as him. He can't even remember my name, for God's sake.

Zero feelings commencing right now. If he wants Maddie Macon—have at it, buddy.

I angrily toss the rest of my clothes in the basket as I get ready to head to the stadium with Jess and Sarah.

Chapter 19

Kiki

THAT NIGHT I watch Tatum from the side of the stage in a whole new light. He's wearing his painted-on jeans with a plaid button-down and cowboy boots and a black cowboy hat.

I mean, okay, he's still extremely sexy…like melt-your-frozen-panties-off sexy. I'll give him that, but he's kind of making an ass out of himself as he jumps around the stage, gyrating his hips in front of the ladies and taking stage selfies with their phones. He needs to get over himself.

I roll my eyes as he crouches down in front of a group of screaming women and thrusts his hips up in the air. Um, hello? I thought he had a "wholesome" image to uphold? What he's doing doesn't look very PG.

He tried to flirt and talk with me before the show in his dressing room, but my half-smiles and short answers made it clear I wasn't in a good mood. I mean really, what is there to say? He never said a word about the whole Maddie thing, so maybe he did hook up with her. Maybe if I hadn't bolted he would have suggested a three-way with her.

Ick.

And then when I was stocking the side stage with water and towels, I saw him flirting with a pretty female fan before the show, laughing and showing his damn dimples.

The *same way* he flirted with me.

I feel so stupid, thinking our back-and-forth teasing banter might have been something special between us. I'm such a moron for being a star-struck idiot. I mean, he even flirts with the old lady pushing the trash cans at the end of the night, for Pete's sake.

I chew my thumbnail as I watch him bring one screaming female up on stage, propelling her to sit on a stool. She's sobbing like she can't believe her luck. They take a selfie together and then he gives her a G-rated lap dance as he sings.

Barf.

She slaps his ass and the crowd goes wild.

Really, Tatum Reed? How had I not noticed this repulsive performance in Boston and New Jersey? Oh wait, because I had my head up my ass, captivated by his charm and good looks. So what if he fills out those jeans so perfectly it makes my mouth water? So what if his smoky green eyes give me goosebumps every time they lock with mine? So what if I had a dream about him last night where coffee was accidentally spilled down my front and he had to help me peel my clothes off?

I shiver. That *was* a really good one.

But, so what, Tatum Reed?

"Hey, earth to Kiki. You okay, hon?" Sarah waves a hand

in front of my face.

"So what?" I shout out loud. I quickly put a hand over my mouth. Did I seriously just shout that?

"Whoa, there, take it easy. You okay? Did something happen?"

"Oh my God, please tell me I didn't just yell that out loud. I'm so sorry." I really need to work on my groans and outbursts.

"Yes." she giggles. "It's okay, no one heard you. What's going on?"

"Nothing. I'm just seeing Tatum in a whole new light tonight, and I guess it's pissed me off."

"Ah, yes. When the lust clears, the true man is revealed," Sarah says in her Buddha-like wise voice. "I'm actually surprised. It usually takes a couple months for girls to see past all the good looks, charm, and star power. You did it in a week." She winks at me and elbows me in the arm as we watch the performance. "I'm just kidding. He's actually a really nice guy."

"Hmph. He looks like a douche out there. Is he seriously waving his arm like a rapper right now?"

Sarah snorts. "Yeah, he is. What can I say? The chicks dig him."

We both laugh over the line Tatum likes to say often.

"I heard through the rumor mill he was hooking up with Maddie. I'm so disappointed in him. She's just, ugh... He could do so much better...like you," she mutters. "Anyway, I hope it's just a rumor."

Sarah's revelation causes a burning sensation in the pit of my stomach. So it's true. They *are* together. Even though I never really had a chance with him, it still hurts. I mean, he was just in my bed two nights ago. Granted, all clothes were on and we were just listening to music, but I could have sworn we had a connection. Reality hits my chest with an ache. It must have just been me who felt something more.

I guess this is why they call them crushes.

"Maybe you're wrong. Maybe they're perfect for each other." I swipe my eyes as my nose begins to smart. I feel like such a fool.

"Hmm, we'll see about that." Sarah side-eyes me as I busily pick up towels. "Oh, hey Maddie, we were just talking about you."

Oh no. She's the last person I want to deal with right now. I inwardly groan as I turn my back to the stage to see Maddie approaching.

"Hey, Kiki, I need to talk to you." Maddie saunters up to me, completely ignoring Sarah.

"Uh, sure, what's up Maddie?"

"Can we go into my dressing room?"

Sarah slinks away before I can grab her to go with me. *Traitor.*

"Um, let me make sure it's okay with Jess to leave."

Maddie snorts. "I think Tatum will survive the next ten minutes without you standing here, watching his every move."

I glance over at her bitter expression. Geez, who peed in her Wheaties?

"Um, okay. Well, I need to check anyway because this is my *job* to stand here. I'll meet you there." I tap my earpiece and speak to Jess as Maddie stalks off to her room.

"Jess, it's Kiki. Maddie needs to talk to me in her dressing room, so I'm leaving backstage. Is that okay?"

"Okay, thanks, Mackenzie. I've got it covered. Let me know if you need help with her."

"Will do."

I make my way to Maddie's dressing room and knock softly on her door.

"Come in."

"Hey, what's up?"

"I'm not liking this look for the next show." She pulls out a skimpy, sequined dress from the rack.

Really, we're doing this in the middle of the show tonight? The next show is in three days.

I take a deep breath. "Okay, tell me what you don't like about it."

"Well, I mean, I know it's blingy…"

"And short, and shows cleavage."

"I know, but why can't I wear this?" She twirls in her high-waist, denim cutoffs with a midriff-baring, bedazzled football jersey.

"Because you're not a Dallas Cowboys cheerleader?" I deadpan.

She huffs. "Are you calling me fat?"

"Um…no. But you're short, and those look better on women with really long, lean legs." I gesture toward her shorts. "Besides, I can see up your shorts."

"Well, I was going to pair it with these lace thigh-high boots. They have, like, five-inch heels."

Jesus, this girl is clueless. Maddie isn't overweight by any means, but she's five-foot-two and curvy. She can't pull off that style.

"If you were Rihanna or Taylor, you could probably pull off that look."

"Well, why can't I be like them?"

I sigh. "Your body shape is different and your style is all over the place. I'm trying to give you your own look that compliments your body, so girls can look at you and say, 'I want to be like Maddie Macon!'"

She huffs. "And why can't girls say that when I'm wearing this?" She points to her cutoff jersey.

"Because no one wants to be caught on *US* magazine's worst-dressed list." Shit. Did I say that out loud? I sigh in frustration. "Listen, Maddie, I'm only trying to help you. Think of me as your girlfriend who will always tell you the truth. Does this make me look fat? Should I buy these boots? Is this a good color on me? I'll give you an honest answer every time."

I'm met with stony silence. *Hmm, this is awkward.*

She folds her arms over her chest as she sizes me up and narrows her eyes. "So...what's up with you and Tatum?"

"Um...what do you mean?" How on earth did we go from clothes to Tatum?

She juts out her chin. "Well, are you guys together?"

I give her a confused look, because I'm truly confused. "Um, no. He's my employer. Aren't you two together?"

"Oh...well, yeah, we've started hooking up lots since the tour started. But I'm not blind. I see the way you moon over him." She tosses the sequined dress on a chair. "I think you're lying about Tate. What were you doing on his bus yesterday?"

An uncomfortable silence blankets the room. This girl is not my friend, and I definitely don't trust her. I don't want to be talking about Tatum's hookups, especially if Maddie is involved, and who is staring at whom. She just confirmed they hooked up, so there's my answer in black and white.

I sigh, ignoring her question. "So, what do you want me to do about your clothes?"

"I guess...tell me the truth about what I'm wearing."

Jesus, do I have to spell it out for this idiot? I bite my lip. "I kind of already have."

"Well, as my 'girlfriend,' tell me again." She air-quotes obnoxiously.

I shrug. "It's not the right look for your body shape."

"In all honesty, I have enough friends right now. I'm not looking for a new girlfriend to tell me the *truth*." She twirls around and flings the door open. "Oh, and you're off the tour. I'm firing you."

My mouth hangs open in complete disbelief. Did she really just fire me? Can she do that? Oh my God, Jess is going to have a cow. How did this go so wrong?

Un-fucking-believable.

I grab the sequin dress and quickly walk out of the room before I say something I'll regret. I touch my ear piece. "Um, Jess?" My voices wobbles, I'm on the verge of tears for the second time in less than an hour.

"What, Mackenzie?" she snaps.

"Where are you?"

"I'm in Tate's dressing room."

"Okay, I'll be there in a second."

I open the dressing room door and fling myself into a

chair, still clutching the sequin tank dress. Sarah's cleaning up her station and Jess is hanging clothes. The concert has wrapped up and the guys are meeting with backstage ticket holders.

She looks over at me from the clothes rack. "What did Maddie want?"

I swallow. "Um…she just fired me. Can she do that? Can she fire me?"

"What?" Sarah screeches. "She can't do that!"

Jess gives Sarah the stink eye. "Why did she fire you?"

"Apparently, she doesn't want someone to tell her the truth about what clothes look good on her body type. She wants to continue to dress like Britney Spears during her meltdown days. She even said this isn't slutty enough. I took three inches off of it this morning!" I hold up the skimpy dress in my hands.

Sarah shakes her head. "The only reason that girl is on this tour is because she has two hit songs on the radio. She has zero good taste. She asked me the other night if I had any black lipstick and could I tease her hair up a little higher."

I grimace and nod in agreement with Sarah. I look at the dress and examine the hemline. "Oh my God, she put safety pins in this to make it shorter. Ugh, she's ruined this!" I throw the dress down. "Then she accused me of having a fling with Tatum, because apparently they *have* been hooking up. I think she's pissed because I walked in on her naked in Tatum's bed the other day."

"What?" Sarah screeches. "*Hello?* When were you going to tell me this?"

"Sarah, please stop screeching like that," Jess chastises

her. "Well, are you fooling around with Tatum? Because you did sign a nondisclosure." She arches an eyebrow at me.

I hold my hands up in exasperation. "I've only shaken hands with the guy. She's delusional!"

Jess doesn't need to know about him grazing hot kisses along my jaw. I haven't even told Sarah or TJ.

"Okay, well, I'll talk to her agent and Lee. She can't fire you, Mackenzie, but she can make your life hell. She can wear whatever she wants and make a fool of herself onstage. She's not our problem anymore. Let her answer to Lee and Tatum. You just do your job and try to stay clear of her."

"No problem." I frown as I formulate ways to avoid her. For the first time since I started this job, I'm grateful for Jess being in my corner. I quickly roll a rack of Tatum's clothes back to the bus before I run into any members of the band or evil bitch Maddie. If Tatum wants to hook up with her, then fine by me. I'm here for a job, not to have sex with my employer.

Besides, he's just being friendly to me. He's a professional flirt, and I fell for it hook, line, and sinker. Of course he wouldn't be interested in his stylist's assistant—the coffee errand girl. Maddie's in the industry. They understand each other's lifestyles.

Meanwhile, I am *way* out of my element.

TJ Lame: Hey
Me: Hi

TJ Lame: *We okay?*

Me: *Absolutely.*

TJ Lame: *You've kind of gone radio silent…*

Me: *Just trying to do my job. It's been hectic. I'm fine.*

TJ Lame: *It has. Ok, just checking in. Let me know if I can help you out.*

Me: *R u always this helpful to the assistant to your assistant?*

TJ Lame: *I like to see you smile.*

Me: *Well, I do laugh when I see you doing those awful dance moves onstage…*

TJ Lame: *Hey! Those dance moves have taken me years to perfect. And guess what?*

Me: *Yeah, I know. The chicks dig it.*

TJ Lame: *I can't help it that the ladies love me;).*

Me: 🙄🙄.

Chapter 20

Tatum

TONIGHT WE'RE IN Atlanta, and it's hotter than the devil's dick. Why Jess gave me leather pants to wear tonight is beyond me. I don't get how Lex wears these fuckers all the time. I was sweating profusely throughout the whole show and had to peel my shirt off on stage. I wish I could have peeled off these fucking pants too. Now, I'm back on my bus lying on my bed trying to take these damn things off of me, and they won't budge.

Jesus, if the guys caught wind of this they would never let me live it down. I'm going to have to call Jess to come and help me. I reach for my phone.

"Jess, it's Tate. Can you come over to my bus? I need help."

Jess sighs. "Seriously? I just got my dinner. Can't you call Jimmy?"

"I am paying you, am I not? Jimmy isn't available," I grumble. I fucking hate being the asshole, but this is a dire situation and I do not want anyone walking in on me to see this. "It's kind of an emergency. The bus door is unlocked."

"Okay, give me a minute," she grumbles.

Ten minutes later I hear a knock on my bedroom door. I'm still lying on the bed with my pants unbuttoned. I should have changed in the dressing room while the girls were in there right after the concert, but I wanted a hot shower, and some peace and quiet.

Besides, Kiki has been weird. She's friendly...professional, but it feels like she's drawn an invisible line between us. I'm trying to keep my distance as well because of all the Savannah-breakup-drama, but I miss how at ease we used to be with each other. Absent is the flirty banter and blushing smiles. I didn't realize how much I miss them now that they're gone.

The door slowly opens and Kiki peeks her head in.

Speak of the devil.

Her expression goes from annoyed, to surprised, to concealed laughter as she takes me in, spread-eagle on my bed, shirtless with my pants unbuttoned.

"Oh my God. Um, hi, Tatum. Jess sent me over to help you. I didn't realize you and her were a thing, so...I, um, I'll just pretend like I never saw this and send her back over."

"Wait! Kiki, it's not what it looks like."

"Um, pretty sure it looks like you're waiting for...Jess? Or I can call Maddie if you wish." She smirks as she starts to shut the door.

"No! Wait! I'm stuck."

"Huh?"

"Shit, don't make me repeat it."

"Well, you're going to have to because I don't think I

heard you correctly." She rests one arm on the doorjamb and her other hand grips the door knob like she can't wait to shut the door and run.

"I'm stuck," I say weakly, totally humiliated.

She opens the door wider and walks towards the bed. "What do you mean, you're stuck? Stuck to the bed?"

I growl because this is utterly mortifying. I'm going to ream Jess a new one for sending Kiki in her place.

"I'm stuck in these pants. I need help taking them off."

She starts howling with laughter.

"Can you help me or not?" I snap, growing impatient with the whole situation.

"Oh my God, wait, hold on. I just need to wipe the tears from my eyes." She's bent over crying because she's laughing so hard.

"Kiki, come on, this is serious, and embarrassing enough without having you laughing your ass off about it. Can you please be professional?"

"Oh Jesus, I needed that. I haven't laughed that hard in a long time," she snorts, wiping tears from her eyes, and then quickly composes herself and looks around the room. "Okay, okay, I saw this on *Friends* once. We'll need some baby powder. Do you have any?"

"What? No, that didn't work! It made Ross all pasty."

"You watch *Friends?*"

"I have an older sister who loves that show," I say contritely. "Besides, I don't have any powder. Just help me pull them off!"

She bites her lower lip and crosses her arms, pushing her boobs up. Oh God, my dick just jumped. *Not now! Down boy!* I cannot have a hard-on right now when she's trying to take these pants off.

Grandma Pat and her hairy mole... Grandma Pat and her hairy mole...

"Did you say something?" She bites her lower lip again as she scans the room looking for something.

"Will you stop doing that?" I grumble.

"Stop doing what?"

"Biting your lip. It's distracting. Can you please try to help me peel these off?"

She smiles and walks toward me. "Keep your pants on, Tatum, I'm coming. Ha! Keep your pants on. See what I did there?"

"All I heard was that you were coming." I smile back at her.

"Hysterical," she deadpans. "I don't think you're in a position to be cracking jokes." She sighs and then kneels on the end of the bed and tries tugging the pant leg off.

Nothing.

She tugs harder. "Son of a bitch. What are these, glued on?"

She hops on the bed and straddles me. God, she's beautiful. Her gorgeous chestnut locks cascade down over her luscious breasts. She's wearing a black tank top that makes her tanned skin glow. I can see her hot-pink bra strap peeking out, and that little bit makes me want to strip her shirt off to see more.

When she leans close she smells like flowers in a meadow. Her long dark hair brushes my chest, causing my skin to break out in goosebumps. She is thoroughly concentrating

COFFEE GIRL

on the task at hand, but I can't help her because all I can see and smell is her. She bites her lower lip again in concentration and grabs the top of my pants.

Yep, I'm hard again.

"Lift your hips up. I'm going to tug down."

I do as I'm told and she slides down my legs, peeling the pants down over my ass. Shit, I forgot I was going commando.

"Oh my God, Tatum James Reed, seriously?" she screeches as she looks down at my hard cock.

He twitches because he's excited he can finally breathe and there's a hot girl right above him. "Shit, I'm sorry. I forgot, but it's not like there's room for underwear in these fuckers," I say sheepishly.

"I don't get paid enough for this shit," she mutters as she looks away, tugging harder, but the pants suddenly stop. She loses her grip and the momentum causes her to fall backward off the bed, landing with a loud thump.

"Shit! Kiki, are you okay?" I sit up, but I'm still stuck in the damn pants so I can't move.

"I'm fine. Just great," a muffled reply comes from the floor.

Laughter rumbles from my chest and I can't stop.

"Tatum James Reed, you are in no position to be laughing right now!"

I chuckle. "I'm sorry, I'm sorry."

"I'll be right back."

God, her scolding me, using my full name is so hot. I lie back against my pillows and think of Grandma Pat again as Kiki crawls out of the room. No need to scare the poor girl

133

off with my fucking hard-on. She comes back in with a pair of kitchen scissors and a hand towel.

I swallow and cover my manhood. "What are you going to do with those, Lorena Bobbitt?"

"Tempting, but I'm going to take your pants off for you, and I figure this is the easiest way before I break an arm or cause a bloody nose."

"I'd hate for anything to happen to your cute little nose."

"It's not *my* arm or nose I'm referring to."

She averts her eyes to my ridiculous hard-on as she throws the towel over it, and sits down on the bed next to me. It's cute how prim she's acting. I'm used to girls who would take full advantage of this situation and jump right on my dick. As weird as it sounds, it's a turn-on she's not.

"Besides, these pants are revolting. I mean, they have rhinestones on the side. Seriously Tate? What was Jess thinking?" She nervously babbles as she cuts away the material. "You know, you can say no to her, right? This gives new meaning to the term 'rhinestone cowboy.' Hideous. I never want to see these pants in the dressing room again. You're a jeans kind of guy, not leather pants. I mean, they weren't bad on you...you can make anything look good, but these are like New York City club meets the bedazzler gun at Walmart. Did Jess make these for you? Have you worn them before?"

She cuts the last shred of material from my leg. She's so fucking beautiful. I take the scissors from her hand and throw them to the side. She immediately stops talking as she hesitantly watches me.

I take her face in my hands and pull her down to meet

my lips. Her eyes go wide, but they flutter to a close as I touch her soft full lips to mine. God, I've wanted to do this since the moment I laid eyes on her. I start slowly, feeling the soft texture of her lips. I suck on her top lip and then her bottom. I run my tongue along the seam, begging for entry. She opens her petal-pink lips and I taste her for the first time. She tastes like heaven. I stroke my tongue with hers, and she whimpers as I groan. I thread my fingers through her hair and deepen the kiss, bringing her down on top of my chest. My heart is beating a wild dance of pleasure as she moans against my lips. I could seriously get lost in this girl.

I sit up, pulling her with me, still kissing her thoroughly as she straddles my lap. I want to touch her. Everywhere. I skim kisses across her jaw and down her neck. She smells so good.

"Tatum, I... Oh my God, you're really good at this," she breathes as I skim down her neck.

I chuckle as my thumbs skim across her breasts. I want to cup them and feel their heavy weight. I'm so rock-hard right now, I ache.

"You're stunning, Kiki." I capture her lips again in a hot kiss as I start to pull her shirt up when there's a knock at the door.

"Yo, Tate. You in there, man?" It's Lex, my lead guitarist and best friend.

Worst. Timing. Ever.

She immediately breaks the kiss, springing off the bed like I shocked her with electricity. Her eyes dart from me to the door, to my naked body on the bed, the leather pants in shreds, and the hand towel on the floor.

135

"Ah, hold on, dude!" I shout. I do not want Lex to see this scenario, even though he's seen a lot of weird shit. It's pretty fucked up if you're just walking in on it. Scissors, shredded pants, Kiki…my dick in full salute.

Kiki looks like a deer caught in headlights. Hair mussed, eyes dilated, her lips swollen…so sexy.

Yeah, we're fucked.

"Um, could you toss me a pair of shorts?" I ask her. "Top drawer on the right."

"Um, uh, yes, sure no problem." She fumbles with the drawer and whips a pair of athletic shorts my way.

"Thanks." I quickly pull my shorts on and think of Grandma Pat's mole for the third time tonight. "Listen, Kiki…"

"No, don't! I, uh, I mean, I get it. Don't say anything. I'm just going to let Lex in and let myself out. Oh my God, Maddie…" She grabs the shredded pants and scissors.

I look at her confused. What the hell does Maddie have to do with this? When she gets to the door she turns back to me.

"I, uh, don't worry. This"—she holds up the pants—"stays between us."

I'm not sure if she's referring to the pants, or the kiss. Maybe both. Before I can respond she opens the door to a surprised Lex.

"Oh, hey, Coffee Girl…"

"Hey Lex!" She breezes by Lex as he gives me a curious look.

I wave a hand dismissing her departure. "It's not what you're thinking. It's nothing."

"What am I thinking?" The cocky bastard arches an eyebrow. He knows me so damn well.

"CG was just bringing some concert T-shirt designs by for approval." I make it up on the fly. For some unknown reason, I'm not ready to share what just happened. Not even with my best friend. I want Kiki to myself a little bit longer and I need to sort out what I'm feeling toward her.

"Ah, cool. Let's see them."

"See what?"

"Let's see the T-shirts. I want to see the new designs."

I look desperately around the room. "Um, I don't have them. She must have taken them with her."

Awkward silence beats between us.

"She's a nice girl, dude. Not a one-off."

I give Lex a cool gaze. "What are you talking about?"

"You know what I mean, mate. She's not a one-night stand. Now get your wanker washed off. The guys are waiting."

So much for keeping it a secret.

Chapter 21

Kiki

IT'S NOT WHAT it looks like. It's nothing. CG was just bringing some concert T-shirt designs by for approval.

His voice echoes in my head as I run for my bus. Humiliation washes over me like a tidal wave. Tears stream down my face as I reach for the door, but I stop myself because I don't want anyone to see me in this state. I wipe my face off with the bottom of my tank. Oh God, it smells like him. I take a deep breath and open the door. Sarah and Jess are eating dinner at the tiny dining table. I brush past them as quickly as possible with my head down. I toss the leather pants in the trash.

"Hey, wait! What did he want? What was the *big* emergency?" Jess shouts from behind me as I enter the hallway.

"Um, he wanted one of those new soft T-shirts to wear out tonight," I lie, my voice sounding unnaturally high.

Jess snorts. "That was the emergency? God, he's being such an asshole on this tour."

I open our partition and close it shut. Tears fill my eyes

again. I feel so confused. Oreo meows in greeting. I kick off my shoes, climb up into my bunk, and crawl under the sheets. Oreo tries to headbutt my shoulder.

Sarah pops her head in. "Hey, you okay?"

"Yeah," I croak.

"Liar. What's wrong?"

"I guess I'm not feeling that well. Probably that sushi I ate earlier."

"Oh no, yuck. So I guess you don't want to go out with the band guys to the house party?"

With Tatum.

"Um, no thanks, just feeling out of it."

"Aw, I'm sorry, Kiki. Can I get you anything?"

"No, I'm good. Just want to sleep."

"Okay, sweets, I'll try to be quiet when I come back in. Feel better. If you change your mind, we're leaving in a half hour." She pats my leg and leaves.

I replay "pants-gate" in my head. I almost peed in my pants laughing when he told me he was stuck in those leather death-traps. Serves him right for wearing such tight-ass clothes. But it took all my concentration not to look at his perfectly chiseled body as I tried to strip them off. My fingers itched to glide over his washboard abs and the silky, dark-golden line of hair that went from his belly button down into his pants.

And then, all of a sudden, I was staring at his cock. *Tatum Reed's cock.* It was glorious—smooth, hard, and big. I wanted to take it in my mouth and bring him to his knees. I can feel my cheeks blush just replaying the memory in my head.

And then I fell off the bed.

I was so embarrassed, especially when he started cracking up. Then he gave me his shy dimpled grin when I came back with the scissors, making butterflies erupt in my stomach all over again. I was nervous as hell, babbling as I tried not to look at his beautiful body while I cut his pants off.

I lost my breath when he suddenly captured my face in his hands and brought my lips to taste him. And taste him I did. I knew it was a bad idea. I mean, he's hooking up with Maddie, but, holy cow, is he an amazing kisser. I lost myself in that kiss, and for just a weak moment, my heart opened for him. I wanted him, badly. I wanted to be his.

But then the spell was broken, and the look on his face when he was about to tell me that kiss should have never happened. I couldn't bear to hear it. It was humiliating to be another girl on his proverbial belt. Way worse than finding Maddie in his bed.

The thing is, I'm not really sure why I'm so upset. It's not like Tatum and I are an item. He's a major country star. Hell, he irritates the crap out of me with his cockiness on stage and his sexy dimples. But that kiss...that kiss melted the icy wall I tried to fortify around my heart.

And then he built that wall right back up in a matter of seconds. He can have any girl he wants with just a snap of his fingers, and I fell right for it. The humiliation of just being passed off as something unimportant kills me. I'm nothing to him, just another errand girl at his beck and call. He's a player, plain and simple.

Ugh, I hate that my feelings are all over the place! Stupid hormones turning me into a total train wreck.

I slide my cell phone out of the back pocket of my jeans and hit TJ's name.

"Hey, assistant to the assistant to the gorgeous, I-want-to-shake-his-booty, be-his-Bey-Queen country star!"

I start to cry again. "TJ…"

"Oh my God, Kiki, I was just kidding. What's wrong?"

I tell him the whole story, and by the end, he has me laughing.

"You had to *cut* his pants off? And he wasn't wearing any underwear? And you were practically sucking his dick?"

"Whoa, I did *not* say that. I said I kissed him."

"Whatever. We both know you would have done that next."

"Okay, maybe."

"I would have."

"Yeah, I know you would have, you little slut. But seriously, what am I going to do? I'm so embarrassed. He basically dismissed me like I was a nothing groupie to his guitarist Lex."

"And you said they're all going out tonight?"

"Yeah, they're going to some local house party. One of Lee's friends has a house on the lake."

"Then you know what you have to do. You get your ass out from under the covers, pull yourself together, put a hot little dress on, and make Tatum wish he never let you walk out of his room tonight."

I sigh. "I'm tired, TJ. Besides, he's with Maddie. I was just a convenient piece of ass."

"Don't sell yourself short, honey. You're a hot piece of ass, convenient or not. You can sleep when you're dead! Go.

Out. Tonight. And you're a bazillion times prettier than that hose-bag Misty Bacon." He sniffs.

I laugh. "It's Maddie Macon, not Misty Bacon!"

"These details are *so* bourgeois to me. Besides, Oreo just texted me and told me you were hogging his covers and he wants you to go out."

"Oreo can't do that, he doesn't have thumbs." I sniffle.

"*Hello*. He used the microphone to text for him."

"Hey, TJ?"

"Yes, Kinky Doodle?"

"Thanks."

"I love you too."

It's not what it looks like. It was nothing. CG was just bringing some concert T-shirt designs by for approval.

Fucking Coffee Girl. That's what I am to him, another willing girl who was there for him at an opportune time. Well, fuck that. I'm a person with feelings and desires. I may not have celebrity status, but I'm just as worthy, and if Tatum can't see that, then he can suck it.

"Hey, Sarah?" I shout down the hall a few minutes later.

"Yeah?"

"I'm suddenly feeling better. Can you do your magic and make me look irresistible?"

"Hells yeah! Meet me in the back room. I'll grab my stuff!"

What's that saying? Eat your heart out?

Here I come, Tatum Reed.

Chapter 22

Tatum

LEE HAS A friend in Buckhead who lives on a large piece of property on the lake, and he mentioned they wanted to throw us a little get-together tonight. It sounded like a good idea earlier, but now I'm tired and it's late. I mentally and physically rally because I don't want to be rude to Lee or his friend, or let the guys down since they're excited to go out.

Lex and I drive up to a gorgeous, cedar-shingle house right on the lake that must have been over twelve thousand square feet. Torches are lit on the enormous back patio and continue down the flagstone path to the dock. They have a firepit and plenty of people around it who are drinking, which means the booze and women will be plentiful.

"Wow, I could get used to a place like this," Lex says in awe as he steps out of the car.

"Lex, you have a place like this." I laugh.

"Not this big. And mine doesn't have a torch-lit pathway with beautiful girls lounging about."

"I'm sure you could make that happen any day of the

week," I say drolly. "Besides, you live alone. You don't need a bigger house."

Lex shrugs and grins. His house is really amazing. A five-thousand-square-foot horse ranch with panoramic views off of every patio. His parents are landscape designers and stayed with him for months redoing the grounds. *Home and Garden* has been begging him to do a spread, but Lex refuses. His house is his sanctuary. He doesn't want to share it with the world.

We greet Matt and Will at the door and chat with them a bit before heading towards the firepit. There are a lot of people here and lots of women. Lex sits down and two girls immediately sit on his lap. I shake my head in amusement. Lex is definitely a free spirit. He may not want to share his house, but he'll share everything else. To say he isn't the monogamous type is putting it mildly. Lex's idea of being tied down to a woman is preferably on a bed with ropes or silk ties, possibly handcuffs. He thought I was nuts for getting involved with Savannah. The asshole might have been right about that one.

To him, women are like ice cream. You can't pick just one flavor. You have to sample them all. Pathetic thing is, everyone thinks I'm the hound chasing down the girls. If I even wink at a girl, the next thing I know, it's been said I slept with her.

I like being in a relationship. I like knowing everything about the other person, but still finding out little surprises down the road. I want meaningful conversations, knowing what makes her laugh, holding her when she cries. The one-night stands get old quickly. They're just tension-relievers.

But not to Lex—he is terrified of relationships.

I leave Lex to the girls and find Lee talking to a tall, middle-aged guy. He introduces me to the host of the party, a guy named Derek Banks. Derek went to college with Lee at Georgia Tech and now owns a surgical equipment business. Lee excuses himself to grab some drinks and I continue to talk to our host about the hardships of constantly being on the road when something catches my eye...or I should say someone.

Maddie sidles up next to my side, dressed in what looks like a skimpy outfit made out of tinfoil. Her boobs are practically hanging out, and it's so short it cuts right under her butt cheeks. Derek's eyes bug out when she wraps her hand around my arm. She turns her back to him as she looks up into my eyes and juts her bottom lip.

"Tatums, I'm *bored*! Want to blow this lame conversation off and walk me down to the dock?" she whispers loud enough for Derek to hear.

"Maddie, I'm in the middle of a conversation with Derek. He's our host tonight," I say irritably as I detach her hand from my bicep.

"Oh! I'm so sorry." She sounds anything but. "I just thought you might want to be rescued. I didn't know you *actually* wanted to talk to a fan." She runs a manicured nail down my chest.

"Maddie! Derek, I must apologize for her. I think she might have drunk too much."

"What? No, I haven't." She pouts and crosses her arms over her chest like a petulant child.

"No worries, no worries. I don't want to take up too

much of your time. I know there a lot of people here who would like to talk to you. Thanks for stopping by. I thoroughly enjoyed our chat and thought the show tonight was awesome."

I shake Derek's hand. "Thank you so much, man. Your house is beautiful, and we really appreciate you opening it up to us tonight. I'll tell Lee to hold a private box for you for our Nashville date. We'll fly you and your guests there for the show. Maybe we can even get in some fishing at my lake house while you're there."

"Wow, that's really awesome, Tatum. Thank you!" Derek walks away and I steer Maddie away from the crowd.

"What in the hell is wrong with you?"

"Ow, you're hurting my arm!" she whines.

I loosen my grip as I spin her around to face me. "That was incredibly rude and distasteful. We don't treat our fans that way, especially not the host of this party. That's Lee's best friend from college," I chastise.

Her face crumples and she sobs. "Are you mad at me? I didn't even see him standing there."

I look around to make sure we aren't causing a scene, trying to rein in my temper. "Maddie, I was in the middle of a conversation when you walked up. Don't ever do that again unless someone is dying. And a little word of advice? Your fans will make you or break you, so you better start treating them better."

Maddie nods agreeably. "Okay, okay, I promise I won't interrupt you again." She flips her hair and then glances over to the main house. Her face contorts into an ugly frown. "Ugh! What is *she* doing here? I thought I fired that bitch."

I swivel my head around to see who she's talking about. Walking down the back steps toward the patio and firepit are Sarah and Kiki. But Kiki looks different. She was gorgeous before in her casual tank tops and jeans, but tonight she looks stunning. Heads turn as they make their way toward Lex and the boys. I swallow as I drink her in. Her hair is down and curled in loose waves. She's wearing a slinky, strapless, silk coral dress and gold heels that wrap up her tan calves. The glow emanating from the fire makes her look incandescent.

I ignore Maddie's bitching and walk toward her, smiling. Her eyes collide with mine and heat simmers in the pit of my stomach. They flicker to over my shoulder and then she quickly looks away, not returning my smile. My mood deflates like a balloon. Just over an hour ago she was straddling my naked body kissing the hell out of me, and now she's pretending like she doesn't know me? *What the fuck is that about?*

I reach Lex and the guys and grab two beers for Sarah and Kiki. "Hello, ladies. Want a beer?"

"Yes, please. Thanks, Tate." Sarah grabs the beers and hands one to Kiki, who barely acknowledges me.

After a couple minutes of standing silent next to her while the guys banter back and forth, I lean towards her. "Uh, hey, Kiki. Can I talk to you for a minute?"

She turns her face toward me and I breathe her in. Her eyes look like storm clouds tonight and the anger simmering in them make me mentally take a step back.

"I'm not doing coffee deliveries tonight, Tatum, if that's what you're looking for."

"Damn!" Matt crowed. "Coffee Girl just gave it to Tater Tot!"

I slide him an annoyed look and turn my attention back to Kiki. "That's not what I meant," I whisper.

Sarah elbows her and whispers in her other ear.

She hands Sarah her beer. "K, I'll give you a minute." She walks past me, heading for the pathway that leads down to the docks.

"Kiki, Jesus, wait up!" I grab her arm once we reach the path and spin her around. She shakes her arm free of my grip. "What the hell is wrong with you? One minute we're sharing an incredibly hot kiss and the next you act like I've got some untreatable venereal disease."

Her eyes go wide and she steps back. "Oh my God, do you?"

"What?" I run my hand through my hair in frustration. "God, no, it's a fucking metaphor. I like you, Kiki. I want to get to know you better. Look, I know you have a boyfriend, but I want—"

"I don't have a boyfriend," she says quietly, cutting me off.

Uncertainty mixes with relief as it pumps through my veins. "You don't? Who's TJ, then?"

"My best friend. My *gay* best friend." She smirks.

Relief washes through me. I take a step toward her and give her a lopsided grin. "I'm really happy he's your gay best friend."

She crosses her arms and her boobs push up, looking like ripe peaches nestled in her top. Unlike Maddie, she is fucking irresistible. I want to run my hands all over her body and feel her silky skin underneath me, begging me to touch her. My dick is instantly hard.

"Why, Tatum?"

"Why what?" I'm so lost in my wet dream of her I lose the thread of the conversation.

She huffs. "*Why* are you relieved that I'm single, and *why* do you want to get to know me?"

I'm stunned into silence. "Why? Because you're funny and sexy as hell. I love making you laugh, and I especially love making you blush. And maybe it was just me, but I felt a connection when I kissed you."

I step toward her and tenderly tuck a lock of hair behind her ear, putting my heart on the line. "Shit, I think I've felt a connection to you when we first shook hands in my dressing room. My attraction to you scares the hell out of me."

She looks down at the ground, but when she looks back up, it's not heated desire simmering in those beautiful, stormy eyes. It's a scorching death blaze.

"Uh-huh. So if you felt such a connection, then why did you tell Lex it was nothing? That I was just 'Coffee Girl'? And what about Maddie?"

Damn, she heard me. I run my fingers through my hair in frustration. "Kiki, you have to understand. I just got out of a relationship with Savannah a few months ago. It's splashed all over the gossip magazines right now. I can't so much as take a step off my tour bus without getting my picture taken or having some nasty headline written about me. Savannah has managed to paint me into a pretty ugly corner, and I constantly have to defend myself to the media. I want to protect whatever this thing is…could be…might be…between us. Tell me you feel it too."

"So you want me to be your dirty little secret?" she asks darkly.

I scrub my face. *Why is this coming out all wrong?* "Shit, no…that's not what I meant. It's just—"

"I don't understand. If you just got out of a tumultuous, high-profile relationship, why would you want to jump right back into a new one with *me?* Am I just a rebound fuckbuddy? And then there's Maddie. I'm not understanding this…" She gestures between us.

"Tatum! I've been looking everywhere for you!" Maddie stumbles up from the dock, panting.

I growl, "Not fucking now, Maddie. I'm having a *private* conversation."

"With who? Fucking *nobody Coffee Girl?* Didn't I fire you?" she snorts as her eyes rake viciously over Kiki.

Kiki takes a step back and holds up her hands. "I don't know what's going on between the two of you, but I'm not getting involved. Tatum, as for your question, maybe there was something…I just…I don't know. I'm sorry, I can't do this." She waves her hand between Maddie and I. "Sounds like you all need to work your shit out."

Kick in the fucking gut.

"Kiki, please don't go." I reach for her but she's too far away from me. She holds up her hand to prevent me from following her as she walks back to the party. I can't take my eyes off her retreating form.

"Well, now that she's gone. Maybe we can get back to me and Y. O. U." Maddie leans forward against the railing, allowing her boobs to spill out of her dress. I'm so disgusted and annoyed by this girl I can't even pretend to be nice.

"Maddie, have a little decency and put your boobs back in your dress. No one wants to see that shit. You've also drunk too much. You better go find Lee."

"You know, Lex wouldn't turn me down. I could always have him. In multiple positions."

"It's true, Lex doesn't turn down much, but honey, I'm pretty positive you are one girl he would happily refuse."

Her mouth gapes. I turn and head back to the party to find Lex.

Chapter 23

Kiki

BOSTON, NEW HAMPSHIRE, New Jersey, New York, Virginia Beach, Charlotte, Raleigh, Hotlanta, Jacksonville, and now back in Nashville for two nights before starting the West Coast half of the tour.

Clean cool sheets, space to sleep in a bed that isn't the size of a coffin, and blessed quiet. Oh, thank the Lord! Even Oreo won't stop running from room to room chasing his catnip toys. He's so excited to be off the tour bus.

I haven't had a conversation with Tatum since that night in Atlanta, unless you count yes/no answers as talking. He mostly deals with Jess, honorably giving me my space, and I'm fine with that.

Totally fine with that.

I'm *fine*.

I mean, I kind of miss our joking, flirting, texting, and yes, I totally miss wiping him down. I'm now in charge of wiping down Lex and it just isn't the same, although Lex can make me giggle with his horrible knock-knock jokes.

Fortunately, he doesn't jump around as much as Tatum, so I don't have to do it every three songs. It also makes me feel like I'm cheating on Sarah by wiping down Lex's chest, although she's never said anything to make me feel that way.

Maddie is her typical, spoiled, bratty self, and whoever's dressing her—*ahem*, Maddie—is doing a piss-poor job.

She's furious I still have my job, but because of Lee (and frankly, because of his friendship with my brother), I'm not going anywhere. I like my job, and I do it well. I actually think Jess is beginning to warm up to me. And when I say warm, I mean a frigid forty-five degrees. But hey, it's better than freezing, right?

I know. I can't believe it either.

We aren't there on a personal level, obviously. I don't think Jess gets up close and personal with anyone. We're still in a dark closet on that front, but professionally, we're making progress. She's beginning to ask my opinion on things and letting me take charge on what the guys should be wearing. Don't get me wrong, it's not like I'm dressing Beyoncé every night, but the guys have a rock-country look they're going for, and we're making it happen.

I like my job, and as much as I try to convince myself I don't have any feelings for Tatum Reed, the truth is...I do.

I miss my fun banter with Tatum and his teasing, dimpled smile. I sometimes catch him staring at me, and it makes my skin break out in goosebumps, but he always keeps it professional. I want to kiss him again. Who am I kidding? I want to do much more than that. Just daydreaming about it makes my toes curl. Some days I wish I could take back what I said that night in Atlanta, but I feel so humiliated by Maddie and the whole "Coffee Girl" situation I shut him down. Self-preservation and all that.

I'm the one who shut that door and locked it, and I don't know how to find the key again.

MY BROTHER FLEW into town yesterday and is taking me out to breakfast this morning before I have to head over to the concert venue. He's narrowing down his search on locations for his new bar and is super excited to be in Nashville. Who knew my brother is into country music? I always assumed he was a punk rock kind of guy.

Lee secured him two VIP tickets for tonight's show. I'm wishing I could have flown TJ in this weekend, but he's swamped with work. Apparently, Jonathon, the guy who took my place at *Cufflinks*, is a real diva and refuses to do much of anything. TJ and Darren hate him. I also suspect TJ might have a boyfriend he isn't sharing info about...perhaps Trent from accounting. He sent me a dozen different outfit choices the other night for a poetry reading. Loud, obnoxious TJ and poetry? I made him choose the outfit that sported an ascot.

"Earth to Kiki?" Cam stares at me across the table.

"Oh, sorry, I must have spaced out for a minute. Did you say something? I need coffee."

Cam smiles and shakes his head. "You look good, Kiki. You liking this new gig? Worth the cross-country move?"

"Aw, thanks, Cam. Yes, most definitely. I mean, it's not

what I want to do for my career, but I think it's a good resume-builder. Being on the road has been exhausting, though, I'm not going to lie. It feels like being with a traveling circus, constantly packing up and moving."

"Yeah, that would be rough. Mom sent a care package with me. It smells like flowers."

"Oh, good! It's body lotion and shampoo from La Lucent, Aunt Bobbie's spa. I can't find anything close to it here."

Cam rolls his eyes and smiles. "Women." He scratches his jaw. "Um, Brooke told me to tell you her nanny position is still open if you wanted to grow up and stop playing the role of country-music-hillbilly-groupie. Her words, not mine."

"God, she sucks." I chuckle. Is she ever going to get over me telling her no? "She's just pissed because she can't find a French nanny who'll wipe her ass for her." I take a stab at my French toast.

"Uh...well, she found one who tried to wipe her husband's ass."

"Huh?" It takes a minute for Cam's words to sink in, my fork frozen in midair. "No!" I'm totally dumbstruck. "Graham? Really?"

Cam solemnly nods his head.

"What happened? What's she going to do?"

Cam shrugs. "She was supposed to be at a tennis lesson, but wasn't feeling well and came home to find them 'cleaning' the shower together. Graham actually had the balls to tell her the showerhead wasn't working properly." He takes a bite of his egg sandwich and shrugs. "She's probably not going to do anything to upset her perfect marriage."

"Shut up! Oh, poor Brookey." I kind of feel sorry for her. I mean, as horrible as she can be, I'd never wish that on anyone. "Her perfect fairytale marriage is now…shit."

"Oh, I wouldn't say 'poor Brookey.' I mean, she's hanging onto this marriage with everything she's got. She made him burn the prenup, and they're going to some new-age, fellowship, church-revival worship together. She's convinced they need more Jesus in their lives now."

"Whoa! He burned the prenup?"

"It doesn't really matter if he shredded it or burned it. There's always a copy with the courts. But he's scared of her. She's got him by the balls, and she's squeezing hard."

I wince. "I'd be scared of her too. How are the boys doing? Do they even know?"

Cam shakes his head. "Mom and Dad don't even know."

"What? How on earth did you find out?"

"She called me right after she found them. She said she couldn't trust any of her friends, and she knew Mom would freak out. So, I came to help mediate. That shit was intense. She had the nanny immediately deported."

"Only Brooke would actually have the *cajones* to deport someone for having an affair with her husband. Geez, church-revival worship? So unlike her."

"Apparently, it's the new thing to do in her group of friends. Tennis is out, Bible study is in. And then she posted some cheesy Instagram pic the next day of the two of them canoodling at worship. Hashtag *I'm the luckiest*, hashtag *It's Jesus time*." He rolls his eyes as he takes a bite of his bacon. "Anyway, she'll be fine. She's Brooke, the queen of 'my life is blissfully perfect.' Enough about her. How are you doing?"

I casually move the food around on my plate. "Ha. Definitely *not* the queen of perfect, but I'm hanging in there."

"So, is it exciting working for a major country star?"

"Eh, I mean... Would you really say *major*?"

"Kiki, the guy sells out his concerts to football stadiums. Yeah, he's major. He's nominated for Entertainer of the Year. Lee told me they may have to go right back out on the road after this tour because it's been a complete sellout. But that stays between you and me."

"What? No! I-I don't think I could do another bus tour."

Cam laughs. "That bad, huh?"

"Yes and no. I wasn't kidding when I said it's like a traveling circus. It was exciting at first, but now hearing the same song set every week, sweaty guys, doing their stinky laundry, being in tight quarters with someone who doesn't really like you, it's definitely not *Lifestyles of the Rich and Famous*."

"Yeah, but you said you really liked the makeup artist."

"Sarah? Yeah, she's awesome."

"She hot?"

"Cam, seriously, you have enough girls in your little black book."

He chuckles. "What about you?"

"What about me?" I take a big gulp of coffee.

"Lee said you may have turned a few heads in the band."

I nearly spit my coffee out on my plate. "Lee needs to get his head checked. Besides, it's none of your business."

"Whoa, whoa, calm down. He was just teasing. He's keeping an eye out for you. Making sure you're walking the straight line."

This annoys the crap out of me for some reason. "I don't need a babysitter, Cam. I'm fucking twenty-six years old. I can handle myself."

Cam sits back in his chair crossing his arms over his chest and studies me. "Fair enough, but rumor has it you might have gotten in over your head with the country-rock star."

"Jesus Christ," I breathe, my blood pressure rising by the second. "Something would actually had to have happened for me to be in over my head. Who the fuck is feeding you this information? Lee? He needs to mind his own fucking business, *and* get his facts straight."

"Easy on the F-bombs." Cam looks around the restaurant. "So nothing happened between you and this guy?"

I hesitate for a split second too long. "Nothing." I shrug.

"Mackenzie Leigh Forbes, you're lying. I know when you lie."

"Where's that coffee?" I look around for the server, avoiding my brother's penetrating stare. I sigh in defeat. "So I may have kissed him. But nothing came of it. It was just... a kiss."

He stares at me for a beat. "Not that I really want to know, but you sound kind of sad it was just a kiss."

"Cam, drop it. I'm not really into sharing my love life with my brother," I growl.

"Okay, okay, but I'm here if you need me. I'm your big brother and it's my job to look out for you. I just don't want you getting in over your head. And besides, I'm a fucking fantastic mediator."

We both laugh.

"Thanks, Cam. I'm actually in a really good place right

now. I'm…content."

"Good."

"You bringing a date tonight?"

He blushes and looks sheepish. "Maybe."

"Ha. Only you could be in a new city for a couple days and have a hot date lined up."

Cam shrugs. "There's this girl…"

"A girl? What girl?"

"Lisa. You'll meet her tonight."

"That's it? You're just going to give me a name? I need details!" I whine as my brother picks up the check.

Cam gives me a smirk as he pays the tab and we exit the restaurant into the late-morning sunshine.

"You've been hanging around TJ too long."

"Okay, fine, don't answer me. I look forward to meeting this mysterious Lisa. Thanks for breakfast. Text me when you get to the arena and we'll meet up." I kiss Cam on the cheek and head back to my comfy apartment to rest up before tonight.

Chapter 24

Tatum

I THROW THE article down on my kitchen island and run my fingers through my freshly cut hair.

"I don't understand why she's doing this." I'm irritable and upset.

Savannah's interview with *Marie Claire* magazine basically paints me out to be a womanizing, egotistical, verbally abusive, shithead alcoholic. She's even produced a picture of herself with bruises on her arms. I'm sick to my stomach. She told the interviewer she was the one who had to leave *me* because she couldn't handle all the women and booze and me constantly telling her she wasn't going to make it in the music industry. Oh, and that one fateful night I raised my hand to her, the night that ended our relationship for good.

All fucking lies.

It makes my stomach roll, because none of it is true. None of it. If anything, I was a totally supportive boyfriend. I always complimented her on her work and thought she had amazing stage presence. And never, ever have I raised my hand to a woman, child, or animal. The thought of it disgusts me.

This article has totally come out of left field and knocked me on my ass. It's due out in next month's edition. One of Lee's friends over at the magazine sent him a copy this morning to give us a heads-up.

"Ratings, petty revenge, sympathy?" Lee shrugs his shoulders.

I shake my head. "It doesn't make sense."

"Was she this cuckoo for Cocoa Puffs when you were dating her?"

I grimace. "Maybe. Definitely when things got rocky between us."

"Have you tried calling her?"

"Yeah. She won't take my calls. I mean, she's acting like she's the innocent victim in all this when you and I both know she's not."

"We can sue her for defamation of character. Put a gag order on her so she's not allowed to talk about you to any news media, print or otherwise. We can also try to keep this article buried."

I nod my head. "Do whatever it takes. This will kill my career. If any hint of what she's accusing me of gets out, I'm a dead man walking."

"I'll call the lawyers." Lee grimaces and gets on his phone.

I sigh. "Okay, keep me posted. I have to go do sound-check."

How has my life suddenly just turned to shit?

I'M SPEEDING OVER to the arena when my phone dings with a text. It's from Jess.

I have an emergency and can't get over to the arena in time for sound check. Kiki said she could meet you there. She'll get you and the boys set for tonight.

Great. Now on top of Savannah's shit, I have to deal with Kiki, who will barely look at me, much less talk to me. Just fucking perfect. My mood plummets as I pull into the stadium parking spot.

Lex greets me inside, and we walk onto the stage with the rest of the band. "Dude, you okay? Seem a little off today."

"I'll be all right. Savannah's just stirring the pot again, accusing me of some pretty outrageous stuff, and they're all fucking fabricated lies, man."

Lex shakes his head. "I knew that girl was trouble."

"Thanks for the heads-up, dick."

"Want to talk about it?"

"No."

"Eh, well, here's a bit of advice: if you want a decent, level-headed woman with tits that fill your hands perfectly and an ass you can bump and grind against all night long, then you need to go out with Kiki. Now, that girl exudes sex appeal."

Lex has his eyes on Kiki as she stocks towels backstage. She's wearing tight skinny jeans and a tank top, and every time she bends over, my dick jumps. A surge of jealousy roars through my blood, but I tamp it down. I can't stand that we're talking this way about her, but I can't let on I have feelings for her. He'd never let me live it down.

"Lex, dude, she's not a piece of ass. You said so yourself."

Lex chuckles. "Yeah, well, I'm in a bit of a dry spell."

I choke on my water. "You went home with that girl from the bar last night."

"Right. Shit. Hmm…but she was nothing like that ride there."

"You're such an Irish asshole. You know I want to fucking slug you in the nuts right now." I laugh as I put him in a headlock as he pulls me out of my funk. I whisper into his ear, "Talk like that again about my girl Kiki, and I will shove your head so far up your Irish *arse* you won't know which end is up. Got it, Chancer?"

Lex gives me a shit-eating grin as I shove him away. "I knew it."

"You don't know shit." I chuckle.

"She's a good one, mate. Hang on to that one." He slaps me on the back as we head toward the stage hands. I look over at Kiki one more time. I can't hold onto someone who doesn't want me. I swallow past the lump in my throat and shake myself out of my reverie.

"All right, let's get this done!" I yell to everyone before I end up actually making good on my threat and punching Lex in the jaw to relieve some of this tension I feel. "It's going to be a packed house tonight."

I turn back to Lex. "We're pulling the duet I do with Savannah's video."

"Whoa, seriously? That's a crowd favorite. Damn, you must be really pissed. What the fuck did she accuse you of?"

I ignore his question, not wanting to rehash my conversation with Lee. "It's done. I already talked to the production guys. We're going to play that new song we've been working on with the Winston Brothers and Maddie."

Lex shrugs. "All right, whatever you need to do. I've got your back."

"I appreciate it, bro. I'm going to need you to. Let's go tell the rest of the guys."

Chapter 25

Kiki

A TEXT FLASHES across my phone from Jess. She was supposed to be here by now.

Hey Kiki, my mom isn't doing well, so I need to rush her to the emergency room. I've already texted Tatum. His number is 624-899-7232 if you need to reach him before he gets there. You can totally do this, and Sarah will help you. Thanks!

Shit, shit, shit!

"Uh, Sarah? Looks like it's just you and me tonight," I squeak as nerves start to claw their way up my body.

Sarah is setting up her station in Tatum's dressing room. "What do you mean? Where's Jess?"

"I guess her mom isn't feeling well. She's taking her to the emergency room."

"Oh no, I hope she's okay. I'm glad Jess is home to be with her." She turns back around.

"Um, hello? That means it's just *me*. I can't do it all by myself!" I whine, causing Sarah to stop what she's doing and turn back around.

"Oh my gosh, Kiki, you totally can. You no longer have to deal with Maddie, thank God. And the Winston Brothers are super easy, so that just leaves Tatum and his guys, and knowing you, they're already set, right?"

"Well, I mean, yeah, the guys…"

"Oh, I see. You're nervous about having to deal with Tatum one-on-one. You'll be fine. Listen, he usually follows your cues, so if you don't feel like talking to him, he won't push you."

I nod. "Okay. You're right, this is a piece of cake."

"And you get to rub him down again." She winks at me. "Ooh, can I wipe Lex down? Pretty please? I'll do your makeup for a month!"

I laugh at her puppy-dog expression. "Yes, you sicko, he's all yours. Besides, you'd do my makeup anyway." I wink at her. "Dang it, I was just feeling confident again. How on earth am I going to keep it together? Especially when I've had dreams of wiping down his naked body for the past four nights."

"Whose naked body are you wiping down in your dreams?" Tatum walks in wearing a black cowboy hat that makes his dimpled grin more pronounced, a button-down that matches his eyes, snug Levi's, and cowboy boots.

Jesus, I'd like to crawl into a small black hole and never come out again.

"What? No one said that. Wiping down a body. *Pfft*. I said I had a dream of typing with a hot toddy. It was so weird. Get your hearing checked, Tater Tot."

Sarah snorts and Tatum looks me over with a shit-eating grin on his face. "Sounds pretty weird."

"Totally." *Change the damn subject, Kiki!* "Um, oh hey, Tate, so I guess…er, here's a pair of pants to wear tonight." I throw the closest pair of pants hanging over the rack at his face.

Luckily he catches them. "Cool. Thanks, Kiki."

I busy myself looking for a shirt for him while he changes into the other pants. "T-shirt or button-down? What do you feel like?"

"T-shirt."

I hand him a soft cotton tee with a bourbon logo on it. He's shirtless and just as freaking amazing as the last time I saw his chest and abs. His pants are so skin tight you can see a defined bulge. The room suddenly becomes super small and claustrophobic. All I can see is Tatum. And all I can think about is that kiss. My hormones go into overdrive and I get flustered.

"Wow, those pants are super tight. How do they feel? Do you want another pair?" My cheeks heat as I stare at him.

"Nah, these are fine. Besides, the—"

"Chicks dig 'em," Sarah and I both deadpan in unison.

Tatum flashes his dimples at us. "So you've heard."

I roll my eyes. "Oh, we've heard, all right."

He sits down in Sarah's chair and they start chatting about how great it is to be back home for a few days while she styles his hair.

"Dang, Tatum, I'm going to have to use some concealer under your eyes tonight. You not sleeping well?"

I look over at the mirror and see Tatum grimace. He does have shadows under his eyes.

"Just got a lot on my mind right now. Do your magic,

Sunshine."

"You got it." Sarah beams.

My phone buzzes in my back pocket. I pull it out and see my brother has arrived.

"My brother just got here. I'm just...I'll be backstage if you need me," I mutter. They both continue to talk, completely ignoring me as I slip out of the dressing room.

I'm curious to know what's going on with Tatum, but not enough to engage in a serious conversation. Right now, our status is equal to that of casual acquaintances— employee, boss. And sadly, because I'm a coffee-girl loser who can't tell him how I really feel, that's the way it will have to stay.

"Kiki, over here!"

Lee, Cam, and some gorgeous brunette make their way past the security guards. "Hey!" I hug my brother and turn toward the brunette. "Hi, I'm Kiki."

"I'm Lisa." We shake hands and she looks around at all the roadies changing the stage from the Winston Brothers to Maddie's stage. "Wow. This is *so* cool. I'm a huge Tatum Reed fan," she gushes.

"It's really cool. Are you guys going to watch from back here?"

"No, we're headed to the meet-and-greet right now, and then we're going to the luxury box with Lee."

"Oh, well aren't we fancy-pants!" I wink and elbow my brother. "Maybe we can get drinks together after?"

"You got it. We'll have Lee bring us back here after."

"Perfect. Nice to meet you, Lisa. Have fun!"

"You too." They walk away, and all I can think is how in

the hell my brother found a date in the two days that he's been here. And a stunning one, at that.

I stock towels and water on both sides of the stage as Maddie performs. I used to like her voice, but now that I've seen the real Maddie Macon, it sounds like nails on a chalkboard.

The Bridgestone arena fills up as people arrive for Tatum and the guys. I peek out from behind the side of the stage's exit door and am blown away by the amount of people milling about. Maddie sings her last song and fortunately exits the stage opposite of me. The roadies start quickly changing the stage once again for Tatum's band. Guitars are tuned, microphones tested. It's a well-oiled machine.

"Yo, Kiki, this shirt isn't working for me," Tatum's drummer Will rumbles from behind me.

I whirl around and almost bust up laughing. Will is the size of a linebacker and somehow he ended up wearing a T-shirt that would fit my ten-year-old nephew. The bottom of the shirt is stretched tight and rolling up across his midsection.

"Um, probably because that's not your shirt, Will. Come on, I'll find something for you, but we have to hurry. You only have a couple minutes."

I drag him back to the dressing rooms down the concrete hallway streaming with people and after a few minutes, I finally spy the shirt I picked out for him stashed behind a couch pillow. Weird, but I don't have time to dwell on it.

We rush back to the side of the stage and he climbs up on the riser that holds his drum kit. All the other band members, including Tatum, get into position as the sheer screen-drop in front of them rolls upwards toward the ceiling as the music starts.

I love watching the opening song because the crowd goes absolutely nuts when they see the guys. It's such an incredible rush. Even though I'm not onstage, the waves of energy wash over me. I can only imagine what Tatum and the guys feel in that moment.

AFTER THE FIRST set, Tatum quickly exits the stage and hands me his T-shirt, which is soaked. He grabs a water bottle and I quickly pat him down. It's a hot, humid night in Nashville, and his skin is slick with sweat. He doesn't say a word to me, won't even make eye contact, and I must say, it totally sucks.

I hand him a clean shirt, and he gives me the water and gruffly says, "No shirt. It's too fucking hot." And he hops back onstage to start the second set.

I watch him sing to the crowd, swinging his hips seductively and showing off his well-defined upper body. Women try to reach for him, but he stays just out of their reach, only touching their fingertips with his, but they're charmed nonetheless.

Suddenly, he bends over to reach for one fan and his tight jeans split down the rear.

Mary, Mother of Joseph, he's not wearing any underwear.

I quickly look around for the pair of pants I'm supposed

to keep on hand with me for an emergency like this, but I must have forgotten them in my haste to help Will.

Shit. Shit. Shit.

Tatum realizes his pants have ripped and Lex quickly steps to the front of the stage and improvises a guitar solo while Tatum skips backward keeping the rip hidden. Panic completely seizes me and without thinking, I tear off my tank top and throw it at Tatum, who runs in my direction from the stage. He freezes as he catches the tank, drinking me in, his eyes smoldering as I stand there in my white-lace bra. I'm hidden from the crowd, but not from him or the stage hands. I'm miming for him to cover himself with my tank. He holds up the tank and grimaces.

Oh shit, I forgot I was wearing my Mr. Kitty tank. It's a white boyfriend tank with a graphic of a cute fluffy kitten wearing a sparkly bow tie.

Tatum turns back to the stage and lifts his mic up, interrupting the music. "Hold up guys, hold up. We've got a situation here." The music slowly dies as the guys all turn toward Tatum. "Seems I've ripped my pants, and this is what my girl Kiki has given me to cover it up with until she can get me another pair."

The guys slow down the music and Will holds a steady beat as Tatum holds the tank up in total disgust and the crowd goes wild.

"You can put your mittens on my kitten anytime, Tatum!" a woman at the front of the stage screams. Tatum just smirks as he quickly ties it between his legs, holding his pants together.

"I'll be your Mr. Kitty," Lex deadpans into his mic.

"Mee-ow."

Tatum shakes his head as he chuckles. I'm pretty sure he's blushing. The crowd is eating it up, going wild.

"Of all the nights to go commando, huh?" He winks. The crowd roars with approval.

"Let it all hang out, Tatum!" fans hoot and holler.

I just stand there and chuckle because he continues the song like a professional while wearing a kitty in a bow tie, sumo-style, on top of his jeans. Sarah's suddenly at my side with another tank top for me.

"Oh, thanks!" I quickly pull it over my head.

"The roadies were starting to drool. You better go run and grab some fresh clothes for Tate."

"Shit, you're right."

I quickly gather my wits and rush back to the dressing room to grab another pair of pants and a shirt for Tatum. I get back just as the lights dim down and he runs off stage. He whips off the tank and throws it at me.

"What the fuck was that, Kiki?" he says angrily as he strips the ripped pants off.

Yup. Standing in his full glory for all of backstage to see. I quickly avert my eyes before he catches me staring at him. I hold a towel up to block his naked ass from prying eyes backstage.

But he's so mad, I don't think he gives a rat's ass. I swear I've seen this guy naked more times than my last three boyfriends combined, and I haven't even slept with him.

He grabs the pants out of my hands and quickly tugs them on before I can utter a reply. He takes the T-shirt I'm lamely holding and tugs it over his head. God, I could watch this man get dressed for the rest of my life. He quickly downs a bottle of water.

"I'm so sorry, Ta—"

He shoves the water bottle at me. "Save it. I'm too pissed to talk right now. Meet me in my dressing room as soon as we're done."

"Okay," I squeak, but he's already running back on stage. The crowd boos because he's fully dressed again.

Shit. I'm in so much trouble.

I'M IN THE dressing room packing up clothes when the door slams open and Tatum comes stalking in with a murderous look in his eyes. He slams the door shut with a loud bang.

"What the fuck was that, Kiki?"

"Uh..."

"Did you plan that? Was that some sort of twisted revenge?"

"Whoa." I hold my hands up in defense, but he quickly cuts me off.

"Are you not getting enough attention? Is that it? Let's embarrass the shit out of that asshole Tatum in the heart of country music, in *his* hometown, in front of thousands of fans? The press is going to have a fucking field day with this." He paces the room like a caged tiger, practically tearing out his hair. "I have so much shit going on, Kiki. I don't need it from you too."

"Tate, I swear I didn't..."

He advances on me quickly, backing me into a wall, caging me between his arms. "No, Kiki. I don't want to hear it," he growls.

My lips part as I stare into thunderous green eyes.

He swoops down and captures my lips in a dizzying kiss. The kiss is full of frustration and anger. I soak it all in, absorbing the punishing blows his lips give against mine. This is not a tender, explorative kiss; this is Tatum unleashing whatever anger he's kept inside.

And I take it, because I want it. Badly.

I moan as he deepens the kiss, lifting me up against the wall. I wrap my legs around his waist, my fingers greedily tugging his silky hair. He runs his palm over my breast and flicks his thumb over my hardened nipple peeking through the thin tank. He pinches and I moan again. He's got me so hot, so quick. I'm a quivering ball of nerves. His kisses soften and I throw my head back exposing my neck to him as I shamelessly grind against him, gasping for air. I want him to lick me everywhere. As if reading my mind, he runs his tongue from my earlobe down to my collar bone.

"Tate," I moan.

"Jesus, Kiki, you taste so fucking good. I want you so badly. Goddamn, I'm so pissed at you."

I'm practically panting with need, ready to tell him to take me right here against the wall when there's a knock at the door. We both freeze.

"Fuck me," he grinds out.

"Hey, Tatum, you in here?" It's Lee. Which means my brother and Lisa are with him. I unwrap my legs from around him and slide down his body. His eyes burn into mine.

"We're not done here. Not even close," he says gruffly.

He spins away from me before I can say anything and quickly strides across the room and flings open the door. I barely have time to straighten my shirt before Lee pops his head in.

"Oh, hey, Kiki. Uh…so, we're going to have to have a little chat about what happened tonight," he says to the both of us as he walks into the room.

"Yeah, I was just telling Kiki that."

Lee nods as my brother and Lisa come around the corner and walk through the open door.

"Hey! Great show tonight, man!" Cam shakes Tatum's hand and Lisa is practically vibrating with excitement.

"Can I get a picture?" she squeals as she whips out a selfie stick.

Tatum looks from me to Lee and then back to Lisa. "Uh, sure thing."

Cam takes a photo of Lisa practically bear-hugging Tatum and then she takes several with her stick. I'm a little embarrassed for her at this moment, but my thoughts quickly go to the fact that I'm probably fired.

"We ready to head out?" My brother slings an arm around me and kisses the side of my head. If I'd been looking I would have seen Tatum's eyes glaze over with ice.

I shrug. "Where are we going?"

"Whiskey Sky. It's a new bar off Main," Lee answers.

"Are you really going to wear that out?" Cam chides me.

Before I can answer, Tatum interrupts. "She's fine for Whiskey Sky. Trust me, most girls there are practically naked," he growls at Cam.

"See you there, Tatum?" Lee asks, but doesn't get a reply. Lee just shrugs and ushers Lisa out the door. Cam slings an arm around my shoulder.

"Ready?"

I nod, shooting Tatum one last glance over my shoulder as we leave the beast to simmer in his own bad mood.

"Geez, what crawled up his ass?" Cam whispers to me as we head to the limo.

"Um, I think I did."

"Way to go." Suddenly it dawns on him. "Nice tank top by the way." He smirks, and I cringe.

"I really screwed up."

"Eh, you'll be fine. Everyone needs to be seen wearing a fluffy kitten tank. What are twenty thousand people?"

I cover my face. "You're not helping."

He laughs and shouts back to Lee, who's chatting with Lisa behind us. "Hey, bro, is Kiki in deep shit?"

There's a pause and then Lee clears his throat. "Depends on how pissed Tatum is about it."

"Well, sis, you always have the nanny job."

I elbow him in the ribs. "Asshole."

WE GET TO Whiskey Sky a little late because I wanted to go home and change into a cute dress. Tatum is right, though, everyone is scantily dressed, wearing barely there cutoff shorts or minis and cowboy boots. Some are just wearing bralettes. This place is like Maddie Macon's home planet. Ugh, which means she's probably trouncing around here somewhere. The last person I want to run into after tonight is her.

We go upstairs to the VIP lounge reserved for the band. Will, Matt, and the Winston Brothers are already there hanging out. Girls galore in skimpy clothes mill about, rubbing up against the guys like cats in heat. I notice Lisa cling tighter to Cam and suddenly I wish I was tucked into my soft sheets at home, reading a good book.

I pull my buzzing phone out of my purse and see a text from Sarah.

Not going to make it out tonight. Killer migraine. Boo. Keep an eye on Lex for me!

Dang it, now I'll be a third wheel with my brother. I scan the room as I sip a vodka Sprite, looking for Lex. I love Sarah, but the girl is a wee bit delusional if she thinks he isn't going to go home with one of these bimbos. From the stories I've overheard in the guys' dressing room, Lex is a bit of a man-whore.

I finally spot him sitting on a leather couch, and low and behold Tatum is sitting next to him. But they aren't alone. Lex has a girl on each knee and is making out with both of them. Tatum looks bored as the blonde on his lap gabs on about something, running her fingers up and down his leg.

I want to throw up. Jealousy courses through my blood like a freight train, but I can't tear my eyes away from him. I lean toward Cam, trying to hold the bile inching up my throat at bay. He puts his arm around me, and I want to sob into his shoulder. Seeing Tatum with a leggy blonde on his lap has thrown me for a loop. I mean, an hour earlier we were making out against his dressing room wall. This ping-pong of emotions makes me dizzy and confused and angry as hell.

"Cam, I think I'm going to head home. This isn't really my scene."

Cam nods as he looks around, spotting the guys. He knows I have feelings for Tatum despite my angry denial over breakfast this morning.

"Sorry, Kiki, I totally get it. We'll have to hang with Lee, but you can take the limo back. I'll be staying at Lisa's tonight."

"Nah, it's okay, I'll just grab an Uber. I just—I need to leave. Now." I hug him and avert my eyes, feeling the sting of tears threaten to spill over. "I like Lisa, by the way. She's nice."

I look up in his direction one last time as I'm about to set my drink on the bar. His green eyes collide with mine and they flash anger. He turns to the willing blonde and nuzzles her neck, just like he did with me.

I'm so disgusted and pissed, I slam my drink down and quickly walk toward the exit. I tear down the stairs to the private VIP lobby and am just about to open the exit door when a large hand wraps around my bicep.

Chapter 26

Tatum

"WHAT THE FUCK, Kiki?" I growl as I grab a hold of her arm.

Tears stream down her face as she flings her arm out of my grip. "Get the fuck off me, asshole."

"Kiki," I say gruffly as I wipe her tears away from her cheeks. I look into her stormy gray eyes, and the anger that has had me so in knots this evening slowly starts to melt away. I ask, a little gentler this time, "Why are you crying?"

She laughs and sobs at the same time. "Why am I crying? Gee, I don't know. Maybe it's because not less than an hour ago you were kissing me to the point of stripping my clothes off, and then I turn around and you're making out with a blonde bimbo right in front of me! Asshole!" She tries to shove me off, but I hold onto her.

I sigh. God, this night is going from bad to worse. "I didn't kiss her, Kiki. I didn't do anything with her. Come on, I'll take you home."

"I'm not going anywhere with you!"

"Well, I'm not letting you walk the streets. You won't find a decent cab at this hour. And that jackass you came with... First he insults your clothing, and then he lets you leave by yourself while he has his hands all over Lee's date."

She scoffs. "That *jackass* is my brother. And he offered me his limo, but I declined. God, are you always this much of a jerk when you're the one who's in the wrong?"

Suddenly my pent-up anger at seeing another guy with his arm around Kiki dissipates. "Your brother?" I ask stupidly.

She looks away from me. "Yes, that's what I said. He's really good friends with Lee. Now can you let me go so I can go home? I've had enough for tonight."

"Kiki, I... Look, I'm sorry. I got jealous. I thought you were with him, and we just kissed minutes before they came into the dressing room and he had his arm around your shoulder... I just saw red."

"Yeah, kind of like how I'm feeling right now. So, now that you understand, let me go."

"Kiki, those girls were with Lex. I wanted to get a reaction out of you. I knew you'd be there. It was fucking stupid and immature on my part. I wanted to hurt you like you hurt me. Shit, this is all a big misunderstanding." I tip her chin up so my eyes meet hers. "I'm sorry if I hurt you. I don't want those girls. I don't want any girl but you."

"What about Maddie?"

"Maddie? What about Maddie?"

"She told me you guys have been hooking up the whole tour."

Jesus, Maddie Macon has become a serious thorn in my

side. "Are you fucking kidding me? I swear to you, I have never, ever touched Maddie."

"But she was in your bed."

I sigh and run a hand through my hair in frustration. "She showed up there unannounced. I immediately told her to get out. I told her I'd kick her off the tour if she ever attempted something like that again. If you hadn't run off, you would have known that."

I stare into her watery eyes and continue, "You're all I've ever seen since I laid eyes on you that day you had coffee all over your clothes, struggling with the door. When I see you, I can't stop staring. I can't get you out of my head, Coffee Girl."

I wrap her in both my arms so that she can't move. She growls a profanity. I softly kiss her nose and her wet cheeks. I nudge her nose with mine to move her lips up to meet mine. She turns her face in protest, but I continue to place soft kisses along her cheek and throat.

"Kiki, come home with me," I say softly in her ear. "I need you. I want you. Only you. Don't overthink this."

I nudge her cheek again with my nose and she turns her lips to mine to speak, but I kiss her before she can. I kiss her softly and she gradually acquiesces. I can feel the tension melt from her bones as she stops struggling in my hold. Her tongue meets mine as I take and take from her. Her body relaxes against my chest as our lips find solace in each other.

"Come home with me," I echo, rasping softly against her lips.

"No," she whispers, "but you can take me to my home."

I kiss her again because I can't seem to stop. I tuck her into my side and head out the door to my waiting car.

Chapter 27

Kiki

I'm CONFUSED AND tired. My heart's been through the wringer and it doesn't know which way is up or down. But I can't help breathing in the heady scent of Tatum next to me and the new leather seats of the Escalade. I want to be stronger. I want to tell him to go to fucking hell. Instead, I lose myself in his citron-green eyes when he begs me to stay.

I wanted to knee him in the balls when he kissed me after having those skanks at the bar hanging all over him, but instead, my traitorous body melted into his kiss and the warmth of his hard body. The news he's never been with Maddie is so refreshing, it feels like fresh oxygen being pumped through my veins. She's so awful, I'm not sure I could trust his judgment if they had hooked up. Thank God his moral compass isn't totally fucked up.

Right now I'm cozied up next to him, his arm wrapped tight around my shoulder in the back seat as his driver takes us to my apartment. *My brother's apartment.* Shit! I sit up and pull my phone from my purse.

"You okay?" Tatum mumbles sleepily.

"I was supposed to text my brother when I got into an Uber."

"I can't believe that was your brother. I feel like such a prick."

"Mmm." I nod in agreement as I type my brother a message.

Tatum shakes his head and chuckles. "Thanks, Kiki. That makes me feel better."

We pull up in front of my apartment and the driver gets out and opens my door for me. Tatum speaks briefly with him and then walks me to the door.

"Do you want to come up?" I ask nervously.

"Do you want me to come up?"

I fidget and look down at my shoes. I'm not ready to say goodbye to him yet. "Yes."

"Okay. Let me just tell Brad."

He runs over to the parked Escalade and speaks to Brad through the window. He briskly walks back over to me.

"Do you always have Brad drive you all over?"

"Either Brad or Jimmy. Brad drives me unless I want to take out my car to go to the gym or the studios for a quick meeting and don't need him. He acts as my security too, so it's safer for everyone involved if he's behind the wheel." Tatum sighs. "Just goes with the territory."

"Ah, I see." But I really don't. I can't imagine having to rely on someone else to drive me around or to need constant security.

We take the elevator up to my floor and I invite Tatum into the apartment. Thank God it's somewhat clean. I turn on some music and tell him to look around while I run to my bedroom and shove the clothes I threw on the floor earlier into a hamper. I scoop up the half dozen dresses off my bed and throw them into my closet. I stuff a couple things under the bed and quickly glance at my bathroom and deem it presentable.

"Do you want something to drink?" I ask as I breeze back into the living room.

"Water, please."

I get him bottled water from the fridge as he looks at family pictures on my bookshelf.

"This is nice, Kiki."

"Yeah, my brother stays with me when he's in town. He's scouting locations for a new restaurant. He's got two right now in California and one in Chicago."

Tatum sits down on the sectional. "Wow, that's awesome. What kind of restau—Holy shit, what is that?"

Oreo jumps on the couch next to Tatum, and he looks terrified.

Tatum, that is. Not Oreo.

I giggle. "That's Oreo. He's a Maine Coon cat, Tatum. Ever seen one before?"

"That's a cat? But he's gray and scruffy like a small terrier."

"Don't listen to the haters, Oreo. You are a sexy bastard and you know it," I coo at him as I rub him down. I look over at Tatum and he has this bewildered expression on his face. "What?"

"I don't know how to tell you this, but I think that thing ate your cat, Oreo."

I laugh and hand him his water.

"Why on earth would you name a gray cat Oreo?"

I shrug. "Well, he was black with a little white when he was a kitten, but as he got older, he turned silver-gray. You know, like a silver-back gorilla."

Tatum looks at me with a lopsided grin that has me blushing. Like a gorilla? God, I sound like such an idiot.

"Did you just compare your cat to a gorilla?"

I playfully shove him as I sit down next to him on the sectional.

"How long have you had him?"

"Mmm, I found him outside by the dumpster when I was in college, so I'd say, seven years now."

"Are you sure he's not a rat?" Tatum whispers.

I roll my eyes and giggle. I move Oreo over closer to Tatum. He looks at him like he's a giant bug.

"He's not going to eat or attack you, Tater Tot. In fact, Stan adores him."

"Stan, the bus driver?"

"Yeah, Oreo's been on tour with us the whole time. He likes to ride shotgun with Stan." Tatum looks over at Oreo. Oreo, in turn, meows and head-butts his arm. He laughs and relaxes a fraction as he leans back into the couch, scratching Oreo's head.

"Are you not an animal person?"

"No, I am. I'm a dog guy. A big-dog guy. You love cats obviously."

"I love all animals. I hate it that the shelter animals don't have loving homes. I'd adopt a whole shelter if I could."

He smiles at me. "We had a Bernese growing up. He was

a rescue."

"Where'd you grow up?"

He stares at me for a beat. "You mean you haven't Googled me?"

"No, Mr. Big Head. Not everyone immediately goes to Google to find out about a person. I'm just trying to make casual conversation. You know…trying to get to know each other."

Of course I had Googled and Wiki'd him, but he didn't have to know that.

He looks a little sheepish as he ducks his head. "Sorry, I'm just used to everyone knowing every single facet of my life."

"There goes that inflated head again." I wink at him and he pokes my side. I take a sip of water and decide I need to bring up the pants fiasco before I lose my nerve.

"Tatum, listen. About earlier tonight, I didn't mess with your pants. Honest to God, I was so nervous without Jess there, that when you walked in the room I just threw the first pair on the rack. I don't remember pulling those tonight. They must have been with Jess's stuff. Even if I hated you and never wanted to see you again, I would never purposefully tamper with your things like that."

He leans forward and rests his elbows on his knees, scrubbing his hands over his face. "I'm sorry I accused you of that. I've had a really shit day. I was hurt and angry and embarrassed."

I place my hand on his leg. "Nothing to be embarrassed about, the crowd went wild."

He looks at me and smiles. His eyes flicker down to my

lips. We lean into each other and our lips touch. He gently strokes my cheek.

I kiss him tentatively, pushing myself toward him. I thread my fingers through his silky, dark-golden tousled hair and hold on. He takes it all in stride while he continues to punish my mouth. Have I mentioned he's an amazing kisser? Holy hell, where'd he learn this from? Not every guy is gifted in the art of kissing—bless Ethan's heart. But Tatum? He is in total control of this make-out session.

He grabs my hips and lifts me on to his lap to straddle him. I can feel his hardness beneath me and it takes all my self-control not to grind against him. His tongue slides expertly with mine, his lips perfectly angled. When I try to speed things up, he slowly coaxes me back to his steady rhythm. Jesus, if he's anything like this in bed, I'm going to lose my mind. I shiver at the thought.

Tatum breaks the kiss, running his hands down my back. I moan in protest. "Your cat is staring at me, and I'm a little nervous he might attack me."

Oreo is sitting on the coffee table, creeping like a total perv. I smile as I look down into Tatum's glazed green eyes. *God, he's so pretty.*

"Kiki, I really want you, and I can't believe I'm saying this, but we don't have to rush this. We can just sit and talk if you want."

I stare at him, weighing my options. I mean, we've had two very hot kissing sessions. We've basically covered the first two dates, right? I bite my lip as I contemplate. He leans into me and gently kisses my neck.

Oh yes…

"Right." I take a deep breath as he continues to nibble my jaw. "So…listen, I haven't had sex in, like, a year, maybe two. I lost track a while back, and Jesus, I can't believe I just admitted that to you. I appreciate you wanting to take it slow, but I want you, you want me. I'm tired of playing whatever cat-and-mouse game we've got going on. And if I have to get myself off with my vibrator one more time, I might cry. This may not sound very classy, but right now, all I want is for you to fuck my brains out."

Tatum's eyes widen and then he starts laughing, which annoys me.

"Tate, I'm serious!" I pinch his arm.

"Okay, okay! I'm sorry. I just have never had a woman propose sex to me quite like that." He clears his throat. "And it was totally hot as hell."

He places his hands under my thighs and stands up with me wrapped around him. He carries me quickly to my bedroom and slams the door shut with his foot.

"Kiki, I want to say I'll take it nice and slow with you, but I don't think I can."

I draw in a deep breath and kiss his throat. I suck his earlobe and then whisper, "Tatum, please fuck me hard and fast."

Seductress, I am not. Horny for Tatum? Hands down yes.

"Shit," he groans.

He sets me down on my feet and brings my dress up over my head. He runs a finger along the swell of my breast. "I almost went crazy out of my mind tonight when you were standing there on the side of the stage in your white-lace bra.

I wanted to beat the shit out of every guy who was staring at you." He starts kissing my neck as he walks me backward. My legs hit the bed and I fall onto it. He licks his lips as he places a knee on the bed.

"Wait. You need to take your clothes off."

"Not a patient one, are you?" He chuckles as he stands back up and strips off his shirt and pants.

I bite my bottom lip as I sit up on my elbows and drink him in. Lord have mercy, he is one fine specimen. Even though I've seen him strip down 456 times—that's just an educated guess—having him strip in front of me for non-work-related reasons—like mind blowing sex—is on a whole different level of hot.

He's in tight, black boxer briefs, and he looks like a Greek god, all tan and muscular. He leans over me on the bed and kisses my nipple through the sheer lace of my midnight-blue bra. I moan as pleasure ignites in my belly.

"Kiki?"

"Mmm?"

"Are you going to lick, bite, and tug on things?"

My eyes pop wide open. Crap, he remembers the text. "You're never going to let me live that down, are you?"

"Not a chance, beautiful."

"Well, in that case..." I tug his hair toward me and bite his shoulder, making him growl.

"Damn, that's so hot. Are you expecting anyone to-night?"

"Like who?" I ask, confused.

"I don't know, but if we get interrupted for a third time, I might just invite whoever it is to watch, because I don't think I have the self-control to stop myself once I start touching you."

He trails his fingers down to my matching satin panties and slowly rubs his knuckle over them. My body bows off the bed, wanting him to touch me again.

"Don't stop. Don't ever stop," I breathe out. He lowers the cups of my bra, taking my nipple into his mouth as his fingers slide back and forth over my slit.

"You're soaked," he says gruffly as he slides down, running kisses down my belly to the top of my panties. He kisses me through the panties and I moan.

"Oh God, yes, please, Tatum."

He smiles as he hooks his fingers in my panties and slips them off. He slides a finger into me and I moan, needing more of him.

"So perfect," he whispers, as his mouth moves over my clit, sucking me into oblivion with his finger still in me. I shamelessly arch into him as he expertly moves his tongue in and out. The sensation is too much. He moans, and it vibrates against me, almost making me unravel. I grab fistfuls of his hair as I move against him. The wave of pure desire takes me under as I fall apart against his mouth, screaming his name over and over.

He grins wolfishly as he reaches for his jeans and pulls out a condom. "You taste just as good as I imagined in my dreams. And watching you come is the biggest turn-on I've ever experienced."

I'm completely satiated as I watch him roll the condom over his thick length, and I lick my lips in anticipation.

"Ha. I bet you say that to all the girls," I half-kid.

He leans over me, the tip of his cock nudging against me. I push myself up to meet him, I want him in so badly, but he pauses.

"No, Kiki, only you," he whispers against my lips.

I moan. "Please, Tatum…"

He kisses me and plunges into me. "You're so fucking tight."

"I'm sorry," I breathe as I try to get used to the size of his heavy cock in me.

"No, it's a good thing. Really, really fucking good. Shit, Kiki, you feel too good."

I run my hands down his chest, feeling his silky skin with my fingertips. I'm in awe of the feel of his hard, ridged abdominal muscles. He leans down and kisses me as he starts to move in and out and rolls his hips. I match his rhythm, wanting more.

Goddamn, this boy can move. All those hip-thrusts on stage and squats I used to make fun of? Not anymore. Because those hip-thrusts are being used on me at this very moment, and they are killer, hitting that sweet spot perfectly.

My orgasm hits me hard. I buck underneath him as I break apart, screaming his name. His thrusts quicken and become almost out of control as he wildly drives it home, unleashing as he climaxes. Watching him completely let go is the hottest, most animalistic thing I have ever seen.

We stare at each other as we recover from our highs, both of us slick with sweat and panting. There's so much I want to say, and so much I want to keep to myself.

He leans down, sweetly kissing my swollen lips.

"I'll be right back." He gets up, throws away the condom, and lies back down, pulling the sheets over us and tucking me to his side. He props his head on one arm, looking down at me.

"You've ruined me," I murmur. "I can never be with another after amazing sex like that."

"Good." He chuckles. "On a scale of one to ten, how amazing was it?"

"Oh my God, it was like a twelve-and-a-ha—" I side-eye him. "Wait a minute, are you seriously fishing for compliments, Tatum James Reed?"

"What? Who me? No." He drags his tongue over his teeth as he smiles at me, then slowly lowers the sheet down and starts tracing my nipple with his finger. "So...just a twelve-and-a-half?"

I laugh as I smack away his hand. "It just went down to a six for lame after-sex pillow talk."

"A *six*? That's highly unreasonable."

"Okay, how would you rate it, then?"

"Fucking off-the-charts awesome."

I laugh. "Mmm, I like off-the-charts awesome. Okay, I'll upgrade you to an eight."

"Jesus, Kiki, I never knew you could be so harsh." He quickly turns and starts tickling me. Tickling and I don't do well, and I'm scared I might pee on myself or howl like a lunatic monkey.

"Ah! Stop, please don't! I can't...I'm—ah! Stop!" I scream and laugh at the same time.

He stops and rolls me on top of him. I sit up, straddling him, and immediately feel him harden. He cups my breasts, thumbing my nipples. He's looking at me like I'm a goddess, and it does something funny to my heart.

"I've wanted you naked and begging since the day I met you." He gently massages my breasts and I arch my back, giving him more.

I run my fingertips over his chest, unable to keep myself from touching him. "Would that be the day I looked like a coffee rat or the ACM night where I almost threw up on you?"

"Almost threw up on me?" He chuckles. "Uh, why? Were you sick?"

I huff out a laugh. "No, I just wanted to jump your bones that morning in the lobby, and then when I saw you the next night in Vegas, I thought I was going to pee my pants, because there you were. Tatum Reed was the hot guy from the lobby."

His dimples deepen. "So when you saw me, you wanted to throw up on me and pee your pants? I must not have made that great of an impression. But I'm thankful you didn't do either. That would have been embarrassing for you."

I shove him and laugh. "Figure of speech, Tater Tot. You made *quite* the impression."

"I think you're the one who impressed me. Do you realize how funny and beautiful you are?" He skims his fingers over my breasts.

"No," I say breathlessly. Because I really don't. I mean, he has girls like Savannah Freaking Edwards, for fuck's sake. I look away, and he brings my face back to his. "What is it?"

"Nothing."

"Kiki, you're stunning…and kind, and smart, and funny." He kisses my lips after each compliment.

I sigh. "Thank you, but I guess I don't get it. I mean, you've gone out with countless gorgeous women, the last one being Savannah Edwards, who's, like, supermodel-beautiful. I mean, I'm not even in her league. You have girls like Maddie Macon throwing themselves at you." I swallow and look down. "It's just hard for me to believe."

He tucks a lock of hair behind my ear. "Kiki, you're nothing like Savannah. She's all plastic. Literally, from her lips to her tits to her personality. She's also a lot crazy, and trust me, crazy is not appealing."

"Hmm, there must be a lot of unappealing women walking around in the world, because all guys think we're crazy."

"Yeah, true, all women *are* crazy." He slaps away my pinch before I can get him. "*But*, I'm talking about the mean kind of crazy. The spiteful, ugly kind of crazy."

"How do you know I'm not?"

"I don't." He brushes my hair back with his fingertips over my shoulder. "I'm taking a chance and hoping to God you're not, because I don't think I could handle another." He gives me a small, sad smile. "For all I know, you could just be with me because of who I am. It wouldn't be the first time for me."

I take the sheet and pull it up over us as I snuggle down to his chest. "I'm not mean-crazy."

Tatum kisses the top of my head and releases his breath. "Good."

"And I couldn't care less if you were a major country star or just an ordinary Joe. I'm not like those starry-eyed groupies."

He smiles and kisses my lips. "Sometimes I wish I were just an ordinary Joe."

I snuggle into him and squeeze him gently. "The world would miss you."

"Ha. I doubt that."

"What do you think you would be doing if you were just ordinary?"

"Hmm, most likely a male stripper."

I sit up and laugh. "What? That would have been your dream?"

He chuckles. "Oh, we're talking about dreams, not reality? I'd be a country music star."

I playfully shove him. "You do have the stripper moves down. Seriously, though, what would you be doing?"

He sighs. "Probably working for my dad at his accounting firm. Married to Kelly Blakewell with two and a half kids."

"Who is Kelly Blakewell? The love that got away?" A tinge of jealousy crawls up my throat for some poor girl who's not even in Tatum's life.

"Uh, no, not quite." He chuckles. "She was a stage-five clinger. She wasn't even a girlfriend, but she was determined to be. We went to high school together. My mom called it a crush, but I call it obsessed. I was sure she'd follow me to Nashville, but luckily her parents forced her to go to college in Texas."

"Oh no." I giggle, relieved I didn't have to kick Kelly's ass. "Do you ever hear from her?"

"At first she emailed me a lot after graduating high school, telling me she was coming to visit. I would change my email, but she would eventually get the new one. I had to delete my Facebook account because she would send me messages constantly. But they eventually stopped. Pretty sure she's married now with kids, according to my mom."

"I guess you dodged a bullet by not being an ordinary Joe." I smile up at him.

He grins. "A big one. I hate accounting, and Kelly was definitely stalker-crazy. Besides, I would have never met my Coffee Girl if I wasn't on the path I'm on."

I smile up at him and snuggle into his side.

"It's not just physical beauty, Kiki. I feel this pull toward you, and it scares the hell out of me because this is happening so fast. All I want to do is make you laugh and smile. I love your sense of humor, the way you smell, and the way you babble when you're nervous. The terrible music you listen to."

"Hey!" I laugh and playfully shove him.

He grins and kisses the tip of my nose, squeezing me tighter. "I want to protect you and fight like hell for you. There's just something about you that I've never felt toward anyone else. It's hard to explain."

"Mmm, I think I get it. I feel that same pull toward you. It is a little scary." My eyes flutter closed as I breathe in his musky male scent. He sifts his fingers through my hair, causing me to hum in pleasure. "That feels nice."

He kisses my temple and tucks me closer to his side where I drift off to sleep.

"KIKI."

"Mmm…bee."

"Kiki…wake up."

"Go away, Oreo."

Someone chuckles as I slowly surface to the land of living. A scratchy face nuzzles my ear. Lips kiss my jaw. My instinct is to shove it off, but I don't want it to stop.

"Mmm, you better have coffee with those kisses for waking me up at the crack of dawn after keeping me up all night with your insatiable need for sex." He woke me up in the middle of the night, and we made love twice more before we both passed out. I open my eyes and stare in to the most beautiful, smiling, green ones.

"Good morning, sexy." He kisses the tip of my nose. "As much as I want to feed my ravenous appetite for sex at this very moment, I can't. I have an interview this morning with Sirius XM's The Highway, and I need to get going."

I notice he's already showered, dressed, and ready. He drags his tongue along my nipple and sucks it into his mouth. My sex clenches as heat zings through my blood. He returns to my lips and gives me a toe-curling kiss.

"Stay," I whisper.

"I want to, but I can't. Lee will have my balls if I miss this."

"Okay, I understand. Will you… Um, are you…?" I bite my lower lip and blush. Shit, this is awkward.

"I'll call you afterwards." He quickly kisses me again and covers me back up with my duvet. I snuggle into the blankets as I watch him leave the room.

Sex God: *What are you doing?*

Me: *Well, I was sleeping. You?*

Sex God: *Waiting for the interview to start, thinking about you.*

Me: *Aw, you're forgiven.*

Sex God: *For what?*

Me: *For waking me up twice.*

Sex God: *Lots of girls would love to have me wake them up.*

Me: *I'm not lots of girls.*

Sex God: *I know :) Thank God.*

Chapter 28

Tatum

I'M TRYING TO concentrate on the interview, but all I can think about are Kiki's long, tan legs wrapped around mine all night. Her sensuous curves and round, luscious breasts…

"I'm sorry, can you repeat the question?"

"You, uh, seem a little distracted."

"Sorry, Ken, long night last night," I say ruefully scratching my jaw.

"Care to elaborate?" He chuckles.

"Nope."

"Well, Tatum Reed fans, I tried. So what's your reaction to today's tabloid pics?"

He tilts his computer screen toward me, and I grimace at the photo of a fluffy kitty with a black sequined bowtie covering my dick. The caption reads "Mee-Ow!"

Thanks for that, Lex.

I rub a hand down the side of my face and chuckle. How on earth am I going to spin this into a positive? "What can I say? The fans love a good meow," I joke and take a gulp of my coffee.

"Um, that would be mostly your female fans." Ken laughs.

Suddenly, inspiration hits as I think of Kiki's scruffy cat, Oreo. "I'm just kidding. In all seriousness, we did it for charity."

"Really? So it wasn't an accident you ripped your pants?"

"Ah, well, yeah, that was an accident. The shirt was not."

"What charity is it for?"

Lee in the control booth looks to the heavens and shakes his head.

"Dog and cat rescue, of course. We'll be selling the kitten tees at our concerts, and all proceeds will go to dog and cat rescues around the United States."

Lee throws his arms out and mouths *what the fuck?* I just smile and shrug and take another sip of my coffee, formulating my next response.

Ken looks surprised. "Wow, didn't see that one coming. That's awesome, Tatum."

"Yes, well, we weren't planning on releasing that shirt until the next tour, but with the pant snafu last night, it was all we had on hand. Not exactly how we wanted to announce it, but there you have it."

"Well, I know rescues will be jumping for joy over that. There are a lot of animals in shelters that don't make it out. This will help immensely."

"Yeah, it's a cause that's been recently brought to my attention. I wish we could have started it a long time ago."

"Well, no time like the present. Simply awesome. So tell me, what's going on with you and Savannah? There was a noticeable number-one hit song left out of last night's concert. Was that done on purpose?"

I tense at the mention of Savannah's name. Ken was specifically asked not to mention her name or ask any personal questions about us. I take another sip of coffee to calm myself down and arch my eyebrow at Ken, who quickly avoids eye contact. I clear my throat.

"Savannah and I have always been friends and will remain so. I wanted to mix things up a little last night. We'll continue to play that song, but Maddie Macon will be singing it with me instead of the recording Savannah made for us. I want a more authentic feel to the song, and I think Maddie will do a great job."

"Yeah, wow! Maddie will kill it for sure. Well, awesome job last night, buddy. And congratulations on the Entertainer of the Year nomination. I can't wait to hear your next tour announcement and what cities you'll be hitting. Hopefully Nashville will be one of them."

"Thanks man, I can't say right now, but Nashville is my home, so we'll work something out."

"Awesome. Can you announce your latest number-one single before you go?"

"Absolutely. Thanks for listening to the Highway! I'm Tatum Reed and you heard it here first, 'This Isn't a Love Song.'"

The song starts to play and Ken takes off his headphones. "Awesome, man, thanks for taking time out of your busy schedule to talk with us."

"Anytime, Ken, you know that. The guys and I appreciate all the airtime you give us. We couldn't have made it here without you playing our music."

Ken and I shake hands and slap each other's back. I grab my coffee and follow Lee out to the waiting car.

"What the fuck, Lee? I thought we said no Savannah."

He shrugs. "We did. You handled it beautifully."

I grunt in response as we climb into the Escalade.

"I'm not going to even ask what that was about, but what the fuck was that about, Tatum? Do you know how hard it's going to be to get those T-shirts made? I called Kiki. She said it's from H&M. There's no way in hell H&M will release that graphic, not to mention suing us for copyright infringement. We're screwed!"

"So let's do our own graphic. Call Ellen Barr to take the photographs. I think I have time this afternoon before we head out."

Lee throws up his arms. "That's if she'll agree to it! Shit, she might be on location somewhere…or just busy."

"If she's in town, she'll do it for me. She loves me."

Lee makes an exasperated noise. "And where the hell are we going to get a cat on such short notice?"

I smile. "I know the perfect candidate."

Chapter 29

Kiki

I'M TRYING NOT to crack up laughing as Tatum wrangles Oreo out of his carrier. He finally figures out the best solution is to unzip the top and take Oreo out that way. I'm trying to help, but it's way more fun to watch him struggle with a twenty-pound cat. Oreo's wearing a harness and a leash, and watching Tatum walk him around the room has me in a fit of giggles because Oreo isn't being cooperative. He's trying to coax him with soft commands while intermittently dragging him across the floor.

"Oh my God, just give him to me." I quickly scoop up a disgruntled Oreo before he gets rug burn.

"What's wrong with him?"

"He's not a dog, Tatum. He doesn't like his leash, but I was afraid he would dart out of the carrier."

"Do you think he's going to cooperate?"

"Um, sure, if you're nice to him."

"*Pfft.* Of course I'll be nice."

The photographer walks over toward us. "Hi, Tatum.

Can't wait to do this."

"Thanks, Ellen, and thank you for doing this at the very last minute. This is my…stylist, Kiki and her cat, Oreo."

I shake hands with Ellen. "He should be pretty cooperative. Do you want me to put his bow tie on?"

Yes, Oreo owns a bowtie…and a sombrero for Cinco de Mayo, a birthday hat, and the most recent purchase, a cowboy hat. In my defense, TJ bought them for him. He said Oreo needed some more pizzazz in his life. TJ and his damn pizzazz.

"Yes, that would be great. Listen, it will be fine. I'm used to photographing the industry's divas, so I can handle little ol' Oreo."

Oh, photographer Ellen, famous last words there.

When Tatum called and told me he wanted to use Oreo in this publicity stunt, I laughed my ass off, but agreed. Truth be told, I don't know what Oreo will do. He's never modeled before. And he isn't used to Tatum, or all the people and camera equipment in the studio.

Ah, well. His funeral, I suppose. Tatum's, that is.

Ellen sits Tatum down on a stool. He's wearing a plain, white button-down with jeans, and he's barefoot. He's sitting in front of a muted backdrop surrounded by large lights covered with umbrella shades. Soft music plays in the background as Ellen's assistants adjust the lighting. Sarah has styled his hair to be mussed, and God, if he doesn't look sexy as hell as if he just finished having a romp in my bed. My cheeks heat as last night fast-tracks through my brain. Ellen motions me over after taking a couple pictures of Tatum.

"Okay, can you take his harness and leash off? I can

Photoshop it out if you can't."

"No, that's fine." I slip the harness over his head and Oreo meows in gratitude. I walk over to Tatum and place Oreo on his lap.

"Place your hands on either side of him." Tatum looks like I just plopped a bee's nest on his leg. "Relax, Tate, he's not going to bite you," I whisper.

Oreo meows and sits up, looking for the nearest exit. He's panicking, and Ellen is fidgeting with a camera lens.

"It's okay, Oreo," I coo as I stroke his fur. "Tate, can you tell her to hurry?"

"Um, Ellen? I think we need to get this done. He's clawing my leg."

"Okay, um, Tatum's girlfriend, can you step out of the way?"

"It's Kiki!" I shout a little too loudly quickly backing away. "His stylist, *not* his girlfriend." Oh geez, could I be more obvious?

Tatum chuckles and then grimaces as Oreo flexes his claws deeper into his thigh.

The flash from the camera scares the shit out of Oreo, and he turns toward Tatum.

"Kiki, shit, what's he doing?" Tatum cries out.

Oreo claws his way up Tatum's chest and sits on his shoulder like a damn spider monkey.

"Fuck! That hurt!"

"Tatum, don't scream!" I yell as I look over at Sarah, doubled over laughing her ass off.

"Shit, he just clawed up my chest!"

"Tatum, big smile, hon!" Ellen yells as she continues to

snap away.

Tatum manages a grimace. Oreo suddenly leaps off of Tatum's shoulder and runs for the door.

"Oreo! Stop!" I scream.

"Fucking shit! That cat just made me bleed!"

"Anyone have a first-aid kit?" Sarah yells to one of Ellen's assistants.

"Well, I think maybe I might have gotten one. Think we could get the cat by himself?" Ellen asks, completely nonplussed by all the shouting.

I look at her like she's grown two heads as Sarah starts to apply antibiotic ointment to Tatum's scratches. I corner a meowing Oreo and pick him up. He starts struggling in my arms, so I quickly shove him in his carrier.

"I don't think so. He's done."

"That makes two of us," Tatum says grumpily. "Why on earth would anyone adopt one of those?"

"Tatum! Don't say that. Oreo's awesome. He just got scared."

"Apparently. I've got claw marks all over my leg and chest."

"Okay, well, if we're done here I'm taking him to the tour bus."

"Why?" Tatum looks completely taken aback.

"Um, because wherever I go, Oreo goes," I say crossly and turn on my heel, ignoring Tatum. I'm ticked at him for lashing out against poor, innocent Oreo. He couldn't help that he got scared with all these strange people, lights, and flashing cameras. I should have known better.

Lee meets me at the door as I'm about to exit.

"Hey, Kiki, Jess isn't going to be leaving with us today. Her mom's in the hospital, apparently from food poisoning and severe dehydration. She hopes to join us out on the tour by next week. She seems to think you can handle everything, despite the cat-shirt incident. Do you think you can handle it?"

"Oh, I'm so sorry to hear about her mom. Absolutely, Lee. Jess has trained me well. You won't have to worry."

Lee nods. "That's what she said. Okay, well, if you're feeling overwhelmed or need help, let me know before it gets out of hand. And let's not have another jeans-ripping episode. This is costing us a small fortune." He waves his hand at Ellen and all the equipment.

"Well, honestly, maybe you should tell him not to do so many squats and hip-thrusts in skintight jeans while he's onstage."

Lee laughs. "Right. Tell his fans that."

I roll my eyes and smirk as I heft the carrier on my shoulder. "Not a problem, Lee. I can do this."

"How'd the photoshoot go?"

"Um…Tatum got mad at Oreo for scratching him."

Lee snorts. "He's such a baby."

I laugh as I head out the door.

Holy crap! I am the head stylist to Tatum and the band! Woo-hoo!

My grumpy mood is quickly wiped away. I mean, of course I'm sad about Jess's mom. I would be hysterical if my mom were in the hospital. I quickly send her a text and say a prayer for her to get better. But, head stylist! I do a mental fist-pump as ideas start formulating in my head. Sequins, feathers, leather. Ha, the guys would die if I tried that! But with Jess gone for this week, I'm going to try to class up their T-shirts and floral button-downs if they'll let me.

I pull out my phone and call TJ.

"This better be good. It's, like, noon here on a Sunday."

I squeal into the phone. "I'm Tatum Reed's head stylist!"

"You totally slept with him, didn't you?" TJ yawns loudly into the phone.

"What? No! Well...maybe, but that's beside the point. Jess's mom is sick, so she's taking this week off tour. I mean, I'm not replacing her, just filling in, but this will be so awesome for my resume!"

"That's awesome, Kinks. Too bad about dragon lady's mom, but cool you get to show your shine. However, I believe we're skimming over one important point."

"What's that?"

"You fucking slut! You're sleeping with the hottest country star in America!"

"Oh, that."

"Don't *oh, that* me, sister. When did this happen? Last time I heard, we hated that sexy beast. I want the deets."

"Please don't say 'deets'."

"Is he hung like a horse? Is his ass as tight as it looks in his jeans? Does his tongue—"

I chuckle. "Oh my God, stop! I'm not sharing anything you can use to spank with later on, you perv."

"*Please!*" The decimal of his squeal makes my eardrum burst.

"Please don't ever screech like that again. I think you just sucked your balls back into your butt."

"That's impossible, Kiki. Balls can't be sucked into your butt. Maybe licked up…"

"Ugh! No! I can't continue this conversation. All I'm going to say to shut you up is that it was… amazing."

"You're such a buzzcock."

"You mean buzzkill."

"No, Kinky, buzzcock. You just killed my cock's buzz."

I roll my eyes even though he can't see me. "Wouldn't you say 'cock-kill' then?"

"Kinky, no. Then it would be buzzcockkill. Totes diff."

Oh geez, I don't even know why I'm arguing with him over this. I might as well stick hot pokers in my eyes. "Okay, I gotta go. I have a more important call coming in. Love you! Byee!"

"Kiki, you lia—"

I hang up on TJ as I get to my apartment to pack up for the West Coast wing of the tour. My phone buzzes again and I think it's TJ, but it's Tatum.

> **Hottest Country Sex God:** *Where are you? You practically ran out of the studio.*
>
> **Me:** *I'm at home grabbing my things and then heading straight for the tour bus.*
>
> **Hottest Country Sex God:** *Meet me at my bus?*
>
> **Me:** *What if someone sees me?*
>
> **Hottest Country Sex God:** *So? I want to show you my wounds your gorilla inflicted on me.*
>
> **Me:** *Why? You need me to kiss them and make them feel better?*
>
> **Hottest Country Sex God:** *I love it when you talk dirty.*

Me: *Lol, you're so weird. Text me when you get there.*

Hottest Country Sex God: *I'm on my way now, just let yourself in.*

Me: *K... R u going to be stuck in leather pants again?*

Hottest Country Sex God: *You promised you would never ever mention that.*

Me: *Never said that. I said I wouldn't mention it to anyone else.*

Hottest Country Sex God: **Sigh* just get your cute little ass over here.*

I smile as I pick up my mail. I sift through some bills and some magazines and pause when I glimpse the cover of my *US Weekly* magazine. The featured picture is one of Tatum and Savannah with a big Photoshopped page rip in between them. *I am not going to read this, I am not going to read this.*

I set Oreo's carrier down on the floor and let him out. I flip through my mail and then pick up the magazine again. I'm just going to look at the "Who Wore it Best?" section.

Oh shit, who am I kidding?

I quickly flip to the article and begin to read about the "King of Heartbreak." Five minutes later, all my self-doubts come right back to the surface. It's like our conversation last night ceased to exist and I was back to being Kiki the Coffee Girl. Because, wow, this article made Tatum and Savannah seem like they were minutes away from saying their "I do's" before he called it quits and broke her heart.

The greatest love affair between two country stars since Tim and Faith. Sources close to the pair say he's been dating several women since the split, but he's still pining for Savannah. All he thinks about is her, and he can't wait for this tour to be over so they can be back together. Another source close to her says he's planning a trip to Tahiti with her after the tour is over. Maybe wedding bells will still be ringing in their near future! Perhaps a destination wedding? Please don't say it's over for Tatum and Vanny!

I stare at the pictures in the layout of the beautiful couple. There's one from the night at the ACMs where they are holding hands. I run my finger over the glossy picture. They look so happy, and dammit if he doesn't look sexy as hell in his suit. I hate feeling this self-doubt all over again. One of the little boxes in the corner has a poll of whether they want a single Tatum or Tatum and Savannah together. Eighty-five percent of the public want them back together.

Ugh.

I throw the magazine down and chew on my thumbnail. Was it all an act last night? Was I just a quick fuck with a little bedroom talk afterwards? Or is this story totally fabricated?

I don't know what to believe anymore. I pack the magazine because I need answers from Tatum, and grab my stuff to head to the tour bus.

Chapter 30

Tatum

KIKI LEFT THE studio before I could pull her aside and talk to her. I gingerly touch the gouges Oreo made on my chest and shoulder. Dang, that cat is lethal.

Lee and I look over Ellen's shoulder at the images she took. They actually turned out pretty good. The one of Oreo on my shoulder is actually pretty decent and we decide to go with that one for our T-shirt graphic.

Lee's in a tizzy because I promised them this weekend for our show in Kansas City. We have to hire a graphic designer on short notice, which will cost a small fortune, but the T-shirts will be in production and ready. I told him it'll be on my dime, not the label's, so that seemed to appease him a little.

After leaving the photography studio I pick up a few things from my house and head back to my bus to work on some songs while I wait for Kiki.

"TATUM?"

"Back here."

Kiki knocks softly on my bedroom door. God, I'll never get tired of looking at her. She's changed from the jeans she was wearing at the photoshoot this afternoon to a long, soft tee and leggings. Her dark chestnut hair falls in soft waves, and her eyes glitter with desire.

"Hi."

"Hi, gorgeous. Come in." I pat the bed beside me. I'm sprawled out in just my athletic shorts working on a new song. I have my guitar next to me and notes scattered all over the bed.

"Oh, Tate, I'm so sorry." Kiki shyly touches the red angry scratches on my chest and shoulder. "I thought you were just overreacting like a big baby, but these are pretty bad."

I chuckle. "It's worse than it looks. If I can't survive a few scratches from Oreo, then I'm a pansy."

"Ah, taking the macho route." She grins.

"Always. Come here, sexy, I've missed you."

I move aside my guitar and the papers as she sits on the bed. She hesitates before gently pressing a chaste kiss to my lips.

I raise an eyebrow, sensing her apprehension. "What's wrong?"

"Nothing!" she says, overly brightly.

I sit up straighter. "Kiki, talk to me."

She covers her face with her hands. "God, this is so embarrassing."

"It's okay. Just talk."

"Okay, um, well… What are we?" She gestures between us.

"What do you mean?"

She groans in frustration. "Dang it, Tate, you're going to make me spell it out?"

I stare at her, unsure of where she's going with this.

She sighs in frustration. "God, I'm trying to play this casually, but it's so complicated with me working for you. What are we doing? What am I to you? Am I just a casual fling? Are we friends with benefits? Your fuckbuddy? Your coffee girl? Was it just a one-time thing? And it's totally okay if it was. I'm not some crazy stalker-fan or groupie. Definitely not a groupie, ew. I'm not really into sharing or group sex. I mean, I get it, I totally get it if that's your thing, but… I guess what I'm asking is where do you see this going? Because I can't just bumble along not knowing what you're expecting. Knowing what I'm expecting…what I want out of this. I want to make sure there's no miscommunication or hurt feelings. In particular, *my* hurt feelings. I guess I just want to make sure we're on the same page." She takes a deep breath and closes her eyes.

I find her nervous babble totally endearing. I stay silent, memorizing her beautiful features. Her soft, pink lips, the blush slowly creeping up her golden skin, her long dark lashes, her cute little nose. One eye lifts open and her brow arches.

"Well? Don't give me that sexy smirk."

I chuckle. "I know what I want. Why don't you tell me what you want?"

"What I want? Jesus," she breathes out as I twist a lock of her silky hair around my finger, brushing her boob in the process. She squirms, batting at my hand. "Quit, you're distracting me."

I sigh. "You're overthinking this. Kiki, all I want is you. However I can get you. It's up to you to tell me how far you want this to go. You're in the driver's seat. I'm just a happy, horny passenger."

"Tatum, that's not fair."

"Sure it is. You can have me for one night or until you get tired of me. I'm not going to lie, it'll hurt my heart a little if you want to go back to being Coffee Girl, but I'll understand. There's a lot of baggage that comes with me."

"So I'm not just a rebound after Savannah? Because—"

"No." I cut her off before that ridiculous idea germinates in her head any further. "Savannah can't hold a candle to you. Were you sleeping when we talked about this last night? I've never felt this way with anyone before. You have some kind of pull over me, and it's only you I want. I'll take you any way I can get it."

She grabs something from her bag and throws it on the bed. I pick up the magazine and stare at the cover. I fucking hate tabloids. "What's this?"

"It's an article about you and Savannah. I wasn't going to read it."

"Good, don't."

"But I did. Were you guys really engaged?"

I snort. "Fuck no." I open the article and skim through

215

it.

"Are you dating other girls?" she asks quietly.

I lift an eyebrow up at Kiki and she has the grace to look embarrassed.

"Well, Jesus, Tate. Last night I walked into the bar to see some girl sitting on your lap molesting you."

"Not only do I regret that, but I already explained it." I sigh, running my hands through my hair. "Kiki, this is all bullshit. You can't believe everything you read and hear. I am not engaged to Savannah, I'm not dating other girls, and I'm not going to Tahiti anytime in the near future, and if I were, it definitely wouldn't be with her. This was probably planted by Savannah's PR team to make her look like the victim and make me miserable, which is working. All I want is you."

"But Tatum, you don't even know me." She stands up and starts pacing the room. "We've had one incredible night of sex—"

I roll to my side and prop my head on my hand, watching her pace and fret. "So let me get to know you."

"But, but…"

"But what?" Why the fuck is she making this so complicated?

"But I'm Coffee Girl!" she yells, exasperated. "You're Tatum Reed! A bigger-than-life superstar! What the fuck are you doing with me—a fashion stylist who totes her cat everywhere?"

I stand up, grab her hand, and look down into her beautiful, stormy gray eyes. "I was serious when I said there's a lot of baggage that comes with me. I'm constantly in the public eye, as you can see." I throw the magazine in the trash can. "My breakup with Savannah has turned nasty. When her fans find out about you, they won't be very nice to you. We can hide whatever this is between us until you're comfortable."

She starts to speak and I stop her by putting my finger to her lips.

"And no, I'm not keeping you a secret, but you're right. There will be a big spotlight cast on you if and when we become public. If you don't want that, it's okay. I get it. Most days, I don't want it. But if that's the case, then you need to tell me now, and we'll go back to Tatum Reed and his assistant Kiki."

"The Coffee Girl," she says flatly.

I give her a half smile and tilt her chin up. "For what it's worth, I really, really like that stained-T-shirt coffee girl. She's funny and sexy as hell. She makes me laugh, and she drives me crazy." I gently rub my thumb along her jaw. "I've tried to fight my attraction to you. To be honest, it's not really a great time for me to get involved in a relationship, but now that I have you, I don't want to let you go."

I kiss her temple and whisper hoarsely into her ear, my emotions getting the best of me. "If it helps, I really hope you'll choose me."

I kiss her as she wraps her arms around my neck. She sighs into my mouth and I deepen the kiss. I turn her around and push her on to the bed. I hover over her as she lies underneath me, panting with need.

"What's it going to be, Coffee Girl? Are you going to let me get to know you better?"

"Yes."

I kiss her nose and lips, and her luminous eyes shutter closed. "Good. Let's start right now."

"Tatum, I, uh…I'm gonna get crazy here for a hot minute."

I still, not sure where she's going with this. "What kind of crazy?"

She bites her lip, worry reflecting in her gaze.

"What is it, Kiki?"

"I don't… I mean, I…" She groans in frustration. "I don't share. I'm not okay with girls coming back to your bus, or sleeping with you when I'm with you. I'm not okay with Maddie having her hands all over you. Call me a jealous bitch, but it's how I feel. I know this is all so new, but…if we aren't on the same page, then—"

"Kiki." I lie down next to her and prop my head on my hand as I gaze down at her. "There's always going to be a Maddie thinking she can throw herself at me for attention. But I assure you, she will not be getting it. Look, I know you've heard the rumors, which are just that—rumors. I don't bring girls back to my bus after every concert. But some of these fans are crazy. I've had every garment of clothing thrown at my feet. I've had girls ask me to Sharpie my signature on parts of their bodies that would make Hugh Hefner blush. I've had to deal with false paternity tests from women I've never even laid eyes on."

I sigh and rub my forehead. Kiki reaches over to me and runs her fingers over my arm. I scoot up against my headboard and pull her into my lap.

"It's crazy. I've had women propose to me, sob on me,

laugh with me, and get drunk with me. They grab my ass, my dick, any body part they can get a hold of. And I hate it. I hate it so much, but often I can't control it. I've accepted it's part of this lifestyle. You can't think I'm sleeping with every girl who looks my way, or you'll go crazy." I tenderly tuck a lock of hair behind her ear. "I'm going to be honest with you. I wasn't exactly a saint after I broke up with Savannah, but I haven't been with anyone since I laid eyes on you that afternoon at the studio."

Kiki sighs as she runs her fingers over my bare chest. I swallow as I continue to drive home how much I want her. "I flirt. I flirt a lot. It's just who I am. If it gets to be too much for you, you need to let me know, but it's innocent. My fans have come to expect it and love it. I'm half-joking when I say the chicks dig it. Some of them really do."

I smile wryly, earning a bemused eyeroll from her. "Do you want to know where my head is twenty-four-seven? It's with you. I'm always thinking about you, wondering what you're doing, where you are, if you're happy, sad, bored... It's just you, Kiki."

"Thank you for that," she whispers as she looks down at me. I trace my finger along her jaw.

I start to softly sing "Just the Way You Are" by Bruno Mars my finger skimming down to her collarbone.

Her eyes get glassy as she leans into me and gently kisses my lips. I deepen the kiss and groan as her scent wraps around me. How could I ever even think about another? She tastes like heaven and I don't think I'll ever get my fill of her.

I lift her shirt up above her head and toss it to the ground. She's wearing a black lacy bra that makes my heart quicken with desire.

"I like this." I skim my fingers over the lace and satin. "But I need to remove it."

"Wait, what if Lee or Lex busts through your door?" Her eyes widen in panic.

"They won't."

"But they could. They have!" She laughs.

With a groan I quickly set her on the bed and get up, slam, the door to my bedroom shut and lock it. When I turn back around she's spread out on my comforter like a fucking delicate flower in her bra and matching lace panties.

"You are exquisite, Kiki. I have never wanted someone as much as I want you."

I lean over her and kiss her silky skin right on the swell of her breast. She threads her fingers through my hair as I trail kisses down her chest, to her navel, and then quickly slide her panties down to reveal her sweet, glistening pussy. I lick her slowly and her fingers tighten in my hair as she moans. No melody I've ever heard is sexier than listening to her sweet little purrs and cries. I suck on her tender bud as she arches into my mouth, panting. I deftly stroke my tongue, tasting her like she's a fucking dessert, the best I've ever had. There's nothing better than tasting Kiki. It has become my new favorite thing to do.

Her moans get louder until she shouts my name over and over. And she comes hard. She's fucking unbelievable.

I'm so hard my dick hurts as I strip off my shorts. I quickly roll a condom on and tell her to turn over. I lift her ass in the air and slap her perfectly round bottom, causing her to gasp. I gently run my hand over the smooth skin to quell the sting. I quickly thrust into her from behind. Shit, she's so tight, I almost come undone.

"Oh my God, Tate, oh my God, you feel so fucking good," she pants, turning me on even more.

I thrust into her hard and pull almost all the way out before plunging back in. I circle her clit with the fingers of one hand as I take her. She's mewling and whimpering, which turns me on even more. She looks over her shoulder at me, our eyes connect, and I can tell she's about to hit her peak.

"Harder, Tate. Fuck me harder." It's the sexiest command I've ever heard. I pump into her harder and she explodes around me as she orgasms again, milking my dick. The sensation is so awesome I can't hold on for much longer. I pump a few more times as I hold tight to her waist and come hard quickly after, shouting like a fucking roaring freight train.

"Jesus, Kiki, unbelievably good." I lie down next to her as she rolls over to face me.

She tenderly runs her fingers along my cheek, touching her finger to my dimple. She stares into my eyes and smirks.

I chuckle. "What?"

"That was amazing. You're amazing," she purrs as she stretches out next to me.

"Keepie?"

She snorts. "Yeah?"

I snuggle her closer to me and kiss the tip of her nose. "Tell me something about you," I murmur as I trail kisses along her collarbone.

"That tickles. Um, what do you want to know?"

"When's your birthday?"

"March twelfth. When's yours?"

"December sixteenth."

"Favorite color?"

I stare into her eyes. "Dove-gray with flecks of purple. Almost like storm-cloud gray. Yours?"

She blinks. "That's pretty specific. I like blue." She shifts and places her hands under her cheek as she lies facing me. "Can I ask you a deep, personal question?"

"Shoot."

"Does it bother you when you read the crap people make up about you in the press?"

"I don't read it anymore. When I first started out, I followed it and it drove me crazy. It was insane seeing my picture on the front of a tabloid for the first time. Kinda made my head explode for a little while."

"Explode as in angry?"

I smirk. "Explode as in my head got too big. I thought I was the shit."

"Um. I hate to break it to you, but you still do."

I tickle her until she cries mercy, which is about five seconds later.

"How did you get started in singing?"

"What planet do you live on?"

She chuckles and blushes. "What do you mean?"

"Well, if you followed me at all, which clearly you don't, and I'm not sure if I'm proud of that fact or totally disgusted—" She reaches over and pinches my nipple. "Ow! You would know I was runner-up on *The Voice*."

"I'm more of an *American Idol* fan," she says dryly.

I roll my eyes. "Anyway, that's how I met Savannah. We were paired together on the show to do a duet."

She lifts her head up. "For real? You were a *Voice* contestant?"

I chuckle. "No, I'm just messing with you. It's refreshing you don't know everything about me."

She playfully shoves me as I continue. "I moved to Nashville to write songs, hoping to break into the industry, playing small venues around town. One night, I listened to this band and liked their vibe. I talked to them after the show and they were looking for a new lead singer. They had a following, so I thought what could it hurt? That's how Lex, Matt, Will, and I started out together. We got a lucky break one night when Lee walked into the bar to hear another band. He loved our sound so much, he offered to rep us, and the rest is history." I shrug. "That's how I met Savannah. She was at the same label as me. We met at a label party for new talent. I wrote a few songs for her, she sang with me on some of mine. I mean, as much as I hate to admit this, she helped my career as much as I've helped hers."

"Did you love her?" she whispers.

"No. I thought I did, but love doesn't make you hate. I think in the beginning I loved the idea of her, but my career was just starting. I didn't need or really want a serious relationship. We were trying to navigate Nashville together, and we formed more of a partnership bond than anything else. No, I didn't love her."

I sigh as I reflect on the past. "Enough about her."

"Okay...thanks for your honesty." She smiles and taps her fingers to her lips, thinking. She's so adorable. "What's your favorite thing to do on a day off?"

"Summer or winter day?" I circle her nipple with my finger, which she quickly flicks out of the way.

"Quit it, that tickles. Um, summer."

"Head to my lake house and go fishing with the boys. Grill out."

"Of course he has a lake house," she scoffs.

I arch my eyebrow. "I've got lots of things, Kiki, get used to it. So, I've met your brother. Is he your only sibling?"

"No, I have an older sister too. But we aren't very close. You?"

"I have an older sister and a younger brother. My brother is at the University of Tennessee, and my sister lives in Texas. We're all very close."

"You said you moved to Nashville after high school. Where are you originally from?"

"Born and raised in Dallas, Texas. You?"

"California. Outside of San Francisco."

"Why aren't you close to your sister?"

"She's not a very nice person."

I kiss her nose. "How could anyone not be nice to you?"

She smirks. "I think you're a little biased right now."

I roll my finger over her nipple, watching her bud tighten as I draw lazy circles. "Maybe." I lean down and take her nipple in my mouth. She rakes her fingers through my hair and sighs. "I want you again, Kiki."

"I'm yours," she whispers as she arches into me.

We make love languidly, getting to know each other without talking.

Me: *What's the song that plays in your head when you think of us?*

Keepie: *Hmm… "I Was Made for Loving You" by Tori Kelly and Ed Sheeran.*

Me: *I haven't heard that one yet.*

Keepie: *Listen to it. You?*

Me: *Mine would be "Look What God Gave Her" by Thomas Rhett.*

Me: *You there?*

Keepie: *Hold on, I'm listening to it…*

Keepie: *Aw…you're laying it on pretty thick there, cowboy*

Me: *TR's a friend of mine, so go download it.;)*

Keepie: **sigh* I should have said Dolly Parton's "Why'd You Come in Here Lookin' Like That."*

Me: *Nope, no seconds. Nice one, by the way.*

Chapter 31

Kiki

So Tatum Reed and I are together! Holy shit, how did that happen?

I want to tell someone, but I can't. I'm dying to tell Sarah, but I keep my mouth zipped. I can't even call TJ. He knows we've slept together, but not that we're an official couple. That whore would call *US Weekly* and *TMZ* before I even got off the phone with him. He's already trying to get me to convince Tatum to pose naked on the cover of *Cufflinks*, despite the fact that it's an upstanding men's magazine, not *Playgirl*. He swears up and down it would be classy. I believe that as much as I believe him suddenly turning straight.

I've got to keep this on the down low until we figure out what we're doing. And I'm good with that. I'm not quite sure I'm ready to be pushed into Tatum's spotlight just yet. I've been thinking a lot about what he said to me the other night and his fame kind of intimidates me.

The scary thing? I think I'm falling in love with him.

Quick, I know. I can't help myself. He's gorgeous and charming, sweet and funny. He's got a sinful body and the sex is really fucking fantastic. And when he sings? Holy cow. I get why women want to take off their panties and throw them at him. Especially when he sings to just me, it's a total turn-on.

Who am I kidding? His dimples alone turn me on. I'm trying to slow myself down and not throw all my heart's cards into the proverbial pot, but it's hard not to take the gamble. I've let my guard down and my heart belongs to Tatum. I think it has since the day I sloshed coffee all over myself outside the studio.

I walk toward Tatum's dressing room in Kansas City, the next stop of our tour, carrying his clothes for tonight. I've dressed Lex in a tight, black T-shirt and leather moto jacket. Matt's in a Robert Graham button-down and jeans, and Will and the rest of the crew are in Ames Bros T-shirts. I've got Tatum in blue jeans—tight, of course—with a tight-fitting, black button-down that'll look killer on him, especially against his tan skin and black cowboy hat.

Granted, the budget for clothing has drastically gone up with these changes, but I don't think the boys mind. They were all preening in the mirrors when I walked out.

Jess? Well, she's not here to complain, so tonight, it's my show. I knock on the door and peek my head in. Sarah's styling Tatum's hair.

"Hey, here are your clothes. I'll hang them up right here."

"Hey, girl! You look cute tonight." Sarah beams.

"Yeah, you do look pretty cute," Tatum echoes and

warmth blossoms my cheeks. He winks at me in the mirror.

"Um, thanks. Nothing special...just jeans and a shirt." I busy myself so I don't stand there and stare at Tatum.

"I like that shirt. Bring it over here?"

I walk over to Tatum and hold up the button-down. I'm nervous I'll slip up in front of Sarah, so of course, I ramble like an idiot.

"It's lightweight cotton, so you shouldn't get too hot in it, especially on a cool night like tonight, but just let me know. I'll bring a back-up T-shirt in case. I really like the material. and I think it'll look good against your tan skin. But, we can always go back to those floral shirts Jess was putting you in if you want something more traditional. I mean—"

"Kiki, it's fine. I like it just fine," Tatum says softly, grabbing my wrist and giving it a squeeze.

"Oh, okay, great." I smile at him and walk back over to the rack.

The dressing room door suddenly bangs open and Lex walks through it like he's a goddamn king.

"You're not dressed? Let's go! Chop-chop. We've got to meet with what's-her-name about the duet. Hey, Sunshine. Hey Kiki." Lex falls onto one of the lounge chairs and starts playing an air guitar. He's so weird. Hot, but weird.

Tatum stands up and grabs the shirt from me, winking as he buttons it up. I run my tongue over my lips as I imagine undressing him and he gives me a low, warning growl.

"What did you say, man?" Lex drums his fingers on the chair as he watches Sarah put away her makeup.

"I didn't say anything," Tatum barks back. He quickly

takes off his shorts, slides his pants on, and pulls on a pair of Chelsea leather ankle boots.

"All right, let's go. Let's go! She's driving the guys nuts."

"Who is?"

"That yoke. What's her name?" Lex snaps his fingers. "Taken... No, that's not it. Macon. Maddie. She's waiting for you in our dressing room."

"Why the hell is she waiting in there? And how can you not remember her name? She's been on tour with us for over two months."

Lex shrugs. "Who the fuck knows? Just come on. See you on the flipside, ladies." He winks at us and I can feel Sarah swoon next to me.

"Bye, Lex!" Sarah yells with a note of longing in her voice.

Tatum looks over his shoulder at me as he exits and winks again. I give him a lopsided grin and he's gone.

"Oh my God!" Sarah sets the hair pomade down with a slam. "You guys are fucking, aren't you?"

So much for keeping it a secret.

"What? No! Sarah!" I feign horror.

"Oh, save it, Kiki. You're the worst liar, and you ramble when you're nervous. And the dead giveaway was Tatum. He couldn't keep his eyes off you. I was watching him in the mirror."

"He couldn't?" I smile dreamily as I sink down into the chair Lex just abandoned.

"I knew it! Oh my God, when? Spill it. I'm so happy for you both." Sarah squeals with delight, doing a little jump.

"Um, okay, when? After the Nashville concert. After we

went to Whiskey Sky Bar, that night. And then we've been trying to hang out when we can, but we want to keep it a secret for a while."

"Kiki…a secret?" She frowns at me through the mirror.

"I know, it sounds bad, but it's my choice. I don't want to be thrust into the public eye yet. I want to keep this little, happy bubble we have at the moment. Can you understand?"

"Yeah, I understand, but eventually it's going to come out. Someone's going to find out. Especially with the way he stares at you."

"I know, I know. But it's so *new*. I want to see where it goes without being under a microscope."

"Well, that's fair. But it's going to be hard. That boy's got it bad for you."

"You think?"

"Uh, yeah! He can't keep that stupid, goofy, love-grin off his face. And I hate to even breathe her name, but he never had that look with Savannah. Not even in the beginning."

I quirk an eyebrow. "Really? I don't know. He says she's crazy, but she's so beautiful."

Sarah rolls her eyes. "So are you, but the difference between you two is that she has the personality of a loofah sponge."

"Oh, and don't forget that eensie-weensie bit about how she can sing."

Sarah sighs, shoves me in her seat, and starts to vigorously brush my hair. "Stop being so insecure. You're going to have to get over comparing yourself to Savannah or any other girl if you want this relationship to survive."

"Ow! That hurts." I grab my scalp where she just murderously ripped my hair out with the brush.

"Sorry. I'm getting frustrated with you. You need to believe in yourself and stop comparing yourself to the likes of Savannah and Maddie. Not all girls are like them, but how would you know that? You've surrounded yourself with men for the last five years. Hell, even your best friend is a guy."

"That's debatable."

She softens her brushing as she smiles and begins to fishtail my hair. "My point *is* that you've built this wall of men around you to hide behind because it's safe. I think it's made you insecure around other females. Men are safer to be around in your world because they can't tear you down like a woman could."

"They can tear your heart apart."

"True, very true, but we can usually recover from that. But when a woman tears you down, it's just mean and hurtful. It's hitting below the belt. It's like we're supposed to be in this together and supporting one another. I think you're scared all women are like Maddie."

"I support you—I'm not scared of you."

"Because I'm not a threat to you. I'm not a mean bully. There's always going to be a Maddie or a Savannah out there in the world who wants to tear you down. But you can't let them, Kiki. You are funny and smart. You know I think you're beautiful inside and out. Use those assets, girl, don't hide them."

"I know you're right, it's just really hard. I hate it when I'm insecure, but she's a superstar, for fuck's sake, and he has girls constantly around him, ready to step in to be his one-nighter."

"Yeah, and he chose *you*. Remember that. He could have easily gone back to her a couple weeks after the ACMs, but he wants you. Haven't you dated good-looking guys in the past?"

"Yeah, but not like Tatum. I mean, he's on a different level of good-looking. The guys I dated were cutesy college guys. Tatum is all man."

"Yeah, I know what you mean. It's like Lex. He's definitely all man." She sighs.

"Okay," I relent, "no more comparing to Savannah or letting Maddie get under my skin."

Sarah nods. "And no more putting yourself down. You're smart and funny, Kiki. You have fabulous fashion sense, and you're going to rule the world someday."

I laugh. "And you? You're not going to rule the world?"

"Ah, well, yes, I'll co-rule it with you. You do the fashion, I'll do the hair and makeup. Nothing can stop us."

I laugh. "I like where this is going." I chew on my lip as an idea starts to germinate.

"God, I'm good at fishtail braids." Sarah ties off the end with a clear band.

"Wow, it looks amazing! How do you do that? And so quickly!"

The door bangs open, making us both jump. Lee comes in, carrying a large cardboard box.

"Kiki, I need you to distribute these 'Rescue Me' shirts to the vendors. More are on their way for the next few shows. Tatum needs to wear this onstage during 'Kick This Town.'"

He opens the box and passes me a black T-shirt with an image of Tatum on the front with Oreo sitting on his shoulder. On the back it says "Rescue Me" and then a list of the cities that have been on this tour.

"These look awesome!" I cry out. "I can't believe she got a good shot out of that session. Oreo looks like a stud!"

"That's why she gets paid the big bucks. Remember, 'Kick This Town.'"

"Got it." I give him a thumbs-up as he leaves.

"Let me see one." I throw Sarah a shirt and she starts to laugh. "Oh my God, the look on Oreo's face says it all! Tatum looks like he's a cat-loving fool. Does he ever take a bad pic? I mean, the man just got scratched all to hell and he's smiling that cute, dimpled smile."

"She had to have superimposed a different picture of his head, because there was no way he was smiling like that after Oreo freaked."

Sarah laughs. "I don't remember. I was laughing too hard. But it is a great pic. Oreo's a superstar!"

"Yeah, well, don't tell him. He's already making Stan feed him kitty caviar when he rides shotgun." I pick up the heavy box. "All right, I'll be backstage after I drop these off if you need me."

"I'd help you, but I need to go stand on Lex's side of the stage to help wipe him down."

I laugh. "Sarah, the show doesn't start for an hour."

"I need to make sure I get a good spot."

"Oh, geez, Sunshine, you're hopeless." I shift the box on my hip as I head toward the door.

"Hey, Kiki?"

"Yeah?"

"I'm really happy for you guys. You both deserve it."

I run over and give her a quick hug before I head out the door.

TATUM IS FINISHING up his first set, and he looks damn fine in his new Boss button-down and Rag and Bone jeans. I'm looking at him differently tonight. Not like the hip-thrusting fool or the one I couldn't have, but the man I'm falling in love with. And as the thousands of fans scream and sing his songs, I'm blown away. He takes it all in and gives the fans what they crave right back. He's funny and loving, sexy and powerful. He controls the crowd with his voice and his talent and it's an intoxicating experience to watch. The song ends and he jogs off stage toward me.

I grin cheesily at him as he saunters up to me, unbuttoning his shirt.

"Hi." I hand him a water and take his shirt after he peels it off.

"Hi beautiful." He winks at me as he gulps the water down.

Heaven have mercy. I want to lick him from head to toe.

He laughs. "Don't look at me like you want to eat me, or I'll bend you over the amp over there and have my way with you in front of everyone."

I wipe him down. "Ooh, that sounds really naughty," I purr in his ear.

He growls as I finish up and hand him the new T-shirt. "What's this?"

"This is the new Rescue Me shirt Lee wants you to wear for your next song."

He stares at the T-shirt and laughs. "She did a great job."

"I'm thinking she superimposed your face on there because I don't remember that shot quite looking like that."

He laughs again. "Nah, Ellen's just that good." He pulls the T-shirt over his head. "Hand me a few more and I'll throw some out into the audience. Wait for me on my bus after the show? Security knows to only let you in."

I nod as my cheeks heat. He winks, and the music starts for the next set as he runs back onstage. The crowd goes wild as he starts to talk about the shirt and his good friend Oreo. My heart melts a little more. He's going to help a lot of rescue animals tonight.

Chapter 32

Tatum

I PACE BACK and forth on my bus as I listen to Lee on my cell phone. He flew back to Nashville after the Kansas show because we've had some issues regarding the gag order. Apparently, it's not possible to block the *Marie Claire* article unless we want to sue the magazine. If it comes to that, this could turn into a media circus. We have five shows left and then I can get back home to deal with this shit in person. I'm livid with Savannah and this bullshit she's trying to throw on me, especially while I'm out on tour. It's hard for me to wrap my head around the fact she's being so hateful and ugly.

I look around my empty bus and think of Kiki. I've decided that once we get back home I'm going to ask her to make our relationship public. I'm tired of hiding it from everyone. Jess has rejoined us for the remainder of the tour and it's making sneaking back and forth to my bus more difficult for Kiki. I don't want to jeopardize her job, but at the same time, I selfishly want her at my side, sharing pieces of our lives with each other, her soft warm body pressed against mine in our bed. Or the simple act of walking down the street with her hand in mine. I want both sides of the coin—the public and the private, and I want it all with her.

"Hello? Tatum, did you hear me?"

"Shit. Sorry, Lee, repeat what you just said?"

"I said, if we can't get the lawyers to stop the article, we can at least have them push it back a couple months. I've already started the process for that."

"That's bullshit. None of it is true!"

"I know, but by that point maybe things will have died down, and you guys will be old news."

"Or I can sue her ass for false accusations and we can really get the party started."

Lee sighs. "Or that." He's quiet for a moment. "Um, this is a really bad time to bring this up, but her agent contacted me. She'll be in Portland the night before you're in Seattle. She's willing to stay another night and come to Seattle to do the duet with you."

"Are you fucking kidding me? Hell no!"

"Listen, I get it, man, but to have you guys onstage together singing your song will be really good publicity for you and the album. In fact, it might even make her story look bogus if it ever does get out. Why would she willingly step out onstage with you if she's accused you of these heinous things? Who knows, man, maybe this is her way of a truce. Maybe you can charm her into retracting the article."

"I can't believe you're even putting me in this position, Lee. I don't want to breathe the same air as her," I seethe.

"You have a couple days to decide. But if I were you, I'd do it. It's positive press. The label thinks it's a good idea too."

I grunt into the phone because I'm too pissed to talk.

"On a brighter note, sales for T-shirts have tripled since we introduced the Rescue Me one. You'll have to figure out which rescues you want to donate to."

"Put Kiki in charge of it. She'll have a better idea than me," I say gruffly.

"Okay, will do. Kill it tonight in Denver."

"Wait. I need to tell you something. It's about Kiki." I take a deep breath. I've debated whether or not Lee needs to know, but in the end, honesty is the best policy, and I want him to hear it from me. "She and I have started dating."

Lee groans. "Fuck, Tate, seriously? With all the Savannah shit we have going on? You couldn't keep it in your pants? What if she goes to the press with this?"

"It's not like that. I trust her…you know that's not easy for me."

"Look, I like Kiki. Her brother is a good friend of mine, but now is not the time to start dating the towel girl, for fuck's sake."

"Careful, Lee. She means something to me."

"You've got Entertainer of the Year on the line!"

I look down at my cell in disbelief. Is that all he cares about?

"Our relationship will have no bearing on whether or not I get it, and you know it." I grind my teeth in annoyance.

Lee sighs heavily into the phone. "Well, all I can say is she better be worth it. If Savannah gets wind of this… Shit, what am I going to tell her brother?"

"She won't. We're keeping it quiet for now. Let Kiki

handle her brother."

"I hope you know what you're doing. Keep it very quiet, my friend. We need this new development like a hole in the head. And don't forget to give me an answer about Savannah joining the tour."

I hang up on him and throw my phone across the bus. I'm so pissed off I can't even think straight. Something about this stinks. Savannah's setting me up for something, but I can't figure out what. I don't trust her one bit. And I hate how cavalier Lee is being about my relationship with Kiki. I mean, I wasn't expecting him to accept it with a cigar and a fine malt whiskey, but the least he could have said was, "I'm happy for you, man."

All he cares about is good press and me getting Entertainer of the Year. What about my fucking happiness? I retrieve my phone and text Kiki.

> **Me:** *Meet me at the front of the stage in ten.*
>
> **Keepie:** *Are you having a wardrobe issue?*
>
> **Me:** *What? No, this isn't job-related. It's personal.* ;D
>
> **Keepie:** *Well, make something up that sounds work-related, preferably in the wardrobe department so I can escape Jess's glare.*
>
> **Me:** *Okay, I'll text her, just get your cute butt down here.*
>
> **Me:** *Jess, I need Kiki's help, so I asked her to come to the stage.*
>
> **Jess:** *What? She can't. I need her to finish getting the T-shirts to the vendors.*
>
> **Me:** *She can do it after. This won't take long, I promise.*
>
> **Jess:** *Fine, whatever.*

I watch Kiki approach the front of the stage. She's so cute in the Rescue Me T-shirt tied in a knot at her waist paired with white skinny jeans and Chucks. Seeing her is like sunshine peeking out on my cloudy day. I immediately put the problems with Savannah to the back of my brain.

I crouch down at the edge of the stage. She glances around nervously. The guys behind me are tuning their instruments, not paying attention.

"Hey, sexy girl."

"Hey, sexy boy."

I grin. "Have you ever watched a concert here at Red Rocks before?"

"No, this is my first time in Denver."

"We'll have to come back here. Denver is a really fun city, and the mountains are amazing."

She grins. "I've always wanted to try snowboarding. And drink hot chocolate by the fire in a mountainside chalet."

"Well, that would be fun to do in Steamboat or Aspen. Maybe Christmastime we could come out here."

"Maybe your birthday."

"Okay, we'll make it happen." My heart thuds faster in my chest as I stare into her luminous eyes. It suddenly slams into me that there's no one else I'd rather spend my birthday with then her.

She looks over my shoulder. "So, what's up? Jess was not pleased you wanted me instead of her."

"You let me worry about Jess. So, Red Rocks is a very special place to watch a concert. You're surrounded by all of these beautiful, red stone boulders overlooking the city. A thousand stars light up the sky, and you're outside with nature and music. It's an awesome experience. Since Jess won't give you the night off, and it's not the same experience watching us from the side of the stage, I figured you could watch us practice right now. Your own little private concert."

She swallows and turns around to look at the rows of wooden benches which will soon be filled to capacity with adoring fans. "Just me?"

"Just you. So I suggest sitting about ten rows back." It takes all my self-control not to reach for her and smash her lips to mine. I need her touch so badly right now.

"Wow, thanks, Tatum. I'm honored."

I wink at her and she gives me a megawatt smile as she turns, jogging up to the tenth row with her box of T-shirts. She slides onto the bench seating and props her feet up, resting her chin on her hands.

This sneaking around is getting difficult, especially with all the prying eyes. I stand back up and signal for Lex to start the opening set.

Chapter 33

Kiki

OH MY GOD, this is amazing. Red Rocks is amazing. Tatum is amazing.

I never really got to experience the power of his performance watching it from the side of the stage. This afternoon, he's not jumping all around the stage, thrusting his hips at the ladies. He's just singing his songs to me, and it's completely intoxicating.

Tatum Reed's bedroom eyes while he sings just to me? It turns my knees to jelly.

"How does it sound?"

I know there are a dozen tech, sound, and lighting guys around me, but he's looking directly at me. Lex smirks and shakes his head. Shit, I wonder if he knows. Are we that obvious? I self-consciously shrug and give him a thumbs-up. He flashes me his panty-melting smile with his gorgeous dimples and I mentally shake myself, my inner tween screaming, *He's so gorgeous and he's with me!*

On the outside? Totally cool, calm, collected.

Minus the drool on my chin.

"Let's do the acoustic Shania one we've added to the set, Lex."

Lex nods. Two stage hands bring out two stools and the boys get comfortable on them with their guitars. Wow, the two of them next to each other is just cruel to all the single women out there in the audience tonight. Their magnetism on that stage right now is overpowering. Tatum smiles at me. Lex starts strumming his guitar softly as the two of them launch into an acoustic version of Shania Twain's "Always and Forever." It's beautiful and mesmerizing, and I'm pretty positive my panties just self-ignited, melting off.

I listen to the lyrics and tears threaten to glaze over my eyes. Listening to Tatum sing this song brings me to my knees. I drink the Kool-Aid that is Tatum Reed, because I am completely captivated. Somehow, I know he's singing this song to me, and I take that little piece of knowledge and tuck it away in my heart.

When they finish, I wipe my eyes inconspicuously on my shirt. I'm so screwed. He holds two fingers up and gives a little wave before he turns and walks toward the guys, talking about a few different cues. My eyes are glued to his ass and I can't help but take in this gorgeous man.

I sigh and shake myself out of my lust-filled daydream. I slowly gather my things. Playtime is over, it's time to get back to the grind and being tormented by Jess.

As I stand, a voice behind me stops me in my tracks.

"You know he's going to get bored with you, right?"

I don't have to turn around to know Maddie's snarky voice.

She continues when I don't say anything. "You'll never fit into his world. You're just scratching an itch right now. He'll get tired of you in a couple weeks. Besides, you'll certainly never hold a candle to Savannah Edwards. She's a star. You're a *nothing*."

I whirl around, her words hitting the mark, the exact insecurities I've been feeling. "Oh! And you think you will? You think he'll be dazzled by *you*? Think again. You're a trainwreck."

A triumphant smile spreads across her face. "I knew it. I knew he was keeping you around for a reason."

Shit, fuck, damn.

"You don't know shit."

"I know more than you think, honey. You're just a flash in the pan."

"Like your career?"

She looks at me sourly and shrugs. "Whatever. It doesn't matter. You're just a distraction. He'll dump you as soon as this tour is over. Like I said, in this business, you're just a body, and you're easily replaceable. You don't understand the ins and outs of the music business. Tatum needs someone who understands him, someone who will fit into his world, and you, sweetie, are not it." She clucks her tongue. "I actually feel sorry for you. It's pathetic you think he's actually into you when he has Savannah dangling from his fingertips. Have fun washing the towels."

She quickly gets up and walks toward the exit without a backward glance as my mouth hangs open. A million retorts come to mind, yet I stand there frozen to the spot, shocked at what a mean bitch she really is.

I quickly walk back to the dressing room and grab an-other box of new Rescue Me shirts to drop off at the vendors. Sarah grabs a box to help.

"Hey, Kiki, wait up."

I dash the tears from my cheeks before she can see them.

"Hey! Hey, what's wrong?"

"Fucking Maddie Macon is such a bitch!"

"Oh well, we knew that. What'd she do now?"

"She told me I'm a big, fat zero. That I'm a distrac-tion…and Tatum will dump me after the tour is over."

"Oh please, do you really believe that?"

"No. At least, I don't want to think that. But she said it, and all my insecurities came right to the surface."

Sarah sighs. "Remember what I said last week?"

I nod.

"It's Maddie Macon. I mean, come on! The girl is an ugly bully, and a badly dressed one at that. She's super jealous of you. Just ignore the hate. You and Tatum will be fine."

I sniff. "She said I couldn't hold a candle to Savannah."

"Well, she's just…she's melted wax! Who the fuck wants melted wax?"

I laugh as I wipe away tears. "A kinky guy during sex."

"Well, there you go. Right up Maddie's alley."

"Tate invited me to watch them during sound-check. It was pretty amazing."

"See?" She bumps my arm with hers. "I've never heard of him doing that for anyone before. Tatum wouldn't invest his time and effort if he didn't care about you."

I think of him singing the Shania song and my heart

blooms with hope again.

We drop the boxes off at the vendor.

"Thanks, Sarah…for talking my head through the bull-shit. I let her get to me, and I need to stop feeling so insecure. You were right, I need to stay strong or this will never work."

Sarah pulls me into a side-hug as we walk backstage. "That's what friends are for. We build each other up, not tear each other down."

LATER THAT NIGHT I sneak off my tour bus and head toward Tatum's bus before the caravan heads out of Denver.

He grabs my hand as soon as security lets me on his bus. "I've got a surprise for you. Close your eyes."

I smile as he guides me to his couch and sits me down. My eyes are closed as he lays a plastic, rectangular-shaped box in my hands.

"K, open them." His smile shows his perfect white teeth and dimples. It's so infectious I automatically smile back at him.

He chuckles. "Kiki, you can look now."

I look down to see three DVDs in my hand. *Pitch Perfect 1, 2* and *3*. Tears glisten in my eyes. "You got me *Pitch Perfect*? All three?" I squeak.

"Yeah, you said you liked them. I was so thrilled to see there were *three* movies!" he says sarcastically and smirks. "I got popcorn too. We can have a movie night."

I laugh, wiping my eyes. "I can't believe you got me all three and you're going to watch them with me." I fling myself into his arms and kiss him hard.

"Well, if I knew this was how you'd react, I would have gotten them for you way sooner."

He carries me down the hallway into his palatial bedroom. He walks over to the bed and tosses me on to it, climbs over me, and kisses my lips.

"I've waited all day to be alone with you. The buses are pulling out soon and won't stop until dawn. How are you going to explain you're not in your bed in the morning? Not that I'm complaining."

"Sarah said she'd cover for me. I'm not sure what she's going to say, but right now I'm in bed with a migraine, so we're good until morning."

"Well, I'm glad you're here. I've missed you." Tatum squeezes me and kisses my lips again. "Let's watch your movie. Then we'll have hot sex until you scream my name." He smiles, his dimples winking at me.

I arch an eyebrow up at him. "Maybe I'll be the one making you scream my name."

He laughs as he gets up and pulls me with him. "Baby, please do your best. I'm always open for a challenge."

I laugh as I go to the kitchen to grab the drinks while he makes the popcorn, and we snuggle back in his bed. I catch him smiling at me as we watch the movie. "What?"

"Nothing. You're just so cute."

I playfully shove him. "Nothing's going to distract me from watching this, not even you." I laugh, throwing a piece of popcorn at him, which he deftly catches with his mouth.

"Showoff," I mutter.

"This movie is pretty bad." He side-eyes me.

"Which part?"

"All of it."

I laugh. "It is pretty bad, but I love it for some reason. What movie do you love that you would never admit to anyone?"

"*Die Hard.* It's a classic. But I would tell anyone that. I'm not ashamed."

I roll my eyes. "I think you're covering, like you secretly love *The Notebook.* You've already admitted you watch *Friends.*"

He throws a piece of popcorn at my head. "I said my sister watches *Friends.* She forced me to."

"Shush, you're missing the good part. This is when—"

"They kick butt, win the competition, and the guy gets the girl?"

"Ugh, you're going to ruin it!"

He laughs. "You've already seen this, probably a hundred times." He starts to nibble my neck.

I sigh. "Are you going to watch?"

"I'm watching," he teases as he licks my neck. He kisses my collar bone as he moves his hand from my hip down south. He glides a finger into me and I moan in pure pleasure, forgetting all about the movie.

I SNUGGLE UNDER the blankets after I brush my teeth.

"Thank you."

"For what?"

"For getting me the movies, for watching them with me even though I know they're lame…and for the hot sex."

"You're welcome. Thanks for making me scream."

I laugh as I hit his face with a pillow. "You did not."

"I know, but I wanted to. Thought I might lose my man card if I did though." He kisses me as he climbs into bed next to me. "So, tell me what you were like as a kid."

"Me?" I squeak. "Um…I don't know. I was a headstrong tomboy. I used to run around in just shorts with the boys in the neighborhood until one day, my mom wouldn't let me go outside unless I put a shirt on. It drove my mom nuts, because my sister was Little Miss Perfect and I was kind of all over the place. She would wear the bows and pretty dresses, and I had snaggly hair and bruises."

Tatum laughs. "You? I have a hard time believing you were a tomboy."

"Oh, big time. I never wore dresses. Once my boobs finally made an appearance at sixteen I discovered it was fun to dress up. Jesus, did I really just tell you when my boobs developed?"

He grins. "You did. I love these boobs." He circles a nipple with his index finger and pinches.

"Stop!" I bat his hand away. "K, your turn. What were you like?"

"Me?" He looks up at the ceiling as he puts his hands behind his head. "I was super cool."

Silence beats between us.

"What?" I sit up in disbelief. "That's it?"

"What else do you need to know?" He flashes me his killer dimples.

"Ugh, I hate you." I push away from him, but he quickly gathers me back into his arms, laughing.

"No, you don't, you love me."

I go completely still in his arms. What do I say to that? *Yes, you're right, I'm totally in love with you? No, I hate you?* Crap. We're in that weird stage of being too early to confess our love for each other, but far enough along that we're more than just friends.

I turn in his arms and smile up at him as he looks adoringly down at me. I trace my finger along his chiseled jaw, taking in his strong features and soft lips.

"You're right," I say softly, opening my heart to him.

"About what?" His eyes are a deep apple-green.

"All of it."

He smiles and kisses my lips softly. "Mackenzie Forbes, I think I'm falling in love with you." He swallows, looking incredibly vulnerable. "Want to fall with me?"

Cue my heart flip-flopping in my chest. Too many emotions clog my throat and I'm afraid I'll cry out of happiness, so I just nod and kiss the hell out of him.

He laughs as he rolls me on top of him. "I love you, Kiki," he murmurs as he nuzzles my neck. I almost didn't catch it, he said it so quietly. "I wasn't expecting you, but here you are, and I've fallen hard for you."

"Say it again."

"I love you, Coffee Girl."

"I love you too, Tater Tot."

His strong arms circle my waist and he lifts me up and

brings me into the bathroom. I look at him curiously. "You want a shower? Right now?"

He turns on the taps and kisses me as we wait for the water to heat up. "Yeah, I've fantasized about this."

He eases me into the shower and gently washes my hair and body. It's such a simple, everyday act, but having him do it to me has turned it into an erotic and sensual thing. He places my hands against the wall, trailing kisses down my shoulder and back. I moan in response and push back against his hard length.

He quickly sheathes himself in a condom and pushes into me from behind.

"Is this okay?" he grits out as he pounds into me while he rubs my clit in tight little circles. I nod, unable to answer him as waves of sensation take me over the edge.

"Shit, Kiki, you feel so tight and warm. I won't last this time…you feel so good. Come for me, baby."

I fall apart in his arms. My orgasm has me gasping for breath. Stars blind my eyes as I ride out this incredible high.

I love this man with every fiber of my being.

"Yes, baby, yes! Fuck, that's so good!" Tatum comes hard right after me. We pant together in the steaming-hot shower and I lean my cheek on the cool tile. Against me, his chest rises and falls as I come back down from my state of pure bliss.

"Wow," I breathe out.

His chest rumbles. "Yeah." He kisses my neck as we let the hot water stream over us. I gently wash his hair and body, then we wrap each other in warm, fluffy white towels.

"Tatum?"

"Yes, baby."

"Do you always keep condoms in the shower?" I tease.

He smiles devilishly. "No, but I've been dreaming of doing that to you for a long time, so I came prepared."

"Ah, okay, I like a prepared guy." I wink at him cheekily.

He playfully snaps the towel at my butt. "Always."

We climb back into bed and he gathers me into his arms, spooning me.

"Okay, I'm tired now. Leave me alone," I tease.

He chuckles as he pulls the comforter over us. By the time my head hits the pillow I'm pretty much on my way to lights-out land. He moves my hair back from my neck and softly places a kiss there.

"I love you, beautiful girl," he whispers as I fade into black.

Chapter 34

Tatum

I CAN'T SLEEP because I have a song lyric running through my head, so I get up and grab my pencil, notebook and guitar. Lex and I usually song-write together, but inspiration's hit, so I need to get this one on paper.

I look over at Kiki snoring softly into her pillow. I smile and cover up her long, tan legs where she's kicked the covers off.

I write, inspired by the lovely muse lying next to me.

I wasn't looking for love, but there you were.
I wasn't wanting much, but you gave it anyway.
I wasn't going to ask you, but you answered the call,
I didn't want to take much, but in the end you gave it all.

Take my hand, take my heart, take my love,
Won't you fall with me?
Tear it up, take a piece, what will be, will be.
Take my love, just say yes...

Won't you fall with me?
Fall with me.

I quietly strum my guitar as the melody plays itself in my head. Kiki stirs a little but doesn't wake. I write down the notes and add the lyrics, singing softly to the gorgeous girl who has captured my heart.

I gaze down at her. How on earth did this woman wrap me so tight around her finger in such little time? I've never had these intense feelings for another woman before. I thought I loved Savannah, but it wasn't love. I can see that clearly now. Nothing compares to my feelings for Kiki. I would do anything for her.

I want to protect her, care for her for the rest of my life, have babies with her. These feelings should scare the crap out of me, but they don't. They excite me.

I'm twenty-eight years old, and I've never been in love before. I've been so focused on my career since I left home I never truly gave myself over to someone else. I thought Savannah was it, but I've shared more with Kiki in the short time I've been with her than the two and a half years I was with Vanny.

Huh, what does that say? I never wanted to open up to Savannah and share my dreams and fears with her, but with Kiki, I want her to know everything.

I need to break down these walls I'd built up to protect myself over the years. Everyone in this industry wants a piece of you, from the label to the fans, and it leaves you feeling alone and cold. It wears on you, and you start to distrust people because they'll turn on you in a heartbeat to get what they want. I'm just a means to an end in this industry.

I'm not sure how I know, but with every pump of blood that courses through my veins I innately know I can trust her.

I tenderly swipe a lock of her hair, feeling the silkiness of it between my fingers. She stirs and mumbles in her sleep. I smile as I write down a few more notes and lyrics as the bus trundles down the lonely dark highway.

I can't be the man that I want to be
It's all pretend, happiness eludes me.
You're still a mystery that holds the key,
Until you let go we both won't be free.

Take my hand, take my heart, take my love,
won't you fall with me?
Tear it up, take a piece, what will be, will be.
Take my love, just say yes…
Won't you fall with me?
Just fall with me.
What will be will be.

I look at my phone and can't believe two hours have gone by. It's now four a.m. and I need to get some sleep. I'm pumped, though, and can't wait to show Lex the song.

I put my notebook and guitar in my closet and climb back into bed, pulling Kiki into me. I kiss her shoulder and trail kisses down her arm. She murmurs softly and pushes back into me, and I take this as an invitation. I move down her silky body feathering her with light kisses until I reach her hip. I gently roll her over and place kisses on her sweet, hot pussy. She moans in protest, still half-asleep, until I lap her with my tongue, tasting her thoroughly.

Her fingers thread through my hair and she moans my name. Sweetest song I've ever heard. I slowly suck and lick her until she's arching and screaming my name. *God, I love this girl.*

"Well, good morning to you too," she pants as she sits up, coming down off her orgasm high. "What time is it?"

"It's about four thirty."

"In the morning? Geez, Tatum!"

I shrug. "I couldn't sleep and you just looked and smelled so delicious."

She smirks at me and blushes. "So I'm guessing you want me to return the favor?"

"No, my little CG, I want you to get your beauty rest. I'm good; I just had some energy to burn."

Her eyes soften and turn a calm gray, like a foggy lake in the early morning. "I want to."

"Well, you don't have to."

"Shush it, Pants Boy."

I laugh as she gently brushes kisses down my abdomen and then I quickly sober, because holy shit, the second-best thing to being inside her is having her mouth wrapped around my dick, sucking me to oblivion.

"OH MY GOD, she didn't!" Kiki screeches, making me sit up

straight in bed.

"Wuz goin' on?" I mumble, trying to rub the sleep from my eyes.

"Oh, sorry, did I wake you?" She absently looks over at me as she starts furiously typing on her phone.

"What's wrong?" I ask groggily.

"Ugh. Sarah told Jess I had raging diarrhea and vomiting this morning, and my hemorrhoids are flaring up so I can't leave the bathroom because it's too painful. I've asked to not be disturbed. Goddammit, I thought we were going to say I had a migraine."

I chuckle. "Well, that's one way to go unnoticed."

"What the hell kind of friend says that?" she huffs as she types again. "I mean, she says it's working. Jess won't go near the back room. Thanks a lot, Sunshine."

"So how are you going to sneak back on now?"

"I don't know, we'll have to let Sarah the Genius figure that one out. Remind me not to ask for her to cover for me again."

I laugh as I prop my pillow under my head and watch her. "Okay."

She looks over at me and grins. "I'm sorry I woke you."

"S'okay. I'm going back to sleep even as we speak." I yawn. My eyes shut as I drift off again.

"What! Oh my God, Sarah is *the* worst cover-upper person ever!"

Or maybe not.

I prop my head on my elbow. "What happened?"

She looks at me absently. "Oh shit, I did it again, didn't I?"

"Mmm, I'll go make some coffee and find out where we are in relation to our next destination."

"That would be good to know considering her plan to get me back on is to drape a mannequin with a sheet and 'carry me' off the bus at a rest stop and then I casually walk back on all better."

I slide her a dubious look. "Maybe you should just tell Jess the truth. That you had super-hot sex all night long with the sexiest member of the band and you don't give a rat's ass who knows."

"Nah, she'll never believe Lex and I are hooking up." She smirks as she looks down at her phone as she texts Sarah.

I throw my T-shirt at her face and leave before I kiss her smirk off her beautiful lips.

I wander down the hall and open the partition to the kitchen. "Morning, Mike. Need any coffee?"

"Good morning, sir. That would be great," Mike, my tour bus driver, shouts over his shoulder.

I make the coffee and bring him a cup. The steaming-hot brew awakens my foggy brain. "Where's our next stop?"

"Well, we stopped around five a.m. to refuel, so probably again around noon. We should make Bozeman in good time by this afternoon."

I nod and grab the paper he had picked up for me when they stopped. "Thanks, man."

I bring Kiki a cup back to bed and hand it to her. She's still engrossed in her phone.

"Um, I hate to break the news, but Mike and the crew aren't stopping again to refuel until noon. I think you're going to have to tell Jess the truth. She's not going to fire you. I won't let that happen."

"Ugh, she already hates me as it is, this will just make it worse. What about the NDA I signed? I'm screwed."

"Jess doesn't hate you. She's just particular with her affection. I seriously wouldn't stress over it. But one great quality about Jess is that she's discreet, so I know she won't gossip about us. It's going to be okay. I'll talk to Lee. Don't worry about the NDA."

She nods. "I guess I should text her."

I open to the sports section. "Just like a Band-Aid, rip it off."

"Huh, easy for you to say."

She types away on her phone, and I tell myself I need to take my own advice with her. I've been dreading this, and trying to figure out a way to drop the news that Savannah will be joining the tour in Seattle.

"Um, Kiki, I need to tell you something, and you aren't going to like it."

She looks up from her phone. "Oh-kay. Shoot."

"Lee told me Savannah wants to meet up in Seattle and sing the duet with me at our concert."

"Okay..."

"Well, there's a lot I haven't told you about what she's done in the last couple weeks." I proceed to tell her how Savannah made up the story in the article and how I've had to get lawyers involved.

"Wow, Tate, I'm so sorry. I had no idea." She moves over next to me and runs her fingers through my hair. "So just tell her no."

I sigh. Her head-rubbing feels so good. "It's not that

simple. Lee thinks if I make amends and sing with her I can convince her to drop the article."

"Okay, that's a possibility."

"You don't understand, though. I don't want to even be in the same room as her, much less sing with her. I can't stand her. She's a lying bitch. I tried to be friends with her, but she's crazy."

"Hmm. I understand your feelings, but I think Lee might be right about this. Play nicey-nice with her, and you'll have a better chance she'll retract the article."

"What if I say yes and then she decides to go ahead with the article anyway? Something feels off about all of this."

"You're being paranoid. It's one song, one night. It'll be okay. I'll be right off stage the whole time."

I love this girl. I pull her into my arms and kiss the tip of her nose. "Thank you."

"What did I do?" She smiles and it's better than sunshine.

"For being my reason and for listening…and for not getting upset my ex will be singing with me."

"Well, I'm not going to lie. Savannah is intimidating as hell, but it helps when you call her your crazy, psycho ex." She grins and I choke out a laugh.

"Noted." I kiss her again and push her back against the pillows. "I can't ever get enough of you."

"Same here," she murmurs as she kisses my neck.

We make love slowly, worshipping each other's bodies, shutting out the world for just a little while longer.

Chapter 35

Kiki

I HAVE TO admit, Jess handled the whole I'm-sleeping-with-Tatum thing better than expected. I mean, I didn't exactly word it like that, but she got the gist. Part of me wonders if she already suspected. I think she's happy I want to keep it on the down low and not shout it to the world.

She wasn't happy about Sarah lying to her, but Sarah confessed she might have taken the lie a little too far. I arched my eyebrow at that one, but otherwise kept my mouth shut.

"Mackenzie, I can't say I'm happy about this news since we are strictly forbidden to get involved with the band. There are reasons we have these policies in place. If anything were to happen and the two of you didn't work out, you could go to the press and spew a bunch of lies just to get even."

"I wouldn't do that, Jess," I say quietly.

"Even so, I could have you fired for this indiscretion."

"I'm aware of the non-disclosure agreement. I'm not

261

stupid."

Jess grunts and shakes her head. "Well, at the end of the day, what Tatum wants, Tatum gets. And I guess you're it."

"Gee, thanks," I mumble.

Jess throws her hands in the air. "Don't sass me, Mackenzie. You're walking a thin line as it is. The only thing keeping you here is I like what you've done with the band's look."

"Jess, I'm here to work hard. I'm going to continue to work hard. I just need to know you're okay with our relationship, and I promise not to let it get in the way of doing my job."

"Does it really matter what I think?" she grumbles. "It's not my business, so don't ask for my blessing. But if I were to throw my two cents in, I think you're getting in way over your head. Now, back to work. We've got a show tonight for Bozeman in two hours, and then on to Seattle so let's figure out what he'll wear when he sings with Savannah." She heads toward the back room.

I look over at Sarah, and she rolls her eyes and smiles, giving me a thumbs-up. Not gonna lie, it was a hard pill to swallow when Tatum revealed he was singing the duet with Savannah. I know he loves me, but that old green friend of mine reared its ugly head once again at the mere mention of her name. I know he says he dislikes her and they're no longer even friends, but history is history.

I trust Tatum, but I don't trust her. I didn't want to agree with Tatum yesterday morning and worry him further, but I'm not sure what her motives are, either. Maybe she really does just want to make amends and sing the duet with him. It's good publicity for them to show they're still friends for their fans.

Maybe her popularity has dropped since the breakup. I don't know or really care. I just have to make sure I'm there for Tatum and not let my insecurities get the best of me.

Chapter 36

Tatum

Me: *How are the 'rhoids?*

Keepie: *Lol, shut up.*

Me: *I'm just a concerned boyfriend checking on his girl.*

Keepie: *Oh, please. A concerned boyfriend would be giving his girlfriend a day at the spa.*

Me: *Or a tube of hemorrhoid cream.*

Keepie: *Lol. Too bad I don't actually have hemorrhoids.*

Me: *Hemorrhoids or not, you should go take a day at the spa.*

Keepie: *Are you going to go naked onstage tomorrow night?*

Me: *I can if you want me to. Matt might object. Lex would be a good friend and strip down with me. I could probably convince Will to go shirtless.*

Keepie: *Good to know. I'm currently pressing the band's clothes for tomorrow, so no, I won't be going to the spa.*

Me: *Can't you ask Jess to do that?*

Keepie: *Lol. Ur funny.*

Me: *Only for you baby. But seriously, if you need a break I can tell her to go do it.*

Keepie: *Don't you dare! No need to rock the boat.*

Me: *Can you meet me this afternoon for a little surprise? We'll be leaving the stadium so we'll have to go incognito.*

Keepie: *Like a date?*

Me: *Yes. It's long overdue. We kind of skipped the whole first date thing.*

Keepie: *Are you sure it's a good idea? What if someone recognizes you?*

Me: *We're not in a small town. I think we'll be okay.*

Keepie: *Okay, meet you at your bus at 4?*

Me: *See you then, beautiful. Don't forget, incognito.*

Chapter 37

Kiki

I BYPASS THE security outside of Tatum's bus and knock on his door. He opens it up, and I bust out laughing. Apparently, we have the same definition of going incognito, because we're matching like twins—wearing jeans, a black hoodie pulled up over a baseball hat, and sunglasses.

"Yeah, we don't look suspicious at all."

He laughs. "Maybe you could lose the hat and glasses? Then we won't look like a couple that should be circulated on a wanted poster."

I lower the hoodie and toss my sunglasses on his couch. "Okay, I'll lose the sunglasses, but I'm keeping the hat, because I'm sure I have hat-head by now. So what are we doing?"

Tatum peers at my hat. "Does that really say 'I Love Me Some Country Boyz' on it?"

I smile sheepishly. "TJ sent it to me. I particularly like the rhinestones on 'Country Boyz.'"

Tatum laughs. "Nice. Well, I thought since you've never

been to Seattle I could show you the fish market and we could go up in the Space Needle."

"That's pretty touristy. You sure you won't get noticed?"

He eyes my hat. "You might blow my cover with that awful hat."

I scoff. "Please, people would die for this hat."

He circles his arms around my waist and kisses my lips. "Aw, honey. 'People' implies more than one person. I think you mean TJ would die for this hat, because no other normal person would even give it a second glance."

I grin up at him. "I love it when you get jealous. Don't worry, I'll let you borrow it sometime."

He grins. "Come on, Jimmy is waiting for us."

THE FISH MARKET is packed and loud. It's stinky, but Tatum and I are having the best time. He hasn't let go of my hand since we stepped out of the car, and it's nice not to have to hide our relationship. No one has recognized him and it's made us both upbeat and happy to just hang out like a regular couple. We approach one of the vendors, attracted by the loud banter from the guys behind the counter. They put on a fabulous circus-like routine, tossing the fish back and forth while yelling at one another.

One of the guys points to me and shouts at me to get behind the counter. I look at the crowd around us, thinking he couldn't possibly be speaking to me. Tatum chuckles in my ear.

"You better go, CG, or they might stick a fish down your shirt."

"What?" I ask horrified as Tatum gently shoves me forward.

"What's your name?" the burly bald guy grunts at me.

I lean into him because I'm having a hard time hearing him over the crowd and the shouting. "Uh, Kiki."

"UhKiki?" He bites back a smile as he holds out a yellow rubber apron and matching rubber gloves.

I look at them as if he's handing me a bomb to deactivate. "Um, what do you want me to do with these?"

"Put them on," he says gruffly, leaving no room for argument. "UhKiki is up!" he shouts to the other guys, causing me to jump.

"No, it's just Kiki…" But Baldy has already turned away from me.

I put on the heavy apron and long gloves that are way too big for me. I look up to see Tatum filming me with his iPhone, a huge grin on his face.

I'm going to kill him.

"UhKiki! Think fast!"

What the hell? I look up just in time to see a large, silver fish flying through the air right for my head. I scream as I automatically reach out to catch it. The fish lands with a heavy thud in my arms and I grunt at the weight of it. I automatically bring it to my chest and hug it like a football.

"Throw it, UhKiki! Over here!"

I frantically look around to see which guy is yelling at me. I'm feeling panicked and crazed. The fish stinks and it's slippery and the glassy one-eye is staring lifelessly up at me.

Oh geez, disgusting!

I hoist it to the large guy to my left and he easily catches it. The crowd laughs and claps as he throws it to another guy who wraps it up and hands it to a patron.

"Heads up, UhKiki!" Baldy yells as another fish comes sailing at me. My shoe slips on something slimy on the floor and I think I might barf, but I manage to catch and throw.

This goes on for two more rounds. Just as I'm getting the hang of it, Baldy throws something gelatinous toward me.

"Flying tentacles, UhKiki!"

A jellyfish-squid thing lands on my shoulder. I scream and cringe as I grasp a hold of the slimy creature to keep it sliding to the floor. Thank God it's not alive, or I would have peed in my pants. People are laughing, but I'm not finding the humor in fish guts and sea creatures being flung at me. I immediately gag as I hold the slimy thing by a tentacle. What *is* that? And who ordered it? I glance over at Tatum and he has tears in his eyes from laughing so hard.

"Order up, UhKiki!" the linebacker yells. I walk over to him and plop it into his hands.

"It's been real fun, but I'm done!" I shout to the guys over the crowd.

"Take a bow, UhKiki!" The crowd cheers and I'm pretty sure I'm blushing almost as red as the salmon on the counter. Oh geez, get me out of here! I remove my apron and gloves and hand them to Baldy.

"Nice catching! Order up!" he yells and Tatum reaches for the packaged squid thing.

"What?" I squeal. "Ugh, no! Why on earth are you getting that fish, or whatever that thing is?"

Tatum pays for the squid and turns to me, smiling his gorgeous dimpled smile. "Let's go. We've got to eat on this date, right?"

"What?" I shriek. "I'm not eating that thing!"

Tatum chuckles. "I got it all on video. It's classic." He flings an arm around my shoulder and steers me through the crowd.

"Tater Tot, I am not eating that slimy thing." I stomp my foot to send my point home.

He smiles at me. "It's not dinner, Squiddy, so just relax. Matt and the guys are grilling out tonight. He asked me to pick some up for him when I told him where we were going."

I shudder. "Thank God. That was revolting. Thanks a lot for putting me through that." I roll my eyes.

"Oh my God, it was so awesome, my little fish monger." He leans down and gives me a quick kiss as we walk to the car. He wrinkles his nose. "Ugh, but you kind of smell."

"Ya think? I just had fish guts flung on to me. I'm sure I reek!"

He quickly steers us toward a flower vendor and buys the biggest bunch of the most beautiful wildflowers I've ever seen.

"For you, Coffee Girl. You always smell like fresh meadow flowers to me."

"Aw, you're forgiven." I sigh as I stick my nose into the bouquet and smell the beautiful flowers.

"Hopefully, the flowers will cover up the fish stink. We can't miss the needle at night, so I guess I'll just have to put up with it for another hour." He bites back a smile.

"And... right back on my shit-list." I side-eye him.

"What did I do?" He laughs.

"I'm not sure, but I feel like somehow you had a hand in that. Out of all the people standing there, he randomly picks me?"

"It must have been the hat," He gives me a sly grin. "And you're pretty cute."

I playfully shove him as we get into the waiting car.

"Um, Jimmy change of plans. Let's go back to the tour bus."

I shoot him a questioning look.

He bursts out laughing. "I'm sorry, babe, but I can't. You smell like dead fish. I thought I could handle it, but it's pretty bad."

I give him a pouty smirk and cross my arms over my chest after I get buckled in. Secretly, I'm thrilled to go get this nasty fish smell off of me, but I'll die before I give him the satisfaction of knowing that.

"I love you, though." He grins cheekily at me.

"Whatever."

"I promise I'll make it up to you."

"Hmph."

Jimmy looks at me through the rearview mirror and wrinkles his nose. The partition slowly slides up cutting Jimmy off from Tatum and me.

"Oh great, I smell so bad even Jimmy can't stand to be next to me."

Tatum laughs. "Aw, babe, it means I don't have to worry about other guys trying to steal you away."

I hold up my hand in front of his face, blocking him

from leaning in to kiss me. "Save it."

He kisses my palm instead. "Ugh, rubber gloves and dead fish smell on your hands too."

"Payback is a bitch, Tater Tot. Just want to forewarn you."

Tatum laughs. "I look forward to it, gorgeous." He starts texting on his phone.

"You better not be posting that video on your social media."

"Nah, Jimmy takes care of that, but thanks for the reminder to send it to him."

I make a quick lunge for his phone, but he's faster than me. "Calm down, Squid." He chuckles. "I'm texting Sarah and asking her to bring over some clothes for you to my bus. I figure we'll get you hosed down and then we can go out to dinner. Maybe go up in the needle after."

"That sounds nice, minus the hosing part, because so far your idea of a first date and mine are immeasurably different." I smile to myself as I watch the city roll by out the window.

"Kiki?"

"Yeah."

"Look at me."

I turn my head and he captures my lips in a searing kiss. I groan in protest as he pulls away.

"You still have fish-guts perfume." He laughs as I elbow him in the ribs.

I growl as I undo my seatbelt and grab him in a tackle. I rub myself all over him like a cat, attempting to transfer the fish smell to him.

He laughs as he smashes his lips to mine. "Give it all you got, Squiddy. This just means we now have to shower together."

"Ugh, worst first date ever!" I tease as I giggle against his lips. The kiss becomes more heated as I grind against him.

"You need to stop or I'm going to have to take you right here. We wouldn't want Jimmy posting *that* video."

"I'm not scared." I bite his ear, making him groan.

"I am. Of your lethal dead-fish smell." He laughs as I sit back and pretend to sulk as we pull up next to his bus.

"I'm going to kill Matt for that fantastic little field trip."

Tatum chuckles. "I can't wait to show the guys the video. Come on, my little cranky fishmonger. Let's get cleaned up and I'll show you how a real first date should go." He slings an arm around my shoulder. I cradle the flowers in my arms as we head to his bus, stinky but incredibly happy.

Chapter 38

Kiki

I JUST DROPPED off the band's clothes in their dressing room when arms wrap around me, lifting me off the ground, propelling me toward Tatum's dressing room. I squeal in surprise, but quickly recognize Tatum's masculine, woodsy scent as he nuzzles my neck and I start to laugh.

"Tatum! Put me down. What if someone sees us?!"

"So? I don't care. Let 'em see." He shoulders his dressing room door open and carries me inside. We're alone for a rare moment as he sets me down, cups my face, and swoops in for a dizzying kiss.

"God, I've waited forever to do that," he says, kissing his way up the side of my neck.

"You just kissed me a couple hours ago." I giggle, wrapping my arms around his neck.

"Exactly. Forever."

"Thank you for last night. Best first date ever." I kiss his lips again. Tatum definitely redeemed himself after the fish market by reserving a table overlooking the waterfront where

I had steak, *not fish*, and then we strolled through a beautiful park before we went up into the needle. It was romantic and perfect and so normal.

"Anything for you," he says huskily as he locks his lips to mine. I don't ever want to come up for air.

There's a knock at the door and we break apart as it opens. I head over to the clothes rack as Savannah Edwards stalks into the room.

"Tatum."

"Savannah."

"Ah, excuse me, I'll leave you two alone," I say quietly as I try to scoot by Tatum.

He snakes an arm out and grabs my waist. "No, Kiki, it's fine. Finish what you've got to do."

Savannah's eyes quickly zero in on his hand on my waist and slowly scan up to my face. "Well, isn't this cozy," she sneers.

"Savannah," Tatum warns.

I wiggle away from his grasp. "No, really, it's okay. I'll be back in five minutes. I need to stock towels and water backstage, anyway."

I smile politely at Savannah, which she doesn't return, and quickly exit the room. I don't shut the door all the way, so I can still hear them as I quickly gather my wits against the outside concrete wall. My heart thunders against my chest.

"Really, Tate? So fucking typical. Fucking the *towel* girl?"

"She's not a towel girl and it's none of your fucking business who I fuck," he roars.

Yikes, I've never heard him this mad before. Sarah turns

the corner and sees me. I silence her by putting my index finger to my lips. Her eyes widen as she approaches me. I mouth *Savannah* to her and she arches an eyebrow as she sidles up next to me to eavesdrop.

She tries to placate him. "Tatum, baby, I didn't come in here to argue with you."

"Then what the fuck do you want, Savannah?"

"I forgive you."

Tatum laughs a humorless laugh. "You have a lot of fucking nerve."

Sarah raises her eyebrows at me, and I shake my head. I feel bad eavesdropping on their conversation, but for my own sanity, I have to hear what she has to say.

"Tatum, you and me, we used to be *so* good together. We can make it happen again, baby."

The nerve of that bitch! Sarah pinches my arm and I pinch back.

"Please get your hands off of me. We never had it good. You made sure of that. I can't believe you have the fucking balls to come in here after you've tried to drag my name through the mud with all your lies. I don't even want you here tonight on my tour, but I'm doing it as a favor to Lee. You make me sick to my stomach. I don't want you, Savannah. I never did." I hear something being thrown. "And don't call me *baby* ever again."

She scoffs. "So you'd rather have *her* over me?"

"Every minute of the hour, every day of the week."

Sarah silently jogs in place, shaking me in silent glee. I pinch her again to get her to stop.

"It's a joke, Tate. She can't help your career like I can.

She's a nobody. Stop fucking the towel girl and come back to me."

"Help my fucking career, are you kidding me? I don't need help with my career. I'm doing just fine, in case you haven't noticed. My whole fucking tour has been sold out. The next one probably will be too. Entertainer of the Year will be mine. And I did it all without your help. You've done your best to ruin my career, not help it. We'll do our duet tonight because I gave my word to Lee, but then we'll be done. I don't ever want to step on stage with you again. And I don't ever want to hear you mention Kiki's name again. Are we clear?"

"This isn't over. You and me? Not over!" Savannah pushes the door open and glares at Sarah and I standing on the other side as we pretend to be engrossed in our phones. She makes a noise of disgust and hurries off to her dressing room.

"Holy. Shit," Sarah breathes out.

"No shit. Do you think we should go in?"

"Maybe you go first, I'll give you guys a few minutes?"

"I…" The sentence dies on my lips as Jess rounds the corner.

"Well? Come on, you two. Stop gossiping like hens out here. We've got a damn concert happening!"

She shoves through his dressing room door and Sarah and I reluctantly follow. Tatum is seated in Sarah's chair when we walk in. He's already dressed in a blue heathered Henley and jeans with a belt and boots. His bright-green eyes pierce mine in the mirror. I give him a lopsided encouraging smile, but he doesn't return it. His lips are sealed tight and I can see his jaw tick. Sarah starts styling his hair and Jess and I pull clothes from the rack to take backstage with us. Lex saunters in and nods to Jess and me.

"Ladies. Hey Sunshine."

"Hi Lex," Sarah gushes.

"You ready for tonight, man?" Lex flips a guitar pick between his fingers.

"I'm good," Tatum says darkly.

"You sure about that?"

"I said I'm fucking fine."

Lex shrugs and saunters across the room to where I'm standing. "What the hell happened? I just saw him fifteen minutes ago and he was smiling," he murmurs to me as Tatum and Sarah start talking about random things.

"Savannah and Tate just had a fight," I whisper and he nods in understanding.

Tatum gets up as soon as Sarah is finished and he and Lex head out without so much as a backward glance.

"Damn," Sarah exhales as she starts to clean up. "He's super pissed."

"Uh, yeah. He wouldn't even look at me," I say quietly. Jess shakes her head but we ignore her.

"Don't worry, Kiki, he loves you." Sarah gently squeezes me into a hug. "She's a snake in the grass."

"I wonder how Maddie is taking it, having Savannah sing the duet," I grumble.

"You didn't hear?" Sarah gasps. "Apparently, Savannah wouldn't come if Maddie was still on the tour. She made up some bullshit about artist disagreement over singing her song. Tatum apparently agreed to the terms and they sent her back to Nashville."

"Whoa. No way! I bet that made her super pissed. So it's just the Wake Brothers opening?"

"Yeah, they had some local band open before them."

"It happens all the time," Jess pipes in.

"Not to have another country star kick you off the tour!" Sarah scoffs.

Interesting. I raise my eyebrows at Sarah. "Karma's a bitch, huh, Sare?"

"I thought the *exact* same thing when I heard." She smiles at me with an evil little glint in her eye.

I head backstage with Jess, feeling a little uneasy, but not quite sure why. There's a different vibe tonight, and it's pretty obvious Tatum isn't his usual, happy-go-lucky self. He's more subdued, as is the band. Tatum smiles at me when he comes off stage, but it doesn't reach his eyes. He doesn't say much to me and I give him his space because he looks stressed. He changes shirts and then heads back onstage for the duet.

Savannah joins him onstage and the crowd goes wild. There's no denying they have incredible onstage chemistry together.

"Seattle, please give a warm welcome to the beautiful Ms. Savannah Edwards!" Tatum smiles at her as he takes her hand and Lex immediately starts the opening notes. They nail their song and the crowd is deafening as they chant their names. She's amazing, and despite the reassurances Tatum gave me earlier about her being a total psycho and the fight earlier in the night, they look friendly under the spotlight. It's crazy to me how they can turn it on for the audience. But

I have to remind myself that he's with me, he doesn't want her. He has to be friendly toward her so she'll retract the *Marie Claire* article.

Tatum pulls her into a side hug. She reaches up and kisses his cheek.

"Wasn't she amazing, Seattle? The beautiful Ms. Savannah Edwards!"

The crowd roars their approval and my heart sinks a little further. It's all an act. *Keep it together, Kiki.*

Keep. It. Together.

My head understands this, but doubt grips my heart. Especially after not saying one word to me back in his dressing room. Maybe Savannah's words finally got through to him and he regrets jumping into a relationship with me. Maybe he realizes she's right, I can't help his career.

"Thank you, Seattle, and thank you, Tatum, for letting me join you tonight. Have a wonderful night!" Savannah waves to the crowd, leans into Tatum, and kisses him on the cheek again. She whispers something in his ear and they both laugh like fond lovers. The crowd goes nuts and she exits towards my side of the stage.

She walks briskly by me with her nose in the air, but at the last minute she looks my way with a smirk on her face and winks at me. The fucking bitch actually *winks.* Her entourage flanks her, and she's gone.

The lights go out and I'm suddenly surrounded by Will and Matt needing towels and water. They quickly guzzle their drinks and run back onstage as Lex starts up the next set.

Dammit, I really need to see Tatum right now. Just a

simple touch to be reassured everything is okay, but I don't get it. After the encore, Lee quickly whisks him away, whispering in his ear, and I'm left to clean up all the towels.

I MAKE IT back to Tatum's dressing room, with my arms full of the clothes worn tonight by the band. Tatum isn't there, but Lee and Jess are in a serious discussion when I walk in.

"Hey, Kiki, got a second?"

I look between Jess and Lee, nerves suddenly making my stomach clench. "Sure."

"Sit down, Kiki. I need to talk to you about something."

I dump the clothes in the laundry bin and sit down on the couch opposite of Lee.

"Listen, I know you're in a relationship with Tatum."

I quickly glance at Jess with annoyance. She shrugs and her eyes go wide. She gathers up her things and quietly leaves the room. Traitor.

"Tatum tells me everything, Kiki. I've known for a while." He links his hands between his legs and gives me a genuine look. "You know, under normal circumstances I would totally support it. He's been really happy and writing new music, and I think you've had an integral part in that...but tonight kind of changed things."

"What do you mean?" I croak, dread filling my lungs.

"I don't know how much Tatum told you about the interview Savannah did a couple weeks ago..."

"I know about it," I say quietly.

"Well, her camp has reached out to me tonight. After the success of tonight's performance she wants to be on good terms with Tatum again."

I blow out the breath I've been holding. "That's great news! So she's going to drop the article? What a relief."

Lee shifts in his seat and leans forward. "I'm glad you think so, but I don't think you quite understand. You see, Savannah's career has kind of stalled since the news of her and Tatum's breakup. Her numbers are down."

"Wait, I'm confused, I thought she was number one on the charts and she was crossing over into pop?"

"Well, that's been put on hold. She's been getting bad press lately. She's had a string of loser boyfriends...some drunken episodes caught by the paparazzi. She thinks that if she and Tatum are back together, it will help her image and her career will take off again."

Wait. What? "She wants to be a couple again? Tatum won't go for that."

Silence.

My heart takes a dip as I swallow past the lump in my throat. I feel like I've suddenly been sucker-punched.

"Well, that's where you come in. I need you to convince Tatum you're on board with this."

"But I'm not on board with this. You're asking me to break up with him and push him towards Savannah? Are you kidding me?" I stand up and start to pace, my hands shaking, my stomach rolling. "There's no way Tatum will go for this. He hates her."

"Kiki, look, I know it sounds fucked up. But at the end of the day it's about his career. Heck, it's about his life. Do you want to put his career in jeopardy because you selfishly want to be in a relationship with him? Do you want that article published? It'll ruin him. And not just Tatum, but all the guys in the band. The fallout will be devastating. Do you want that?"

I flinch as his words beat against me. "Of course not," I whisper.

"Listen, I know this is a hard pill to swallow. But it's not about you and Tatum, it's about the bigger picture. Fans want to see them back together. They're country's sweethearts. They don't want to see him with one of their own because in their fucked-up heads, it could have been them and it wasn't. The fans don't want to root for the unknown underdog. They want Savannah, the star."

"One of their own? The underdog?" I ask incredulously.

"Yeah, a person of the public. A regular girl from San Francisco. You're very beautiful, Kiki, and smart as hell, but you're not a star."

I'm stunned beyond belief.

"You sound like fucking Maddie Macon," I mumble under my breath.

"What was that?"

"Nothing. So, let me get this straight. You're more concerned with Tatum's image than his happiness?"

"Like I said, it's not personal, Kiki. It's my job to do the best thing for Tatum and protect him and the band. If it helps bury this interview that could ruin his career, then…yes. I wish to hell there could be another way, but I don't see any other options. I even thought about you two seeing each other in secret, but it's too dangerous." He chuckles lightly and shakes his head. "If Savannah caught wind, we'd have a more serious issue than a he-said-she-said article. Listen, you know I love you, and Cam is like a brother to me…"

I scoff. "So your way of protecting Tatum is by letting an unbalanced, crazy ex blackmail him to prevent a false article from being published. An interview launched by a total psychotic bitch you're pushing back on him?" I shake my head. "No way. There's no way Tatum will go for this."

Lee clears his throat. "He already has."

The room spins and I quickly sit down on the couch, my heart breaking into a thousand pieces. "What? What do you mean?" I sound a million miles away to my own ears.

"Well, he's talking to Savannah right now. This isn't about love, Kiki. Take your emotions out of it. It's about politics and how to play the game. People's careers are on the line."

"So you just want me to go away," I say quietly as tears track down my face. "And Tatum knows this?"

Lee rubs a hand over his face and nods. How could Tatum do this to me? Just last night he whispered promises of forever to me as we made love. My brain and lungs shut down and I go completely numb, my heart crumpling.

"I guess this is goodbye, then," I say quietly as I rub my clammy hands on my jeans, standing up. I needed to get out of the claustrophobic room, out of this town. I needed to go far away from everything happening around me.

Lee rubs a hand over my back but I move away from him, shrugging him off.

"It doesn't have to be," he soothes. "You can still work

under Jess, just not go out on tour. We have other bands we style for. Or I can set you up with answering phones in the office…"

I laugh a humorless laugh. "Gee, that's so hard to pass up, Lee, but I think my time is up here." I can barely breathe as Lee nods and has the decency to look sad.

"I'll get you a flight to Nashville in the morning."

"Actually, I'd like to go back to San Francisco…first flight out."

Lee nods. "Look, Kiki…I'm really sorry. It's not personal, it's just…business." He clears his throat. "He really did love you, you know."

"Did he?" I ask bitterly as I walk out without looking back.

Chapter 39

Tatum

Me: Kiki, where are you? Why aren't you on my bus?

Me: Did Oreo finally smother you in your sleep? Listen, I'm sorry about earlier tonight. I was so pissed at Savannah, I couldn't even speak. It had nothing to do with you gorgeous.

Me: I guess you're asleep. Sweet dreams, beautiful. I love you.

I place my phone, on my nightstand wondering why Kiki isn't answering or why she isn't snuggled in my bed like she normally is when I get back from doing meet-and-greets after the concert. There's a light tap on my bedroom door.

Here she is, finally!

I'm surprised when Lee pokes his head in. "Are you dressed, man?"

"Yeah. To what do I owe the pleasure of a late-night call from you?" I smirk.

"Can you come out here? We need to talk about some things."

I follow Lee out to the couch, and we kick back after I pass him a beer.

"So, remember what I told you earlier tonight about Savannah's camp wanting to talk with us?"

"Right..."

"She's offering you a deal and I think you should take it."

I shake my head. "What's the deal?"

"She's willing to drop the interview and bury it if you publicly announce you two are back together."

"What? Is she fucking insane? No way. She can go fuck herself. I'm not going to be blackmailed by that crazy bitch."

Classic Savannah. She saw I've finally moved on with Kiki and I'm happy, and she wants to take that all away from me.

Lee blanches. "Would you rather your career go down the tubes?"

"I don't understand...she fucking hates me. What's her angle?"

"Well, her career has stalled out. She's looking to revive it with good publicity, and let's face it man, all of America wants you two back together. Your duet with her hit number one right after we announced the split. The duet about estranged lovers finding their way back to each other. The reality is, your fans want it to happen."

I take a gulp of my beer as I think this over. "That's not my problem. Announcing we're back together is just a minor fix. It's not going to jumpstart her career again."

"She thinks it will. And it *is* your problem, because we have a nasty little interview of she-said-he-said that could ruin your career."

I run my fingers through my hair. "No. No way. Besides, Kiki will never go for this. I'm not going to put her through this."

Lee sighs. "Kiki agreed you should do this."

I'm momentarily stunned into silence. The beer bottle poised at my lips. "What the fuck? You've already talked to her? Is this a fucking joke?"

"Yeah, I did. She cares about you, Tatum. She thinks it's for the best, for you and your career. I wish I were joking, man." Lee sits back and eyes me over his beer bottle.

I need to talk to her in person. I get up and head for the door, but Lee's next words stop me in my tracks.

"She's gone, Tate."

"What do you mean, she's fucking gone?"

"She went back to San Francisco on a red-eye tonight. She's gone."

"What? Well, when the fuck is she coming back?"

"She's not coming back." Lee shakes his head to drive the point home. "It's in your best interest."

Dread fills every fiber in my body. "Fuck my best interest! Get me on the next flight out, *now*."

"You can't leave. You have one more tour stop in LA, and then you have the Fall Fest back in Nashville. You're under contract."

I growl in frustration. "I don't give a flying fuck!"

Lee sighs. "Take your dick out of the equation. Take Savannah's offer, Tatum."

"Get the fuck out!" I smash my beer bottle into the wall as he quickly exits the tour bus.

Chapter 40

Two Months Later

"Do you want to go back to Nashville with me?" Cam asks as he pours a glass of wine.

It's Thanksgiving Day, and we're in my parents' kitchen celebrating with the whole family.

I sigh. "Not you too." I grab his glass and he gives me an annoyed look.

"You can't hide out at Mom and Dad's forever, you know."

I've been living with my parents for the last two months since I left Seattle. I was a complete mess on the plane, bawling my eyes out on the poor guy next to me, and then I cried in bed for the first two weeks, scaring the hell out of my parents. It wasn't until TJ came over and literally pushed me into a shower and a change of clothes, and told me if I listened to another song by the Wreckers or Adele, he'd disown me. He dragged me out to a wine bar where we got shitfaced together, and that is how I re-entered the land of the living.

Surprisingly, wallowing in red wine and sobbing all over your best friend's brand-new silk Gucci shirt is way better than professional therapy. Nothing like a great Pino and laughter from your best gay boyfriend to pull you out of your funk.

"Cam, I'm a grown woman. I realize this. It's only been a couple months. Besides, we worked out a plan. I'm working at Aunt Bobby's spa until January, and then I'm moving back to Nashville to start a business with Sarah."

"The makeup artist?"

"Yes."

"Why wait until January?"

"Because I need the money, and Dad said it would make Mom happy to have me home for Christmas. So if I stay, he'll help Sarah and me financially with the new business."

"And run this by me again. What exactly are you two doing?"

I roll my eyes. "Do you ever listen to me?"

"Only half-listen." He grins as I swat a towel at him.

"We're starting our own styling company. She'll be doing hair and makeup, and I'll be a personal stylist for Nashville's elite. She has a lot of contacts, and her cousin will be helping us too when she's not on tour. I'm even thinking about maybe designing my own line."

"I don't get it."

I take a gulp of wine. "I don't need you to get it. Just be supportive, okay? Sarah's currently looking for a space, so the ball is rolling."

"Hey, you should look at the loft above my bar. It'll be

nice to have someone I trust close by when I'm not there."

"That would be so amazing. I'll have Sarah look at it. Text me the address."

He pulls out his phone. "I can call Lee—he's offered several times to help you. He's always asking me how you're doing."

"That's special of him," I say sarcastically.

"Have you heard from Tatum?"

I shake my head. "Not since he blew up my phone after I left."

"And why didn't you want to hear what he had to say again?"

"Because he made his choice, Cam. He chose Savannah. Besides, I see he had to do it now. I mean, his career and reputation were on the line. I get it."

It wasn't how I wanted the situation to go, but I got it. Only TJ knows about the article she was blackmailing him with, and I had to make him swear on his new boyfriend's balls to keep his mouth shut about it. I mean, we literally had to have a little ceremony with fire and oath-swearing. My brother and my parents don't understand why our relationship took a sudden tragic nosedive. I lamely keep repeating Tatum's popularity was down and he needs to be seen with Savannah as a power couple.

"Hmph, well, I don't."

"It doesn't matter anymore. We've both moved on."

"Kiki, he's—"

"There you guys are! I've been looking for you two! Why are you hiding out in here?" Brooke sashays into the kitchen, interrupting whatever Cam was about to say. He quickly shuts his mouth and corks the bottle.

"Kiki, the boys need some cheese and crackers, and could you make me a cappuccino? Extra foam. That wine is loaded with sugar. You shouldn't drink that."

I look at Cam and roll my eyes. "Brooke, for the hundredth time, just because I moved back doesn't mean I work for you. Get your own damn cappuccino."

"You know, you really shouldn't swear, Kiki. Jesus is listening to your every word," she says contritely. "Hee-choo! Ugh, is that hairy rat in the kitchen?"

"I believe Graham is in the living room." My brother grins at me.

"Hardy-har, Cam." She sniffs. "Hee-choo! Probably on Kiki's clothes. Did you roller-brush your clothes today?"

"Oh my God, this is ridiculous." I swing open the fridge, grab a block of cheese, and throw it at Cam, who deftly catches it.

"Sweetums! I need help in here!" her husband Graham calls desperately from the living room.

"I'll be right there, brownie pie cakes!" Brooke rolls her eyes as she viciously grabs the cheese from Cam and slams it on to a chopping board. "You would think that fucker could take care of his own kids for two minutes without needing his dick coddled," she seethes.

I look at Cam with wide eyes, trying to hold in my laughter.

And I'm pretty sure Jesus's ears just fell off.

"Brookie? Love bunny?" Graham shouts frantically from the adjacent room.

"Gah!" She slams the knife down onto the cheese and

hacks violently at the poor block. She takes a deep breath and transforms her bitchy aggravated face into a dazzling smile. "Coming, macaroni noodle!" she singsongs as she arranges the cheese tray like Martha fucking Stewart on Red Bull. She throws a sprig of rosemary on top of the table water crackers and stomps back out of the kitchen.

Cam and I burst out laughing as soon as she's in the living room.

Mom comes into the kitchen, smiling. "What's so funny in here, you two?"

"Ah, nothing, Mom. Need help?"

Mom hugs me. "Thanks, I'm good. I'm just happy to see my baby laughing again." She kisses my hair and takes a pot of coffee out to the dining room. "Come on, you guys, pie is ready to eat!"

Just then, a crash comes from the living room.

"Graham!" Brooke screeches, causing my brother and I to bust out laughing again.

Cam winks at me. "It's good to see you smiling again."

"I'm good, I'm doing okay." I put on a false bravado as I carry dessert plates to the dining room.

On the outside, I'm rebuilding my life once again, but on the inside, my heart has been smashed to smithereens.

Chapter 41

Tatum

"Hey Lex, did you have a good Christmas?"

"Eh, stayed home. My family came and stayed with me. My brother was a pain in the arse as usual."

I grin. "Convince him to tour with us yet?"

"Nah, he'll never do country. Besides, he'll never leave Ireland. He gets too much pussy in that bar he owns."

I shake my head and chuckle. "Sounds like someone I know."

"Speaking of, how's all the pussy in your life, man?"

"Nonexistent. You know that."

Lex shakes his head. "That's why I always say, you don't get involved. Too much drama."

I pull off my beanie as we enter my favorite coffee shop on Central and run my fingers through my hair. We quickly head towards our usual booth in the back. Patrons cast us curious glances and excited chatter as we pass by, but for the most part we're left alone in here. Lex and I have been coming here a long time, and the owner, Patty, makes sure we aren't bothered. That would never happen if we went to a Starbucks.

We slide into the booth and give our order to the server.

"So in all seriousness, what's the deal with Savannah?" He blows on his coffee.

I kept the guys in the dark about Savannah's offer. I don't need them hounding me about her, and the less people who know, the better. Kiki was harder to explain. I let Lee handle why Kiki was suddenly off the tour and out of our lives. But Lex knows Savannah was trying to blackmail me, and he hates her almost as much as I do. The last bit of information he heard before the tour ended was that we were trying to work out a deal with her.

I shrug. "I don't like being cornered, and that's how I feel. I told Lee he could go manage someone else if he didn't like what I had to say."

"Which was…?"

"I told Savannah to go fuck herself. Print the article. I don't give a rat's ass what she says. I'm done with her once and for all."

Lex sits back and sighs. "Dude, all for a girl? You didn't even think about the impact on the rest of the band?"

I hold up my hands. "Not all for a girl. My reputation was on the line. Besides, she's not just any girl, Lex. Kiki was…different. I was in love with her." Sudden memories flash flood my brain at the mention of her name, saddening my heart. "But I also did it for my own integrity and pride. I *did* think about you guys, of course I did. You're my family. Telling her to fuck off was the most freeing feeling I've ever had. She was like a chain around my neck. It would have brought us all down."

"Hmm…so what's next?" he hums.

"A few weeks ago I gave an interview with *Rolling Stone* magazine and beat her article to the punch."

Lex starts to laugh. "Brother, I knew I loved you."

"Yeah, well it comes out next week. We told them I'd do it for free if they rushed it into the January issue. The fallout will be pretty big."

"When does her article come out?"

"When word got back to her, she tried to have *Marie Claire* release it at the same time, but Lee's friend over at the magazine said the writer couldn't get it in the January issue in time. They're going to trash it and start over. Thought it would be better for the magazine to get a follow-up piece on my article."

"Ooh, I bet Savannah was pissed."

"I'm sure she was." I grin when I remember Lee saying she was spitting nails and trashed her apartment.

"Good, she deserves it. So what are you gonna do about Kiki?"

I grimace and take a sip of coffee. "Nothing. That's over." My heart contracts in pain.

Lex shakes his head. "You're just going to give up on her? Nah, that's not your style, mate. Besides, I've never heard you say the L-word over a girl." He shudders.

"What am I supposed to do? She won't return my calls. I tried to go see her, but her dad told me to leave her alone, that I had done enough damage. She thinks I chose Savannah over her. It's over."

"Why would she think that?"

I sigh. "Lee admitted he made her believe I chose Savannah so she would bow out gracefully. Which she did. Lee said she did it because she loved me and truly feared our careers would be ruined."

"Fucking Lee. I would have fired him."

"I did." I smile ruefully. "But after Christmas I realized he wasn't doing it out of malice. He was trying to save our careers, his included. He offered to bring Kiki back and explain everything, but I told him that ship's sailed."

We sit silent for a beat as the server sets our plates in front of us.

"Word has it she recently moved back here," Lex says matter of fact as he takes another slow sip of coffee, eyeing me over the brim of the cup.

This has my attention.

I quirk an eyebrow at my best friend. "Since when do you have the pulse on Nashville? How'd you hear that?"

"It doesn't matter, but if you'd get your head out of your arse, maybe you can win her heart back. That is, if you still want to. I liked Kiki, and you guys seemed good together." He tucks into his food and snorts. "I can't believe I'm encouraging you to get back together with a girl. Like I've said before, women are trouble, and there are too many fish out in the ocean to get your heart caught on just one."

I shake my head. "Jesus, who did a number on you?"

Lex shrugs. "No one of importance. Just know if it doesn't work out with Kiki you can always be my wingman."

"That's depressing."

Lex chuckles as he chews his pancake. He looks up at me with a wolfish grin. "So then, let's talk about how we're going to win back Coffee Girl."

Chapter 42

Kiki

"Sarah, I know this is small, but you can set up your hair and makeup over there. And over here I can partition this off and can have my office with room for clothing racks."

Sarah looks over the bright space with floor-to-ceiling windows. Honey-stained wood floors meet watery, blue-painted brick walls. "The lighting is really good. It's not too far from where we live."

"There's a bar downstairs…" I raise my eyebrows up and down. "Lots of cute potential guys…free drinks…"

"Ha! That's definitely a plus. Can we afford it?"

"Considering Cam bought the building, I think it's doable." I grin, and she vibrates with excitement.

"Oh my God, Kiki, are we really doing this?"

I grab her hands and we jump up and down together, squealing.

"So I take it that's a yes?" Cam asks, absorbed in his phone as he leans into the doorjamb while we dance around like hyper, Bieber-loving tweens.

We both scream, "Yes!"

"Sweet. I'll need first month's deposit and the keys are yours."

"Deal!" I wink at Sarah and we start talking about what we'll need. She already has two big names in country music coming next month for a black-tie event, and they agreed to let me style them after they heard I worked for Tatum Reed and had a short stint with Maddie. I'm so excited. Our dreams are finally coming to fruition.

"Word will get out. We're going to be the biggest stylists on everyone's must-have list!" Sarah shrieks.

"Um, try to keep it down, though. I do have customers downstairs." Cam smiles over his phone at us.

"Oh! Sorry, Cam. Thank you so much for giving us this opportunity!" she gushes.

I quickly dial TJ's number. "How's my favorite bitch?" I yell excitedly into the phone.

"Kiki, ugh! I hate Jonathon. He's making me bring lunch to the meeting. You know how I hate picking up other people's food." He gags.

"Oh, not this again. It's not like they're making you eat their leftovers. Get a grip. Just have Nelson's deliver."

"Oh my God, you're a serious lifesaver. The cherry kind."

"Aw, I love you too. Want to take a little vacation out to Nashville?"

"Is your brother there?"

I laugh. "Hey! You should want to see me."

"Yeah, yeah, I just saw you. Why would I want to come out to that icebox in the wintertime?"

"To help us decorate our new office space, and maybe my brother will let you guest-bartend at his new bar downstairs."

Cam quickly looks up from his phone and shakes his head no. I laugh and wink at him.

"You got the space?" he squeals into the phone, busting my eardrum. "Yes! I can be there. When? Next week?"

"That works. It'll be so much fun!"

"For shizzle! Can I be Tom Cruise again and you be the old guy? Oh, and Sarah can be the sex-kitten wife?"

I look over at my brother, who eyeballs me suspiciously. "Uh, yeah sure!" my voice suddenly going an octave too high.

"Yass! Okay, okay, gotta run. Will book my ticket pronto!"

I hang up with TJ and bask in the glow of owning our own business.

"He is *not* guest-bartending, Kiki. I can't have another Kokomo incident." Cam points at me.

"Oh Cam, just because of that one episode at your other bar doesn't mean you should blackball TJ for life."

Sarah giggles. "What happened? What's the Kokomo incident?"

Cam huffs. "I let TJ and Kiki bartend one night. He tried to be Tom Cruise from *Cocktail* and ended up smashing ten bottles, then poured shards of glass in some customers' drinks. I had to buy the whole bar a couple free rounds to keep from getting sued."

I roll my eyes. "It's not like he did it on purpose. In his defense, it did look like ice."

"It was green, Kiki," Cam huffs.

Sarah laughs. "Sounds like TJ."

"No guest-bartending. That's final. Listen, I've got to get back downstairs. Here are your keys. Lock up when you guys head out."

"Thanks again, Cam!" Sarah chirps as I hug my brother.

"Yeah, thanks, Cam. You're the best."

"Yeah, yeah. Love you too, Kiki."

I walk over to help Sarah measure the space by the window.

"So...have you heard from Tatum since you've gotten back?" Sarah asks quietly.

"No, and I don't expect to. I mean, he took the deal with Savannah, so he won't want anything to do with me. I wouldn't want to screw it up. Besides, we're over and done. It was nice while it lasted, but I mean, really. It would never work. I'm just a coffee girl at heart, and he's a superstar. Lee was right. The public would have hated me, especially for getting in the middle of two stars like that. No way."

"Kiki, you're doing it again."

"Doing what?"

"Rambling."

"Sorry."

"I don't think he made the deal with Savannah. I mean, I haven't seen anything in the gossip rags they're back together."

"That's weird." I chew on my thumbnail. "The whole point was to splash it across the media they were together. Save her career and all that jazz." I shake my fingers at her. "Have you...seen him?" I'm not sure I want to know, but secretly, I'm craving every tidbit of info I can get.

"No, he's been back home in Texas for the holidays."

"Hmph. Lee told me he took the deal."

"Well, maybe you should find out for yourself. Rumor has it he and Lex are doing a little acoustic deal where they're playing at a few clubs locally over the next month. They're sold out, but I know we could get in."

"Nah, I'm good."

"Kiki…"

I sigh. "Sarah, he broke my heart. He took my trust and snapped it in half. It was pretty harsh for me. I'm doing okay now—I think I've finally put it behind me. But it's taken me months to get here. I just… I'm…good." I shrug, sounding desolate even to my own ears as I look out at the city.

"Okay, well, let me know if you change your mind."

I nod, knowing full well I won't be changing my mind. My heart wouldn't survive it.

Chapter 43

Kiki

IT'S BEEN A month since we signed the lease on our new place, and it looks pretty freaking amazing. TJ has come to visit as promised and in between sessions of flirting with my brother he managed to make this place super cool on a low budget. Not only can he dress a man really well, but he can also dress a working space to the nines. I'm trying to convince him to leave *Cufflinks* and move to Nashville, but I guess things are moving along well with his new boyfriend, Trent. He's promised he would seriously consider it if things didn't end happily...or if Cam decides he's suddenly gay. As much as I want him in the same city as me, I'm really happy for him.

We're gaining more clients for upcoming events and my fashion blog is taking off: *City Girl in the Heart of Country*. During our downtime, Sarah does my hair and makeup and drags me out all over downtown Nashville to take pictures of each other in different outfits for the blog. Turns out she's a great photographer. Not only is it super-fun, but it has brought us closer together and has given me the chance to discover different parts of the city.

Oreo loves his new office space and often curls up in the window sill to look out over downtown Nashville. He has his own IG account and already has two thousand followers. Life is good, and I'm happy as I can possibly be after having had my heart decimated by Tatum.

Sarah talks about setting me up on dates with some local songwriters she knows, but I'm not ready. Just thinking about going out on a date makes my heart bleed. I excuse my lack of enthusiasm over it by throwing myself even more into my work.

"Hey Sare, I'm going to run out and pick up the dress from The White Dove Boutique. Need anything?"

"Nah, I'm good. Oh, unless you stop by a coffee place. I could use a latte, but don't go out of your way."

"Got it." I wrap a scarf around my neck and grab my wool coat. "I'll be back in a few."

THERE'S A LOCAL coffee shop a block over from The White Dove, so I stop there first. Nashville is having a February cold snap, and a hot chocolate sounds perfect on this blustery day. I get Sarah her latte and myself a hot chocolate, balancing them in one hand as I head towards the door. It swings open just as I'm about to push on it, causing me to stumble forward into a tall man.

"Oh my gosh, I'm so sorry!" I cry as I reach for his arm

to steady myself, careful to not drop the drinks.

"Kiki?"

The man grabs my arm to help me balance. He's wearing a black beanie pulled low, but his beautiful green eyes are unforgettable.

I gasp as I grapple my drinks, letting go of his arm as if it were on fire. "Tatum."

"We really need to stop meeting like this." He gives me a crooked, sad smile.

"I...uh, heh," I gurgle.

I can't even form a sentence. I'm completely stunned as I stare into his mesmerizing eyes. My heart is racing a million times a minute and I sway, acutely aware I might pass out. I can't breathe, I can't speak. I can't do anything.

"Hi, I'm Kimberly!" A petite blonde shoves her hand in between us, making me take a step back on the sidewalk. She's cute, perky, and perfect. A wave of intense jealousy strikes a match in my belly.

"Oh, um, hi. I'm Kiki." I limply shake her hand with my gloved one. My eyes flicker back to Tatum's, and we stand there wordlessly staring at each other, ignoring Kimberly.

Memories suddenly surge my brain, causing a tidal wave to grip my heart. I can't move. I can barely breathe as his eyes flicker over my face and land on my lips. He looks at them like he wants to ravish them. I nervously bite my lip when his eyes burn into mine with intense desire.

Kimberly stares at us for a beat. "I'll just grab a table and meet you inside, Tatum, okay? Nice to meet you, Kiki." She's sweet and bouncy, like an overzealous college cheerleader.

"Yeah, you too..." I say absently as my voice trails off.

I knew there was always a chance I *might* run into Tatum on the street, but I never thought it would really happen. I clear my throat and try to sound light, but fail miserably.

"Listen, Tatum, I don't want to keep you from your, uh...date. It was good to see you." I try to slide past him, but he grabs my biceps, holding me in place.

"She's not my date," he growls as he pulls me off to a deserted side patio. "Kiki, why haven't you returned any of my calls?" The hurt look in his eyes crumbles my resistance.

"Tatum, I can't do this right now. Not here."

"Are we ever going to *do this?*" He waves a hand between us.

"I don't know." I look away, over his shoulder.

"I didn't get back together with Savannah, Kiki."

"What? Wait, why not? I mean... I'm confused."

"Because I don't want Savannah."

"But your career...the article. Wasn't that the whole point?"

"I don't want Savannah, Kiki. I only want you. It's only ever been you."

"But I..." *Am completely tongue-tied.* "Lee said..."

"I know what Lee said. He was misinformed." He lets me go and stuffs his hands into his jacket pockets and shakes his head. "I tried to reach you. I even came to see you. Didn't you listen to any of my messages?"

It's my turn to look disconcerted. I shake my head. He came to see me? I had no idea.

He sighs. "Listen, I've got to go. Kimberly's waiting, but Lex and I are playing tomorrow night at The Bluebird. It's our last show. I'd like for you to come."

I look down at my shoes. "I don't know, Tate."

"Bring Sarah. It'll be fun. I'll leave you two tickets at the door." He tilts my chin up with his finger. "Please, Kiki. I know I don't deserve to ask anything of you, but I'd really like for you to be there," he implores, searching my eyes.

"I'll try."

Tatum nods and opens the door. "See ya around, my Coffee Girl," he says barely loud enough for me to hear him over the noise coming from the coffee shop.

The door swings shut and I feel like my whole world is crashing down on me. I head back to the office, tears streaming down my face, the White Dove dress completely forgotten and the coffee now lukewarm.

Chapter 44

Kiki

"OW, THAT HURTS!"

"Oh, sorry, did I burn you?" Sarah unrolls the curling iron and my hair spirals down in a perfect wave.

"No, just pulled on it," I say grumpily.

Sarah ignores my bitchy mood as she wraps another section around the curler. "I love your hair. It does whatever I ask it to. Unlike mine, which just wants to be stick straight."

"No, I love *your* hair because it's funky," I tell her. "I'd look like a dumbass if I had purple streaks in my hair."

"Eh, it's all about how you carry yourself. If you believe you can rock purple hair, then you will."

I look at her dubiously.

"But don't change your hair, it's perfect." She winks at me.

"I'm nervous."

"Don't be."

"I can't help it. I want to throw up. Maybe I shouldn't

go."

"What? No!" Sarah whines. "Besides, Lex is going to be there. I need my Lex fix. I haven't seen him since the tour. Please? Go for me."

"But what am I going to say?"

"You don't have to say anything. They won't even know we're there. We'll leave as soon as it's over."

"Okay, but I'm still nervous."

"This smoky eye I've got on you is killer. If it helps your nerves at all, you look really hot."

I smile to appease her, but what I really want to do is vomit. Seeing Tatum yesterday opened up feelings I kept buried for my own sanity. After seeing him face-to-face, it's apparent I've never stopped loving him, even when I thought he chose Savannah. I definitely hated him for a while, but I never stopped loving him.

I can't believe the bomb he dropped yesterday. He never took the deal? I've been kicking myself over and over for erasing his messages without listening to them and deleting his texts. I have a lot of questions for him regarding the night Lee and I had that little chat. God, this is so messed up. Am I pissed at him? Hell yes. Hurt? Without a doubt.

But seeing him yesterday makes me realize I miss him like crazy.

Seeing him with another woman made me want to hurl, even if he claimed Kimberly wasn't his date. I mean, we aren't together. He can date whoever he wants, but it does feel like a knife to the heart thinking he's moved on.

I want him to be going to coffee with me. I want to be the first person he wakes up to in the morning and the last person he sees at night. I want it all with him, the good and the bad.

I want to be enough for him.

I try to tuck these feelings deep down because I don't want to become an emotional wreck tonight like I was yesterday. I pull on a black, knit cashmere dress and knee-high boots and take one last look in the mirror. My hair is glossy as it falls in loose curls over my shoulders. Sarah did an amazing job with my makeup. The shadow makes my eyes look violet and she's managed to conceal the puffiness from all the crying I did yesterday.

I grab my clutch and we head out into the cold February night.

On the outside I look pretty put-together. On the inside I'm a mess of jumbled nerves.

Chapter 45

Kiki

WE WALK THROUGH the doors of The Bluebird Café and I'm taken aback by how crowded it is. It's packed to capacity. Sarah grabs us two beers as we squeeze between patrons in the back to find a decent standing spot, because forget about sitting. We snag two spots by the bar and I see Lex and Tatum sitting on the small stage, tuning their guitars. I expected the whole band to be here, but it's just the two of them.

My heart beats double-time as I drink Tatum in. His tan, muscular arms are taut as he strums a few chords, his strong jaw sharp. His eyes are serious as he leans in to talk to Lex. His hair is mussed effortlessly and his green eyes scan the crowd briefly before returning to his guitar. His perfect lips form a small frown as he reaches down for his beer, listening to something Lex is saying. He's wearing a muted plaid button-down, sleeves rolled up with his worn Levi's and cowboy boots.

Oh God, I've missed him so much.

But seeing him is like a punch to the heart, because there's too much misunderstanding between us. And Lee's words still haunt me, causing a multitude of insecurities. I'm just a regular girl, and regular girls don't date country superstars like Tatum Reed.

Being here tonight, seeing him in his element makes me realize how different our worlds really are. His words from yesterday reverberate in my head. *It's always been just you.* But all the naysayers' words still sting, leaving their poison to linger in my skin. Can I really fit into his world? The regular, everyday American girl?

It's like I had the most beautiful gift given to me, and I got to hold that gift and admire it, even grow to love it, but in the end, I had to give it back. Now this gift can be mine again if I want it. But my heart is terrified to reach for it. I'm afraid I might break it. That I don't deserve it. It's easier to just slink back into the shadows and lick my wounds.

Tears swell behind my eyes. "Sarah, I don't think I can do this."

She grabs my hand and squeezes it. "We're just two girls going to listen to some music, Kiki. Don't think beyond that."

I nod and swallow my beer as I look around at the crowd. A lot of women are here, of course, but it's a different vibe from his concerts. It's more relaxed and laid back. There isn't a frenetic energy humming in the air like there is when the whole band is together.

I spot Kimberly on the opposite side of the bar and jealousy courses through me again like lightning. I try to squelch it, but I can't. She's a pretty, petite blonde and she's just so perfect. And I know she's here for Tatum.

Before I can obsess over the fact she's here, the lights dim and a spotlight bathes Lex and Tatum in a warm golden light.

"Good evening." Lex's smooth Irish lilt echoes through the room like fine silk. "We want to thank you all for coming out tonight." The crowd whistles and claps.

Sarah sighs next to me and links her arm through mine. Well, at least one of us is happy to be here.

"Tonight, we'll be singing a couple songs, some old and some new, and a few covers. It's a chance for Tatum and I to kick back and relax and get back to what country music means to us and how we first started out."

The crowd applauds with approval. A few hoots and whistles echo through the small crowded bar. Lex strums a few chords on his guitar, adjusting the sound. Sarah continues to hold my hand, probably afraid I'll bolt, which I'm still tempted to do. But I appreciate her strength in my moment of weakness.

"God, he has the sexiest accent," Sarah sighs in my ear. I grin, because despite his womanizing ways, she continues to lust after him. I'm going to make it my mission to help her find a nice, stable guy this summer.

They sing two of their songs acoustic-style and I have to admit, it's amazing. Their voices are pure and harmonize so well together. Watching Tatum sing this way makes him seem so vulnerable, not like the cocky, country megastar he personifies on tour.

"This next song is a favorite of a friend of mine. It's now become my favorite." Tatum strums the opening chords of

Fleetwood Mac's "Songbird." The crowd enthusiastically cheers their approval. He grins and flashes the audience his dimples. "Wherever my songbird may be tonight, I hope she knows I love her." The crowd goes wild, and Sarah squeezes my hand. My heart pounds furiously in my ears as they start to sing the song.

Tears slide down my cheeks as the lyrics sink into my heart. Tatum throws his whole heart and soul into the song, Lex's voice blending perfectly with his. His eyes are closed as the lyrics easily roll off his tongue and I'm completely mesmerized, hanging on every word.

They quietly finish the song and my heart pounds furiously in my chest as the crowd applauds. Is this his way of asking me back? Or is it just a love song? Is it even meant for me?

Of course it's for you, Kiki, I chastise myself. He knows that's my favorite song. I look at Sarah and she silently mouths *Wow* as she wipes tears from my cheeks.

I wish I could get to him, somehow find out what he wants. I want to scream and shout, *I'm back here!* But I don't want to cause a scene.

They launch into one of their upbeat songs called "Kick Start" and the moment is gone. I slump my shoulders in defeat and wipe tears from my eyes.

"You ready to go?"

"What? No! They have one more song after this," Sarah pleads as she shakes my arm. I look at her oddly and roll my eyes. I'm going to have to have a serious come-to-Jesus talk with her about Lex. He's funny, sexy, and charming, but he's still a bad boy who will end up shredding her to pieces.

Besides, I'm having a hard time staring at my own broken heart up onstage. The heart I once had and quickly lost.

"Okay, well, I'm going to go to the bathroom to make sure my mascara isn't running tracks down my face."

"It's not. I used waterproof on you."

"All the same, I need a breather."

"Kiki, wait…"

But I've already moved from our spot, trying to push my way through the crowd on my way to the bathroom. I stop dead in my tracks when Tatum starts to speak.

"This last song of ours, I wrote one night when I couldn't sleep because someone kept stealing my sheets." The audience cheers and Tatum chuckles as he scans the crowd. "It's about finding your heart unexpectedly stolen by someone you realize you're in love with, and trying to convince her to take the leap with you. Coffee Girl, my heart belongs to you."

I turn around as I'm jostled by other patrons, my eyes connecting with Tatum's. His eyes widen in surprise and he quickly recovers, giving me a huge, dimpled smile as he begins to sing.

I wasn't looking for love, but there you were.
I didn't want much, but you gave it anyway.
I wasn't going to ask you, but you answered the call,
I didn't want to take much, but in the end you gave it all.

Take my hand, take my heart, take my love,
Won't you fall with me?
Tear it up, take a piece, what will be, will be.

Take my love, just say yes...
Won't you fall with me?
Fall with me.

I can't be the man that I want to be
Is it all pretend? Happiness eludes me.
You're still a mystery that holds the key,
Until you let go we both won't be free.
Fall with me, baby, please...
Fall with me.

I want to be your man, the only one you see
I want to hear your voice say that you're in love with me,
Can't you hear me calling you baby
Can't you hear my forever plea? Baby fall with me.
Please just fall with me.

Take my hand, take my heart, take my love,
won't you fall with me.
Tear it up, take a piece, what will be, will be.
Take my love, just say yes...
Won't you fall with me?
Just fall with me.
What will be will be.
Fall with me.

The crowd goes wild as Tatum and Lex strum the last chords of the song. He takes off his guitar, handing it to Lex. He jumps off the low stage and the crowd parts like the Dead Sea as he heads straight for me. People touch him as he passes and murmur Savannah's name, but he doesn't take his eyes off me.

Me? I'm a mess. Tears run tracks down my cheeks as I'm frozen in place.

People shoot curious glances over at me as they try to figure out who Tatum is walking towards. He's smiling his beautiful, dimpled grin as he reaches me. He wraps a strong arm around my waist and tugs me to him as I wipe my tears away.

"Coffee Girl."

I sniffle. "Tater Tot."

"Please let me love you. It's only ever been you. Will you fall with me?"

"Tatum, I…"

"Kiki."

I give him a watery smile and lightly thump his chest. "Will you let me finish?" I laugh through my tears.

"You're overthinking it. I know you." He rubs his thumb along my jaw as he cups my face.

I nod and bury my face in his neck, breathing him in. "Yes."

He tilts my chin up so I'm staring straight into his beautiful eyes. "Yes, what?" he says.

"Yes, I'll fall with you."

He tenderly kisses me, wrapping his arms around me as he lifts me off my toes. The crowd around us goes nuts, camera phones flashing, but all I can see and breathe is Tatum.

"I love you, Coffee Girl."

"I love you, Tater Tot."

Chapter 46

WGN TV Nashville

"A MYSTERY WOMAN steals Tatum Reed's heart as onlookers at The Bluebird Café witness his heartfelt confession of love to her. Here's Jessie Lynn with the story."

"Thanks, Tara! I'm standing here outside The Bluebird café where Tatum Reed and Lex Ryan were playing a set a little over an hour ago. Apparently, a little more than just singing went down. I'm here with a local patron, Kelly Briggs, who saw the whole thing. Kelly, can you tell us what happened tonight?"

"Oh my God, it was so amazing! Well, okay, he had just finished his new song, which was beyond perfection. I for sure thought he was talking about Savannah Edwards in the dedication. The whole place was arching their necks thinking Savannah was sitting in the back of the bar. It was so exciting, and oh my gosh, the way he spoke and the new love song he sang, dedicated to her... It was just—oh my God, it was just totally heart-melting."

"The new song for Savannah?"

"No! For this girl. It sounded like they'd been together for a while, but no one's ever seen her before or has any clue who she is. Anyway, he ended his new song, walked off the stage, and he picked her up in a hug and they kissed and she was crying and I was crying…the whole damn place was crying."

"Sounds beautiful. So was Savannah there?"

"I don't know. I doubt it, but who cares? He wasn't looking for her or singing to her. Just to this girl. They left quickly after that with Lex Ryan and another girl."

"You heard it here first on WGN TV Nashville! Check out the video streaming live on our WGN TV website. Tara, back to you."

"Hmm, thanks, Jessie. It'll be interesting to find out who this mystery woman is that has stolen Tatum Reed's heart."

Epilogue

Six Months Later

Tatum: *What are you doing?*

Kiki: *You're not serious.*

Tatum: *As a heart attack.*

Kiki: *I'm sitting right next to you!*

Tatum: *I know. I love waking up to your beautiful smile every morning.*

Kiki: *I'm not putting out.*

Tatum: *Is that a challenge?*

Kiki: **sigh**

Tatum: *If there was a song in your head right now, what would it be?*

Kiki: *You're So Vain*

Tatum: *Haha. Seriously.*

Kiki: *Hmm, Mama, He's Crazy*

Tatum: *Look at you going all country on me! I am crazy for you btw.*

Kiki: *Okay, I'll bite…what song is in your head right now?*

Tatum: *Marry Me.*

Kiki: *Bruno Mars or Train? Oh wait, Bruno Mars is Marry You.*

Tatum: *Kiki put down your phone and marry me.*

"What?" I drop my phone down and look over at him incredulously.

He's sitting shirtless on the bed, facing me with a shit-eating grin on his face, holding a box on his lap. "Open the box, beautiful."

I sit up and look at the box hesitantly. "This isn't a Justin Timberlake thing, is it?"

He huffs out a laugh. "No, this is not a dick in a box. Just open it."

I lean over and slide the top off the box. He reaches down, producing this fuzzy, fluffy, little brown-and-white furball. The furball looks up and meows loudly. Around the furball's neck is a Tiffany-blue ribbon with a beautiful, square-cut diamond ring hanging from it.

"Marry me, Mackenzie Leigh Forbes."

I stare at him, my mouth slack. The kitten meows, breaking my trance.

"But, we—But—Oh my God, Tate!" I squeal. "I can't decide whether to smash the adorable fluffball to my face or the diamond ring!"

He laughs as he places the meowing fur ball in my lap. I hold the kitten up to my nose.

"I love you, Coffee Girl. You've always been my song-bird, and I don't ever want to lose that melody again. So, is that a yes?"

"Yes, yes, yes!" I cry as he slips the ribbon from around the kitten and places the beautiful diamond on my right ring finger. Tears slip down my cheeks as I mash my lips to his.

He laughs and smiles as he kisses me. "Don't squeeze the kitten too hard," he whispers against my lips.

I ease off of him and sit back. "Okay, okay, this definitely deserves some hot lovin'." I glance over at him and wink as I hold my ring up to admire it in the morning light and snuggle the kitten in my left arm.

He smiles his gorgeous dimpled grin. "You make me so happy, Kiki. I'm the luckiest guy in the world. I love you."

"I'm the lucky one. I love you right back." I kiss him tenderly, careful of the meowing kitten in between us.

I hold Furball up to my nose and kiss him. "And who are you? I can't believe you got a kitten!"

He shrugs. "I thought Oreo might want some company. Besides, the Rescue Me fan club kept badgering me about when I was going to get one. Kimberly thought it would be a good idea. Um...I also got suckered into getting a dog. Jimmy is bringing her over this afternoon. There might be a horse too..."

"Tatum!" I laugh at his I-hope-I'm-not-in-trouble expression. "Go big or go home, right, Mr. Reed?"

"You said it best, Mrs. Reed." He smiles his megawatt, superstar smile.

"I think I could get used to being Mrs. Reed." I kiss his lips.

"I wouldn't accept anything less," he murmurs, kissing me back.

Post Epilogue

Kiki

SO, YOU'RE PROBABLY wondering what happened to Savannah. Sadly, nothing she deserved. The interview she held over Tatum's head fizzled out once his *Rolling Stone* article called it all a bunch of lies. *Marie Claire* didn't want to falsely accuse Tatum of anything or attract any lawsuits, so they dropped the article faster than a politician's promise on election day. They didn't even want to mess with a follow-up article, so the whole thing was squashed.

Sarah's cousin spilled the beans—not rice—to us for the real reason behind Savannah's sudden change of heart for Tatum and why she needed him back so desperately. Savannah was pregnant with a big-wig record executive's baby. He, being a faithful married man, denied the whole thing. So, Savannah thought if she could get her relationship back with Tatum, she could play the baby off as his. Or make the executive so crazy jealous he would leave his family for her.

Neither happened. How she thought Tatum would have

gone along with that one was beyond me, but as TJ likes to say, "The bitch be crazy."

She announced she was pregnant in an *US* magazine spread and the father was not going to be involved in the baby's life: *No, it was one hundred percent not Tatum Reed's baby.* Tatum's lawyers made sure she had to vehemently deny any connection with him. Last we heard, she's living in Los Angeles trying to record a pop album. Oh, and she's coming out with her own baby clothing line.

Cue the eyeroll.

I don't think we'll be receiving a wedding present from her anytime soon.

Kimberly, sweet, bubbly Kimberly, ended up *not* being Tatum's new love interest, but the head of his new PR team. He wanted to rework his image after the whole Savannah debacle and try to distance himself from her as much as possible. He also wanted to remove Lee from the responsibility of having to manage the band's personal affairs. She brought in a fresh, new approach that showcased Tatum as the humble-yet-sexy-as-sin country Entertainer of the Year. Her campaign has been on point.

His popularity in the media has soared, and he's constantly hounded for interviews as the hottest star in country music. *People* magazine even wants him for their cover of Sexiest Man of the Year. He must enjoy my dramatic eyerolls because he mentions it every chance he can get. I hope he doesn't quote the chicks-dig-him line. I'll have to warn Kimberly about that.

Kimberly has also successfully turned Rescue Me into a nationwide charity for Tatum, raising over a million dollars in one weekend alone. I adore her.

As for Maddie? Well, her two hits only took her so far. She landed a spot on *Dancing with the Stars*, but only made it a couple rounds. Rumor has it she sabotaged one of the other actresses she was in competition with on the show. Someone backstage supposedly saw Maddie tampering with her shoes. That same evening, the actress twisted her ankle when her heel broke, and she was eliminated. Sarah and I like to call the incident "I, Maddie" after that Tonya Harding movie.

I've learned firsthand you shouldn't believe every rumor you hear, but this one, sadly, is probably accurate. I'm pretty sure she's the one who tampered with the guys' clothes, hiding Will's shirt and doing something to Tatum's pants the night he ripped them in an attempt to get me fired, but we'll never know for sure.

She put out a second album, which received poor reviews. Radio stations didn't want to play it and no one wanted to take her out on tour because word got out she's difficult to work with. She was recently listed as the worst-dressed country singer in *US* and *In Style* magazines.

Karma's a B, Maddie. Karma's a big ol' B.

Tatum and I?

Tatum won Entertainer of the Year and his new song "Fall with Me" just hit number one. He and the guys decided to take some time off, much to Lee's dismay. Strike while the iron's hot and all that jazz.

I don't mind because we are happily planning our wedding here in Nashville on Lex's horse ranch—where our latest rescue, Songbird, now resides.

It's going to be beautiful. Sarah and TJ will be sharing maid-of-honor duties, and of course, Sarah will be doing my hair and makeup. Lex will be Tatum's best man, along with his brother. I thought he would have chosen Lee as well, but he didn't want to, since Lee was the main reason we broke up. I forgave Lee a while back after the truth of what happened was hashed out, but Tatum wasn't a hundred percent there. I understand Lee was trying to protect Tatum, even if it was underhanded and sneaky. I know in time, the trust will be there.

Everyone from the band is coming. Even Jess, which kind of surprises me, but in the end, love them or hate them, they're our family.

Speaking of family, when my sister found out I'm getting married on a horse ranch, she refused to come to a "stinky, hillbilly wedding on a dude ranch" and if she got horse poop on her Jimmy Choos, she would die.

Fine by me.

But, she changed her tune once she mentioned it to her girlfriend Charlotte. Charlotte's so jealous of all the A-list names that are going to be there, so of course, Brooke's coming now.

I just ordered a box of paper shoe scrubs for her to wear around the ranch.

She and Mom have been emailing me wedding ideas hourly and calling my wedding planner and driving her insane though I'm not sure how they got her number. Brooke even proposed I wear her wedding gown, but added I'll probably have to add fabric to it since I'm *très gras* than her with all the red wine I drink.

Gee, thanks, Brooke.

Graham suggested Tatum draft a prenup, and his services were available. TJ suggested maybe he could teach Tatum how to fold his underwear into a perfect square too. Graham's so gross.

Cam will be there, and he's bringing a plus-one. He's been steadily dating Lisa, the girl he brought to the concert. Although I really like her, I may have to have security frisk her and remove any selfie sticks.

Oreo has taken a liking to our new pitbull-mix, Mabel. She's an older girl and just likes to curl up on the couch or sit on the porch in the sun. Oreo likes to snuggle with her, and they end up taking over half the couch.

As for Furball... Well, he's like that annoying little brother who won't leave you alone. He likes to hide under the furniture and attempt kamikaze-attacks on anything that walks by. This includes Oreo, which does not sit well with my buddy. But we love Furball anyway.

Tatum's Rescue Me shirts are still selling like hotcakes and he and Oreo even made an appearance on *Good Morning America*.

I'm still applying antibiotic ointment and kisses to Tatum's wounds.

Understandably, there was a little bit of backlash when it hit the press Tatum and I are an item. Who's this mystery girl and why didn't the public know about me and give Tatum their approval? Where did I even come from? If he wasn't in a relationship with Savannah, then women wanted him to be single. Pure craziness.

There's some hate mail, some not-so-nice blog articles,

and a lot of trolls on social media every time a picture of us is released. It's not easy, but Tatum sticks by me through it all, defending me every chance he can. Eventually the fans have come to see how much we love and care for each other. I had to prove to them I wasn't a fame- or gold-digging whore. There've been some rough moments, I'm not gonna lie, but basking in the glow of Tatum's heart makes it all worthwhile.

It also helped someone—I'm not going to mention any names, *ahem*, TJ—leaked a particularly embarrassing video of me in a bedazzled "I Love Me Some Country Boyz" hat catching fish. Tatum's fans thought it was hilarious and it got over five hundred thousand views in one day. I wanted to kill TJ and Tatum because I'm pretty sure they were in on this together, but Kimberly convinced me to leave it up because it endeared me to the fans. I'm still biding my time, waiting for the perfect moment to get revenge.

Sarah and I have done brilliantly. Our business is booming with clients and we're doing so well we're booked six months out. We've had several mentions in *People*'s best-dressed, and we even have an A-list client for the Oscars. I'm beyond excited. We've also slowly started designing a bridal line on the side. Sarah is a makeup extraordinaire. She's on everyone's speed dial for music videos, parties, weddings… You name it, and she's got it on the books. Even with the increase in demand for her skills, she's still promised to help out the band when they need her. And she does it all with a smile on her face. Have I mentioned how amazing she is?

TJ's no longer with Trent—sad face. Apparently wearing the horn-rimmed glasses 24/7 gave him headaches. He'll be moving to Nashville—ecstatic face—right before the wedding to join forces with us. Cue the happy dance!

As for Sarah and Lex? Well, that's a long story…best saved for another time.

The End

Sneak Peek of

The Makeup Artist

Will you dance with me in the dark?
Take this trip to Never Neverland?
Will you expose my heart?
Do a damn fine job of tearing it apart?

Take my hand, let's dance in the dark
Ooh yeah, let's dance in the dark
This isn't a love song, baby, it's a whole lot of heartbreak.

Not sure how I got here, all you do is take
I'm a closed-off man, unwilling to be a part of your plan
I can't trust you, but baby, I'm a trusting man.
This isn't a love song, it's a whole lot of heartbreak.

Will you expose my heart?
Do a damn fine job of tearing it apart?
Will you dance with me in the dark?
Take my hand, let's dance in the dark
Ooh yeah, let's dance in the dark
This isn't a love song, baby, it's a whole lot of heartbreak.

This Isn't a Love Song written by Lex Ryan, Tatum Reed

Prologue

Lex

"I HAD THE same dream again last night. I'm standing in the middle of an empty stage. It's dark, but I know she's there. I can feel her. My guitar is slung on my back, and I reach for it. I don't need light to strum the chords. I know this song by heart. I can play it with my eyes closed. It's the same song every time. I play a few chords and hum. The sounds echo through the small venue. I'm frustrated because the words won't come to me. Just the melody. I'm filled with so much dread and sadness, I want to cry.

"I just want it to end, and that's when I hear the voice. It's a woman's voice, but I don't recognize it and I can't see her. She asks me to come back. It's strange to me because it's the same thing every time. I don't understand what she wants or who she is. I get frustrated and shout, 'What the fuck do you want?' but all she whispers is to come back. And then I wake up drenched in sweat."

"I think you know who this woman is."

"I don't."

"You do. You just don't want to see her."

"Is it even a woman? Maybe it's the song whispering to me."

"I don't think so. You know who it is, Lex."

"I don't, Doc."

Sigh. "You do, Lex. She's trying to get your attention."

Chapter 1

Sarah

3 Years Earlier

"HI, WELCOME TO Gerry's Coffee House. What can I get you?"

"Well, hi there, beautiful. I haven't seen you in here before. Are you new?"

I hold my bright smile steady as I do a quick sweep of the clean-cut businessman in front of me.

"No, I usually work a different shift. What can I get you?" I continue to smile politely even though I want to scowl as I bend down to retrieve a paper cup.

I deal with jerks like him at least once a day. The kind of guy who thinks he's so charming by calling me dollface, gorgeous, or babycakes. Although some might be flattered by the terms of endearment, I, for one, am not. Especially when they give me that smarmy smile or a wink as they stare at my boobs while I take their order.

As I stand I notice someone else has come in behind Mr. Business Suit. He's looking down at his phone. A ball cap pulled low hides his face. He's wearing a fitted, long-sleeved T-shirt, which is kind of strange because it's, like, a zillion degrees outside. He's got a killer body—that much I can tell. Muscular arms strain against the material of his shirt. Jeans mold to his perfect muscular thighs. Not an ounce of fat anywhere.

Waiter? Yes, I'll take number two, please. Ugh, but first I have to deal with number one. My eyes cut back to the guy giving me a creepy smile.

"Uh…" He looks at my boobs as he pretends to look for my nametag on my apron. "Sare-ah. That's a beautiful name for a beautiful girl."

I internally gag. Where the hell is my co-worker Neil? He's ten minutes late for his shift. "Eyes up here, Chuck. What can I get you?"

The hot guy behind Mr. Suit snorts.

"How about your number?"

Real smooth, asswipe. It's all I can do not to roll my eyes at him. My smile starts to hurt as I hold it in place. "I don't give out numbers. Just coffee. So what'll it be?"

"A date?"

And there goes my smile. Well, I tried.

I blow the bangs I'm trying to grow out in irritation. I'm going to kill Neil for being late, causing me to deal with this wiener head.

"Dude, can you just fuckin' order and leave the poor lass alone? I'm in a hurry," the hot guy says behind jackass. I hear an accent, but I can't quite place where it's from.

Jackass looks over his shoulder at Hot Stranger. "*Excuse me*, do you mind?"

Hot Guy looks up from his phone, and my mouth goes dry. Holy moly, this guy is sinfully good-looking. Dark, rugged, and dangerous. His sharp jawline with a hint of scruff ticks with annoyance. His dark hair curls at the edges under his ballcap. His aqua-blue eyes quickly connect with mine before they return to Mr. Wannabe-Wall Street.

"Actually, I do mind. I have a meeting I'm going to be late for if you don't order. And I'm pretty sure Sarah here would have given you her number already if she wanted to. If you're not ready to order, then please step aside."

Oh my God, his accent is to die for. It sounds Scottish or something in that region.

"Asshole," Mr. Business Suit says under his breath as he turns back to me. "Can you *believe* this guy?" He gives me an incredulous look as he points his thumb over his shoulder as if I haven't been following the whole exchange.

I stare at him blankly as he continues.

"Sare-ah, I'd like a large, skinny latte with extra foam, and a light swirl of caramel with a hint of shaken salt. Two and a half pumps of vanilla with a splash of extra-hot water and one and a half packets of Splenda. Did you get all that, sweetheart?"

He winks at me as he pulls his wallet out. I want to reach across the counter and punch him in the nose, but unfortunately, I'm a lover, not a fighter. My eyes slide back to Hot Accent Guy and once again they collide with his aqua-blues. He arches a dark eyebrow at me. I think he wants to pummel this dude as much as I do.

"Got it," I bite out as I write his ridiculous order on the cup in shorthand. "Name?"

He leans on the counter with his elbow, invading my personal space. "This is going to sound silly, but I've got a super-important business meeting and I want everyone at the meeting table to know I'm in charge. Can you write down 'Captain Amazing'?"

"For real?" I look up at him, my pen poised as I bite my cheek hard to keep from laughing. Hot Accent Guy coughs as he hides his smile.

"Yes, that's my nickname around the office." He winks at me. "And my nickname with the ladies, if you know what I mean," he whispers seductively and chuckles. "Why don't you put your number on there while you're at it?"

Ew, ew, ew.

"Right." I smile at him and roll my eyes as I turn away from his penetrating stare. I write down a name and take his debit card.

Neil rushes in at that very moment. "Sorry, so sorry, Sarah. Oh my gosh, I'm sorry. I hope you're not late for your appointment." He ties his apron, washes his hands, and starts to make the drink I set to the side. I really need to go, but I'm intrigued by the gorgeous guy with the sexy accent.

"I've got one more minute. I'll ring this customer up and then I've got to jet."

"Yes, yes, of course. Again, I'm so sorry. Dang tourists on Music Row stopping to take pictures every two steps had me running late."

"No worries, Neil, it's okay."

I whirl around and come face-to-face with the most intriguing aqua-blue eyes. They remind me of the clear-blue Caribbean ocean I've only seen in pictures—the ones with the white sand, the palm trees holding up a hammock, and that incredible blue-green water.

"Hi," I say shyly, biting my lip. "Sorry for your wait. What can I get you?" He looks so familiar to me, but I can't quite place where I've seen him before.

He stares at my lips before pulling his cap a little lower like he's trying to hide his face. "I'll have a large black coffee, but can you leave a little bit of room for cream? Thanks." He hands me a crisp twenty-dollar bill. He leans in closer and I grab the counter, because it's all I can do not to pull him to me and sniff the incredible smell emanating from him. "You okay?"

I look up from his sensuous lips and meet his eyes, his question surprising me. I let go of the counter and busy myself with getting his change out of the till. "You mean because of the captain over there?"

He nods and gives me the most breathtaking, dimpled smile. "Yeah, Captain Wanker."

I laugh and smile. "Yeah. I eat guys like him for breakfast."

"Ah, so you're a man-eater. Got it."

"I, um, did *not* say that. Definitely not a man-eater. I mean, I date guys, but I don't chew them up and spit them out."

Jesus, just shut up, Sarah! Agh! I quickly close my mouth and hand him his change as I stare at his megawatt smile.

"Keep the change, love." He winks at me and grabs the coffee Neil places on the counter. A wink from the captain would make me queasy. A wink from him has my blood humming with pleasure. I'm so bummed I didn't even get a chance to write down his name. I watch his amazing butt in his Levi's as he walks towards the counter that houses the cream and sugar.

"Captain Poopy Underpants?" Neil calls out, looking shocked, realizing what he just yelled out across the coffee bar. "Uh...867-5309!" Neil looks over at me, thoroughly confused. "Isn't that an eighties song?"

Hot Guy nearly spits out his coffee as he opens the door, laughing.

"Order ready for Captain Poopy Underpants!" Neil shouts over the din of the coffee shop. I bite my laughter back as I untie my apron.

"Gotta run, Neil! Oh, and that coffee belongs to that goober over there on his phone. But since he has his head up his ass, just slip a heat shield on it and hand it to him. It'll be a nice surprise for his *very* important meeting." I smile gleefully as I slip out the back door, hoping for one more glimpse of Hot Accent Guy. My phone buzzes in my pocket as I look out across the street. I'm disappointed when I don't see him. I dig it out and answer it.

"Where are you?" my cousin Heather yells into my ear.

"I'm on my way. Keep your pants on. I had a little incident at the coffee shop. Oh my God, Heather, wait until I tell you—"

"Yeah, yeah, yeah. You're going to be working at the coffee shop for the rest of your life if you don't get your butt down here. I'm putting my neck out on the line for you to get this job."

"Okay, I'm sorry. I'll be there in five minutes. It's not even four. Plenty of time."

"Just hurry. Dragon Princess is pacing and being a bitch."

I hang up with my cousin and quickly get into my dependable Subaru. Heather is a makeup artist for Savannah Edwards, an up-and-coming country singer. Her boyfriend is Tatum Reed, another rising star, and he needs someone to go on tour with him and the band to do their makeup and maybe to do some styling. Even though I'm about to graduate cosmetology school, Heather has been my mentor and is a major influencer. She's been in the industry for five years and said this could be my big break, the one thousands would cut a bitch for. I don't want to cut any bitches, but I do really need this job.

Want to read the rest of *The Makeup Artist*? It's coming in the Spring of 2020!

Stay up to date on future releases!
Join Sophie Sinclair on Facebook and Instagram.

If you have a moment, please leave a review!

Acknowledgements

A big thank you to my anonymous beta readers who fell in love with Coffee Girl and encouraged me to keep writing. To Michelle for having to read and edit this thing a zillion times, thank you for your support. To Julie for being my number one cheerleader on this journey and for loving the hot guy. To Jay for being my voice of reason, my supporter, and for not trying to turn this into a suspense thriller. xoxo

About the Author

Sophie Sinclair runs on lots of coffee, dark chocolate, and wine—after five p.m. of course. She devours all different genres of books, but romance, especially romantic comedies, are her favorite. If she's not writing, she's reading. The rest of the time she's a mom to two amazing girls, a husband that has put up with having to read her romance novels, her three rescue dogs, her rescue cat, and a guinea pig named Fluff.